A CATERED NEW YEAR'S EVE

Center Point
Large Print

Also by Isis Crawford and available from
Center Point Large Print:

A Catered Costume Party
A Catered Cat Wedding

**This Large Print Book carries the
Seal of Approval of N.A.V.H.**

A
CATERED
NEW YEAR'S
EVE

ISIS CRAWFORD

CENTER POINT LARGE PRINT
THORNDIKE, MAINE

*For my mother, my father,
my grandmother, and my aunt.
Thinking of you.*

A CATERED
NEW YEAR'S EVE

Sometimes, you have to throw out the rotten blueberries before the mold starts to spread to the rest of the pint. Otherwise, you'll lose the whole thing.

—Rose Simmons's words
to her daughters

Prologue

Sean stirred another sugar cube into his coffee as he thought about what he should say. Or not say. Not that it would matter. His daughters would do what they wanted anyway. They always had.

It was seven in the morning and the Christmas lights twinkling on the eaves of his neighbor's house pierced the grayness as Sean glanced out the window at the customers parking their vehicles in the lot below and running into A Little Taste of Heaven to get their breakfast sandwiches and/or muffins and coffee before they caught the seven-forty-five Metro-North into the city.

His wife, Rose, had started A Little Taste, had built it up from a coffee and Danish joint to a town institution, a tradition his daughters were carrying on. Sean thought about that as he sighed and reached for the remote. Family. When they were good they were very, very good and when they were bad they were, well, a pain in the butt.

Not his daughters or his wife, of course. He had been blessed in that regard. He was referring to the Sinclairs, a distant branch of Rose's family. At least that's what Rose had said. Actually, Rose had put it a little more strongly. She'd called them leeches, always taking and taking, never giving back. Drawing you in, making you think you could fix things when you couldn't. Sometimes, she had said, with people like that, the only thing you could do was cut off contact. Which was what Rose had finally done.

He understood her point of view. There were the two times she'd lent them her car and they'd totaled it. And then there was the money. They were always borrowing it and the amounts kept getting bigger. Someone was always in trouble. Sometimes legally and sometimes not. *Needy* was the word that came to mind. And dysfunctional. The Sinclairs were always involved in some sort of litigation—probably because they never paid their bills. From what he could make out they always figured they'd find some sort of work-around. The problem was that their work-arounds usually made things even worse.

But it was more than that. If there was a smart way to do something and a not-so-smart-skating-on-the-edge-of-legality way to do something, you could trust the Sinclairs to pick the latter way, the way that would land them in trouble—financial or otherwise. Frankly, he'd been glad when Rose had come home and told him they—meaning her and him—weren't speaking to the Sinclairs anymore, because since he was in law enforcement they were always asking him for favors, favors he couldn't grant them.

He still got all steamed up just thinking about the time one of the Sinclairs—he didn't remember whether it was the wife or the ex-wife—had asked him to talk to McCready, the then police chief in Hollingsworth, to see if he could get him to drop a malicious mischief charge against one of her kids. She'd figured since Sean was the chief of police in Longely he would pull some weight in Hollingsworth. The thing she wanted him to take care of wasn't a big deal. He knew that. Just stupid kid stuff. Still, the request had galled him. He wouldn't even do that for his own kids, let alone someone else's.

He took a sip of coffee and thought about the day Rose had come back from Linda Sinclair's house. It had been a long time ago, over twenty years if he remembered correctly. God, she'd been angry. He smiled, recalling her stomping into the house. He shook his head. Her being angry had always made him laugh, which of course made her even madder, and she'd been really worked up that day.

But when he'd asked what was going on, she'd said that he didn't need to know, that this didn't affect him, and he hadn't pressed the issue. He'd had other things on his plate workwise at that moment. Plus, when Rose got something into her head, there was no changing her mind. If she didn't want to talk about it, she wouldn't, and that was that.

He'd figured it out later, though, when he'd heard Rose talking to the bank manager. And it did affect him, although Rose had argued that it didn't. She'd said if she wanted to loan her family twenty thousand dollars from her bank account that was her business, not his. Which would have been fine with him if she hadn't been so upset. Which was why he'd made it his business and gone and talked to Ada's dad. That had been a mistake because he and Jeff had gotten into a shouting match and then they'd traded a couple of punches before they'd come to their senses.

The question now was: Should he or should he not say something about the Sinclairs to his daughters? Bernie was really excited to have discovered a new branch of the family and he could understand that, considering they didn't have much in the way of one. Both he and Rose had been only children.

He didn't want to rain on Bernie's parade, so to speak. However, he knew this wouldn't end well. The Sinclairs were either going to involve his daughters in some scheme, or ask for a loan and not pay them, or do something else along those lines. Sean pressed the remote. The morning news came on, but he wasn't listening. He was too busy deciding what to do. He knew that this was the kind of situation that required tact, which, unfortunately, was a quality he didn't possess.

Chapter 1

Ada Sinclair walked into the Simmons's flat at four in the afternoon on the dot. It was snowing out and a dusting of flakes clung to her hair and shoulders. "Thank you for agreeing to see me," she told the family. She gave a nervous little laugh as Bernie got up from the sofa to greet her. "I know your mother and my family haven't seen each other in a while." Then her voice trailed off.

Bernie's father stopped petting the cat on his lap for a moment. "I don't suppose you have the money your family owes us?" he asked, raising his voice over the clatter coming from their shop below.

"Dad," Bernie hissed, embarrassed.

Sean turned toward his daughter. "Just kidding," he told Bernie, his expression belying his words, before he turned back to Ada. "But it doesn't hurt to ask, right?"

"Yes. Of course," Ada Sinclair stammered. She colored slightly and nodded in the direction of the door she'd just come through. "I'm sorry. I can go if you want."

"Don't be ridiculous," Bernie told Ada, ignoring her father's scowl and holding out her hand for Ada's coat and scarf. "Let me hang these up for you."

"You're sure you want me to stay?" Ada asked her.

"I'm positive," Bernie said. She threw a warning glance in her father's direction as she watched Ada unwind her long red scarf, take off her navy pea coat, and hand both of them to her. "It's exciting to meet new family, or rather, not new, but family I didn't know we had. Right, Dad?"

"Right," Sean told her, the word coming out reluctantly.

"Here, Ada," Libby said, patting the empty space on the sofa next to her. "Come sit."

"This is a nice place. Cozy," Ada reflected as she plopped herself down and rearranged the pleats of her skirt. Bernie could see that her hands were shaking.

"Coffee?" Libby asked, her voice aggressively cheery to compensate for her dad's rudeness. "A cinnamon bun? They just came out of the oven."

Ada smiled in relief. "Thank you. That would be great." She paused. "I just didn't know who else to come to," she confided after a few seconds had passed. "And you're supposed to be really good at this kind of thing."

"You mean catering?" Bernie asked. Ada's call had come out of the blue and she'd agreed to the meeting because she'd sounded desperate on the phone, even though her father had warned against it. That and the fact that she wanted to meet her.

Ada shook her head. "No. The other thing you do." Then she touched her throat and brought her hand down to her lap.

"Oh, you mean the detective thing," Bernie said as she watched the snow outside thicken and swirl. The forecast had called for two to four inches. She hoped it was closer to two. People tended to go straight home instead of stopping at A Taste of Heaven to pick up dinner when the weather was bad.

"I hate New Year's Eve," Ada suddenly said with a vehemence that surprised Libby and Bernie.

"I'm not a big fan, either," Libby replied, not sure where the conversation was going. She smiled sympathetically. "I don't really like big parties."

"My father died on New Year's Eve," Ada declared.

"Well, that would do it," Libby told her, immediately wishing she could retract the words coming out of her mouth. Talk about insensitive, but in her defense, she'd been taken by surprise.

"I figured you knew," Ada said, looking from one sister to the other.

Both Libby and Bernie shook their heads.

"Sorry," Bernie said. "We didn't."

"Your father didn't tell you?"

Libby and Bernie looked at their dad, who looked back at them defiantly.

17

"I forgot," he told them.

"There were articles in the *Sunset Gazette*," Ada said as she twisted the silver and turquoise ring on her forefinger around and around.

"We don't normally see that paper," Libby informed her.

"Ten years ago," Ada continued as if Libby hadn't spoken. "It happened ten years ago in Hollingsworth." Hollingsworth was two towns away. "We lived there then." She tittered. "I don't know why I said that because we still do." She looked at Sean as if she expected him to contradict her. But he didn't. He continued petting Cindy. Ada turned back to Libby and Bernie. "I'm hoping you can help me."

"It's possible," Bernie said. "But I'm not really sure what you want us to do. You didn't say on the phone. You just said something about hiring us for an event."

Ada poured cream into her coffee and stirred in a teaspoon of raw sugar. "It's simple," she said.

Somehow Bernie doubted that. It never was in her experience. But she didn't say that. Instead, as Bernie watched Ada, she thought about what her dad had said about Ada's family and why her mother had severed ties with them.

Okay, she could see why her mother had done what she had done but that had happened a long time ago. It had nothing to do with Ada Sinclair. Bernie had never gone along with the sins of the father visited on the son philosophy. It was so Old Testament.

"So," Bernie said after Ada had taken a sip of her coffee and a bite of her bun, "tell me why you came."

Ada carefully put her mug back on the tray sitting on the coffee table. She took a deep breath and let it out. Libby leaned over and patted Ada's hands. Ada nodded her thanks. "This is hard," she said.

"So is sticking to your word," Sean observed.

Bernie glared at him. "Dad, didn't you say something about taking a nap?"

"Oh, a nap," Sean repeated. "How could I have forgotten?" And he brushed the crumbs off his lap and pushed back his chair. Cindy meowed and jumped down to the floor as he stood up. "If you'll excuse me," Sean said.

The three women watched as Sean stalked into his bedroom, the cat padding after him, and slammed the door behind them. A moment later, the sounds of the radio drifted out of his bedroom.

Ada bit her lip. "Maybe I should go," she suggested. "I don't want to be the cause of a family argument."

Bernie shook her head. "Don't be ridiculous. My dad isn't feeling well," she lied. She pointed to her forehead. "Sinus headache. It makes him cranky."

"Are you sure?" Ada asked.

"I'm positive," Bernie said firmly. She'd just found a whole new family branch and she was damned if she wasn't going to put the best possible foot forward.

"As you were saying," Libby prompted before Ada could say anything else.

Ada took another deep breath and began again. "Like I told you, my father died ten years ago, on New Year's Eve."

"That must have been terrible," Libby sympathized, making up for her previous comment.

"You have no idea." Ada stopped again. She took a sip of coffee to fortify herself and continued. "My father died from an overdose of pain medication—at least that's what the police said—and, coincidentally, his partner, Joel Grover, died in an automobile accident the next day."

"But you didn't think that's what happened?" Bernie surmised from Ada's tone of voice.

"No, I didn't," Ada said. "A couple of days after Mr. Grover died I called the police. I spoke to a Bill McCready." Bernie and Libby exchanged looks. Their dad knew him. Ada cleared her throat and the sisters turned their attention back to her. "I told him that I thought my dad's business partner had poisoned my dad and then killed himself the next day because he felt guilty about what he had done."

Bernie raised an eyebrow.

"See," Ada said, pointing at Bernie.

"See what?" Bernie asked.

"Your expression. McCready thought that too."

"He thought what?" Libby asked, although she had a pretty good idea what Ada was going to say.

"That I was this crazy twelve-year-old girl." Ada frowned at the memory, as she blinked the tears away.

"Well, I could see where your statement would have given him pause," Bernie allowed, trying to be diplomatic. "That's a pretty big leap."

"Did McCready tell you you were crazy?" Libby asked. She remembered him as being a pretty outspoken guy.

"No. He didn't. He humored me, which was worse. I could tell he thought I was bonkers, though." Ada held out her hands, spread her fingers out, and stared at them, seemingly lost in thought.

"What happened next?" Libby asked Ada, trying to keep the impatience out of her voice after another minute had passed without Ada saying anything. She felt guilty about feeling that way, especially since Ada was so obviously upset, but it was getting late and she and Bernie had to be down in the store for the evening rush in half an hour max. Even if the weather was bad and there were fewer people than normal in there,

21

they still had to man the register and help wait on people. Besides, her sister was more invested in this whole new-family thing than she was.

Ada startled and looked up. "Sorry. I was thinking about that night. Nothing's been the same since."

"I bet," Bernie said, leaning forward to show her support.

"McCready," Libby prompted.

"Right." Ada shook her head as if to clear it. "He came over to my house and talked to my mom, Linda." Ada shook her head at the memory. "Boy, let me tell you, she was really, really pissed when she heard what I'd done."

"I can only imagine," Libby murmured.

"So, you didn't tell her what you thought beforehand?" Bernie asked, thinking of the implications of Ada's action. "You went straight to the police?"

"I didn't think she'd believe me." Ada gave a wry smile. "She always told me I had an overactive imagination. My brother and sister were pissed at me, too. They said I'd imagined the whole thing, that I'd called the cops because I always had to be the center of attention. My stepmom was pretty angry as well." Ada sighed. "So were her kids. Everyone said they didn't see anything weird. The psychiatrist my mom took me to said this was my way of coping with the shock of my dad's death."

"So, everyone was there?"

Ada fell silent and fiddled with the buttons on her navy cardigan. Then she said, "My dad insisted on it. He said he had some kind of business announcement to make and he wanted everyone to hear it at the same time."

"Any idea what it was?" Bernie asked, exchanging another look with her sister.

Ada shook her head. "No. He died before he could tell us. But he said it was a surprise."

"A good surprise?" Bernie asked.

Ada held out her hands, palms up. "I have no idea."

Libby finished the last of her coffee. "Do you think what the psychiatrist said was true about your wanting to be the center of attention?" she asked, reverting to the subject Ada had introduced a minute ago.

"No, I don't, although I began to believe that," Ada answered. "Hearing the same thing over and over again will do that to you after a while. Only, here's the thing. My father didn't take pain medicine. Not the serious kind. He took Tylenol once in a while if his back got really bad, but that was it. And as for his partner, something was going on. Two days before he died, I heard my dad and Mr. Grover arguing."

Bernie glanced at the clock on the wall. "What about?"

"I couldn't make out most of the words," Ada

told her. "But at the end they were shouting at each other and I heard Mr. Grover tell my dad he was going to kill him."

"People say that all the time," Libby pointed out. "That doesn't mean your dad's business partner actually did it."

"That's what the psychiatrist said," Ada allowed. "So did the police. And Linda. And my stepmom, Vicky, for that matter. And my brother and sister." Ada shook her head ruefully. "No one believed me. After a while I thought they were right. I figured I'd made the whole thing up so I just forgot about it and went on with my life."

"And then?" Bernie asked, because obviously there was a then.

"And then last week, I was looking up in my mother's attic looking for something and I came across this box. It turned out my dad's diary was in it," Ada told her. "Or maybe not diary. Maybe more like a notebook. Anyway, I read it and I've been turning things over in my head ever since because you know what? As it turns out, I wasn't crazy." There was a note of triumph in her voice. "I wasn't crazy at all." Ada took a sip of coffee, put her cup down, and asked them what she'd come there to ask.

Normally Bernie and Libby would have said no to her request—they didn't work on New Year's Eve—but their dad was going off to a party with his fiancée, and Brandon, Bernie's boyfriend, had to take a coworker's shift at RJ's, while Marvin, after discussing it with Libby, was going to a family wedding.

"What do you think?" Bernie asked her sister.

Libby shrugged. Ada's request sounded simple enough and it seemed to mean a great deal to her.

"Sure. Why not?" Libby replied. It wouldn't hurt to start off the New Year with a good deed, and even though she wasn't as anxious as Bernie to meet a new branch of her family, it couldn't be—despite what her dad said—a bad thing.

"Thank you. Thank you," Ada cried as she got up and hugged them both. "I knew I could count on you guys. You're the best."

Chapter 2

Sean emerged from his bedroom as soon as he heard Ada's footsteps going down the stairs to the street below.

"You were pretty rude," Bernie observed as Sean sat back down in his chair.

"I was direct," Sean countered as the cat jumped back up on his lap. "I'm just telling you, don't come crying to me when things go south."

"How about if they go north?" Bernie asked.

Sean tried to keep from smiling and failed.

"Don't you think you're being a tad dramatic?" Libby asked her dad.

"No, I don't. Not even a little bit." Sean nodded in the direction of the stairs. "That girl is trouble."

"Woman," Bernie corrected.

Sean waved his hand in the air to signal his annoyance. "Call her what you want, the result will be the same."

"I don't know why you're saying that," Bernie objected as she watched Ada Sinclair get into a nondescript Toyota Camry. A moment later, the Camry's headlights came on, a bright beacon in the early dark of the winter afternoon, and the windshield wipers started going from side to side, clearing the accumulated snow off the glass.

Bernie kept watching until Ada had backed out of A Taste of Heaven's parking lot and was halfway down Main Street. Then she turned to her father and said, "She seems like a perfectly nice person to me."

"Appearances can be deceptive," Sean replied.

"It's not like Ada Sinclair wants us to rob a bank," Libby said and she stood up, brushed cinnamon bun crumbs off her lap onto the tray sitting on the table, and began collecting the dirty plates and coffee mugs to take down to the kitchen. "Or murder someone."

"So, what does she want you to do?" Sean asked. "Since you banished me from the room, I don't know." He'd turned on the radio in his room, and that and a slight hearing loss had ensured he wouldn't hear the conversation in the living room. Otherwise, he might have been tempted to come back out and comment on the proceedings.

Bernie explained.

"Ridiculous," Sean muttered when she was done.

Bernie raised an eyebrow. "So what was the skinny about what happened to Ada's dad and her dad's partner?"

"Nothing," Sean replied. "Absolutely nothing."

"I find that difficult to believe," Libby said. "There's always a story behind the story."

"Not in this case," Sean replied. "If there was

a story, it was Ada, whom everyone thought was nuts."

"Truly?" Bernie asked.

"Yes, truly," Sean replied, remembering. "The deaths weren't a big story back then. The *Gazette* ran a couple of articles about them in the papers—you know, unfortunate coincidence, family tragedy, blah, blah, blah—but that was about it," Sean told her. "Don't forget, the deaths you're referring to weren't seen as homicides. They were seen as a hit-and-run and a possible suicide or accidental overdose. Sometimes, to coin your phrase, things are what they are. And anyway," Sean concluded, "the deaths happened in Hollingsworth."

"Hollingsworth is two towns over," Libby objected. "You're talking like this happened in Cali."

Sean shrugged. "To point out the obvious, Hollingsworth was outside of my jurisdiction. And anyway, at the time I had my hands full with the Long Branch bank robbery." He sighed, remembering how that had gone down. Nothing like having the son of one of Longely's most prominent citizens involved. "And as for being a mess"—Sean shook his head—"wait and see, this is going to turn into a first-rate one," he predicted.

"Mr. Optimism," Bernie retorted.

"You don't get it," Sean replied as Cindy butted her head against his hands.

"Then tell me," Bernie said.

"It's simple." Sean began rubbing Cindy's ears. "The Sinclairs are a bad luck family and everyone who gets involved with them catches it."

Libby raised an eyebrow. "Bad luck? Catches it?" Libby repeated.

"Yes," Sean replied, a defensive tone in his voice.

Bernie rolled her eyes. "Seriously? I can't believe those words are coming out of your mouth. Aren't you the one who says everyone makes their own luck?"

Sean got even more defensive. "To be exact, your mother was the one who called the Sinclairs a bad luck family, but in this instance I think she was correct. Call them whatever you want, though. Bad news would work, too."

"Which is quite a bit different," Libby pointed out. "Since when have you become superstitious?" she asked.

"I'm not, but sometimes superstitions are based on reality," Sean replied. "For instance, if you walk under a ladder, you're more likely to get hit on the head with something. Breaking a mirror was considered bad luck because glass was extremely expensive back in the old days and there are bad luck places."

"Which are?" Bernie asked.

"Places where things don't thrive," Sean replied.

Bernie and Libby looked at each other.

Sean pointed at his daughters. "You two are superstitious," he said. "And don't tell me you aren't because I know that you are."

"That's ridiculous," Bernie told him.

"Yes," Libby said. "Where do you get that from?"

"What about the kitchen witch," Sean demanded. He knew he was grasping at straws but he went ahead anyway. "You haven't moved that." His wife had insisted that moving the stuffed doll from its perch on the window behind the sink would bring bad luck.

"That's out of sentiment, not superstition," Bernie told him.

"So you say," Sean said.

"Yes, I do," Bernie retorted.

Sean kept rubbing the tips of Cindy's ears. She began to purr. "Okay. Let me rephrase this. Your mom was family first all the way."

"Agreed," Libby said.

"So, things had to be pretty bad to make her cut ties with the Sinclairs. Totaling cars, not repaying money. These are not people you want to hang around with."

"Yeah, but that stuff happened a long time ago."

"Not that long," Sean pointed out.

"Long enough," Bernie told him. "People change. People change all the time. So do families."

Sean leaned forward. "Not in my experience they don't," he told Bernie. "Okay," he conceded. "Once in a great while, but it's as rare as a blue moon. It may look as if people have changed, but inside, where it counts"—he hit his chest with the flat of his hand—"everything is still the same."

Libby made a face. She'd heard this all the time growing up. "That's you being a cop and thinking the worst of everyone."

"And it's usually true." Sean threw up his hands. "Hey, don't believe me," he said. Then he repeated what he'd told them earlier. "That's fine with me. All I'm saying is that when things go wrong"—he reached for the remote and turned on the television—"and they will, don't come crying to me."

"Don't worry, we wouldn't," Libby informed him.

Bernie picked a strand of cat hair off her black turtleneck sweater and flicked it away. "I think you're making a big deal out of nothing."

Sean shook his head and stared at the screen in front of him. "Have it your way."

For a moment Bernie watched the snow fall and thought that she or Libby was going to have to shovel the sidewalk in front of the shop if it didn't let up soon. And they'd be smart to pick up the chickens they'd ordered from Odel's farm sooner rather than later because the road leading up to it was bad enough in good weather, let alone in this. She sighed. Sometimes she wondered why she'd left California.

She was thinking about her time there when her dad transferred his attention from the program guide appearing on the TV screen—as per usual, there was nothing much he wanted to watch—to his youngest daughter. "Tell me the truth," he said to her. "Are you taking this job on because I'm going to that New Year's Eve party with Michele?" Michele was his fiancée and his daughters disliked her. "Is that why you're doing this?"

"Don't be absurd," Bernie scoffed, although her dad was partially correct in his assessment. If he'd stayed home, she and Libby would have stayed home with him. Not that she was about to tell him that.

"You could come if you want," Sean told her. "You know that."

"I know," Bernie replied as she finished her coffee. What she didn't say was she'd rather do her laundry than go to that party and she guessed that Libby felt the same way. She looked at her sister expecting her to say something, but Libby didn't. Libby was glancing at the clock on the wall and thinking that it was almost five and that it was time to get downstairs. Libby could hear the voices from the shop percolating up through the floor as customers came through the door.

"Pretty confident of yourself vis-à-vis the Sinclairs, aren't you, Dad?" Bernie observed.

Sean nodded. "Yes, I am."

"Are you willing to put your money where your mouth is?" Bernie asked him.

Sean cocked his head. "Are you saying you wanna bet?"

"You got it," Bernie replied.

"What do you have in mind?" Sean asked.

"How about the usual," Libby said.

"A dollar? Let's make it more interesting," Bernie suggested.

Sean put the remote down. He was intrigued. "I'm listening."

"Me too," Libby said.

Bernie told them. "If the Armageddon you're predicting doesn't occur we buy a new sofa." Their present one was twenty years old and Bernie had been after her dad to replace it for the last five years.

"But I love this sofa," Sean protested.

"Aha," Bernie cried. "So, you're not so sure of yourself after all!"

"I am," Sean retorted. "I'll take your bet on the condition that if you lose we go out fishing for the day."

Bernie and Libby both wrinkled their noses. They hated fishing. They hated everything about fishing.

"Afraid you're going to lose," Sean taunted

when Bernie didn't answer immediately. "Want to back out?"

Bernie stood up straighter. "Not at all," she replied. "We'll take the bet, right, Libby?"

"Wait a minute. What are we betting on, exactly?"

"Good point," Bernie said. "Let's define the parameters."

"Things get really messy at the Sinclairs'," Sean answered immediately.

"That's too general. Define messy," Libby challenged.

"All right, then." Sean stroked his chin while he thought. A minute later he said, "The police get involved, Ada throws a major temper tantrum that becomes some sort of physical altercation, she fights with you and/or her family, refuses to pay her bill, or otherwise sabotages the event she's contracted. Is that good enough?"

Bernie nodded and looked at Libby.

"Works for me," Libby said.

"Okay," Sean said as he and his daughters shook hands. "It's a deal." Then he laughed. "I'm going to enjoy watching you girls bait those hooks."

"And Libby and I are going to enjoy furniture shopping," Bernie threw back at him.

"Not going to happen," Sean told Bernie, picking up the remote and turning up the sound on the TV. As he did he thought about the old saying about a leopard not being able to change its spots. He guessed his daughters would just have to find that out the hard way. Heaven only knows, he'd done everything in his power to warn them.

Chapter 3

Two weeks later

It was a clear, windless night when Bernie and Libby set out for Ada Sinclair's house. They'd warmed up the van first, because Mathilda didn't like it when the temperature hovered in the single digits. Bernie and Libby didn't like it, either, but no one was warming them up—not tonight, anyway.

"At least it's not snowing out," Libby observed, rubbing her hands together to get her circulation going. She had gloves on, but it didn't seem to matter. The tips of her fingers were burning from the cold.

"Not yet anyway," Bernie replied, pointing to the sky. A sliver of a moon was half hidden behind one of the clouds drifting in.

"I thought it didn't snow when it got this cold," Libby said as she watched her breath make clouds in the air.

"Evidently, you thought wrong," her sister replied. The weatherman had predicted another four to six inches of snow later this evening.

"Maybe the weatherman is mistaken," Libby said.

Bernie sighed. "Maybe." But she doubted it. Winter had officially just started and she was ready for it to be over. "Hopefully, we'll make it back before the snow starts." Mathilda didn't do well in the snow, even with snow tires, which was why they carried bags of cat litter in the back of the van this time of year. "At least we don't have to get up early tomorrow morning," Bernie said, trying to look on the bright side.

Libby grunted as she stowed the last of the cartons of groceries into the van and shut the door. The shop had closed at two today—a tradition their mother had started and they'd carried on—and wouldn't reopen until the third of January. "I hate driving on New Year's Eve," Libby grumbled as she walked around to the driver's side. "You never know who's going to be out on the road." Which was why they'd started their tradition of staying in.

Bernie got into the van's passenger side and fastened her seat belt. "Personally, I'm looking forward to this. We're going to meet a side of the family we didn't know we had. How exciting is that?"

"Maybe we don't want to meet them," Libby retorted, thinking about her father's grimaces whenever the Sinclair name had come up. What did he know that she and her sister didn't? "Maybe Mom was right when she cut off contact. She usually was."

"But she could hold a grudge like no one's business," Bernie reminded her sister.

"That's true," Libby conceded, thinking back to the battle with their next-door neighbor over a missing garbage can cover.

"Anyway, Ada did pay us the first third of the bill," Bernie pointed out.

"Yeah. Because she didn't have money for the half we usually require," Libby observed. "That doesn't exactly inspire a feeling of confidence."

"She explained why," Bernie protested. "She just went a little overboard with Christmas this year. Everyone does that."

"True," Libby said, thinking of the present she'd bought for Marvin. Well, for her too. Two tickets to *Hamilton*.

"We should do one of those DNA things," Bernie suggested. "Maybe there are other family members out there we don't know about."

Libby grunted.

"Don't you want to find out?" Bernie asked.

"Not really," Libby replied.

"Why not?" Bernie demanded.

"Because I don't want my DNA on record."

"Why ever not?"

"Because it can be used for other purposes," Libby said as she put Mathilda into reverse and backed out of A Taste of Heaven's parking lot. This morning the lot had been jammed with people picking up last minute orders, but now theirs was the only vehicle in it. "Like facial recognition."

"You're paranoid," Bernie told Libby as her sister maneuvered Mathilda around the pothole near the curb and into the street. "I'd still like to know if there's any other family out there." Bernie stuck her hands under her armpits to warm them up. "And despite what you and Dad say I'm still looking forward to meeting the Sinclairs." Then she looked at the display in A Taste of Heaven's window. They'd done a good job this year. They'd gone with a Rudolph the Red-Nosed Reindeer motif only they'd substituted stuffed puppies for reindeer and loaded the sled with cookies and candies and cakes.

"You know the old saying about letting sleeping dogs lie?" Libby said. "Maybe that should apply in this case. Let's keep things simple. For a change. Let's just do our job and leave."

Bernie leaned over and turned on the radio. "That's what I'm planning, but you gotta admit simple is boring."

"Not to me, it isn't," Libby retorted. "I like simple. I like boring. In fact, I crave them, even revel in them," she replied, looking at her watch. It was five-twenty. They were due at 1302 Danbury Circle South at five forty-five. They had more than enough time to get there.

"Why?" Bernie demanded.

"Because I think we've had enough excitement

39

in our lives up till now," Libby told her sister. "If I never see another dead body it'll be fine with me," she declared, something Bernie couldn't argue with, after which Libby changed the topic of conversation to the chocolate cherry bread she was thinking of making for Valentine's Day. She was trying to decide whether to make the dough out of white flour, whole-wheat flour, or a combination of both.

The sisters were still debating the merits of half wheat/half white flour when they arrived at Ada Sinclair's. They were earlier than expected. Route 48 was usually busy, but not tonight. Tonight, the road had been an empty ribbon of black asphalt paralleling the Hudson River. Except for the gas stations, all the shops Libby and Bernie drove by in Longely and Greenwood were closed for the evening. People were either home or they'd gotten where they were going. They'd passed a total of five cars in the last fifteen minutes. Libby knew because she'd counted them.

"People tend to celebrate at home when it's going to be minus fifteen degrees out," Libby observed.

"Unless they're going out later," Bernie noted.

"Would you? I wouldn't. That's for sure."

"I would when I was eighteen," Bernie told her, suddenly feeling old. When had this happened? When had she decided that staying in was preferable to going out? She thought about when she was eighteen and had gone down to Times Square to see the ball drop with her girlfriends and thousands of random strangers. You couldn't pay her enough to do that now, even if the temperature was warmer.

Libby bit at her fingernail while she stopped at a red light. "I just hope Mathilda starts back up when it's time to go home," she said as the light changed to green.

"She will," Bernie replied with more confidence than she felt as they entered the town of Hollingsworth.

At one time, the town had been the center of a large farming community that had supplied the markets down in New York City with fruits, vegetables, and dairy, but those days were long gone. Now Hollingsworth supplied worker bees to the office buildings in Manhattan. In the last fifty years, the farms had been plowed under, the apple orchards had been ripped up, and four-bedroom, two-bathroom houses had supplanted them. The town had become a bedroom community for The Big Apple, one of many Hudson Valley communities to undergo that metamorphosis. It made Bernie sad. Farmland lost was hard to regain.

Hollingsworth was a little wealthier than Longely, but not by much. The school system was ranked the same, the housing stock was a little bit pricier, and their marina was a little fancier, but other than that the two towns were similar, the only big difference being that Hollingsworth was two stops closer to New York City on the Metro-North and had a larger parking lot adjacent to their train station.

Bernie consulted her phone. Her GPS showed that Danbury Circle South was located on the outskirts of the town, two blocks away from the town's elementary school and half a mile away from a park named Ruby's Nature Walk, a park that had a small waterfall. They were almost at the Sinclairs and she could hardly wait.

Chapter 4

Libby stopped at another red light. She felt silly sitting there, the only vehicle in the intersection. For a moment, she was tempted to go through the light, but then she reconsidered. With her luck, a car would probably come barreling through and T-bone her. Five minutes later, Bernie pointed to a large, imposing Tudor in the middle of the block. Bookended by two smaller ranches, one of whose driveway was empty and whose lights were off, the Tudor stuck out like the proverbial sore thumb.

"Here we are," Bernie announced.

Libby slowed down. "I bet this isn't Ada's house," she surmised as she drove up the driveway. She went by a large, gnarled oak tree in the middle of the lawn. Its bare branches, decorated with Christmas lights, reached out to a sky that was becoming cloudier by the minute.

"I bet you're right," Bernie agreed as vague alarm bells went off in the back of her head. "I bet it's her mom's." Girls Ada's age didn't own houses like this. They didn't want them, and even if they did they usually couldn't afford them. Bernie just hoped there wasn't going to be a problem. She and Libby had talked to Ada about the oven and the number of burners they'd need because they assumed she owned the house. What did her dad always say about assuming?

Libby shut off Mathilda's engine and turned toward her sister. "Are you nervous?"

"A little," Bernie admitted. "I mean it's not every day you meet a branch of your family you never knew about."

"The black sheep branch," Libby said.

"I suppose that's true," Bernie allowed.

"What if they don't want to talk to us?"

"It'll be fine," Bernie told her, disregarding the flutter in the pit of her stomach. "Ada told me she squared it away with her family." She looked at her watch. Time to get going. "I'll see where Ada wants us to unload," she said to Libby as she slipped off her seat belt, opened the van door, and stepped outside. The wind had picked up as she started up the brick path to the house and she could smell the river. She walked carefully, because when she looked down she saw that the bricks were covered with a thin coating of ice, the result of the weather alternating between freezing and thawing for the past week.

Hopefully, we can bring our supplies in through the garage, Bernie thought as she picked her way up the path, imagining how bad it would be if she or Libby fell and dropped one of the cartons they were carrying and the lentil soup spilled or the chocolate ganache roll got smooshed. She held on to the railing as she climbed the three stairs

44

that led to the front door. Then she rang the bell. A moment later, the door was opened by an older, heavier set version of Ada. Bernie assumed the woman was Ada's mother.

"I thought you should know I wasn't in favor of this when Ada told me what she'd done," she announced before Bernie could get a hello out. The woman pressed her lips together and adjusted her glasses. They were black and too large for her face. "Not at all."

So much for Ada's assurances about the family being down with their showing up, Bernie thought.

The woman adjusted her glasses. "We were deeply, deeply hurt by your mother's actions. Of course, you were young when it happened," she allowed. "Very young."

"Yes, we were," Bernie agreed. She had no idea of the time frame the woman was talking about.

"But you can imagine my shock when I heard what Ada had done."

"Do you want us to leave?" Bernie asked. Maybe she and her sister would be spending New Year's Eve at home after all.

The woman in the doorway ignored Bernie's question and continued with what she'd been saying. "The rest of the family wasn't happy either when they heard. They wanted to cancel. I did too at first, but then we all decided that was ridiculous. We're all adults, right? And this happened a long time ago. We're just going to pretend you're a caterer. Agreed?"

"We are caterers," Bernie said.

"I have to say your mother was a good cook, whatever her other failings."

"Excuse me," Bernie said. She could feel her cheeks start to redden.

The woman raised her hand in the air. "I'm sorry. That came out wrong."

"It certainly did," Bernie agreed.

"What I meant to say was that hopefully you've inherited her ability."

"I like to think my sister and I have," Bernie told her.

The woman sighed. "I suppose you're serving lentil soup," she continued, frowning.

Bernie nodded. "Ada . . ."

"Asked you to," the woman said, finishing Bernie's sentence for her. "I hate lentil soup," she told Bernie. "It's such a stupid idea. As if eating that is going to mean you're going to have a prosperous New Year. I suppose you put sausage in it."

Bernie shook her head. "I made it with coconut milk and lemongrass."

"That should be a little better," the woman conceded, brightening. A smile flitted across her face and died. "You know this is only going to open up old wounds," she stated. "No amount of good cooking is going to make up for that.

46

Especially now. Especially when we're finally on the verge of success."

Bernie wanted to say that didn't make any sense. She wanted to say in that case the family should be in a celebratory mood. But she didn't. Instead she watched Ada's mother sigh a long dramatic sigh, her breath visible in the night air.

"But that's my daughter for you," Linda Sinclair continued. "Snatching defeat out of the jaws of victory. Every. Single. Time. I understand she's had a hard time, but who hasn't?"

Bernie started to reply, but before she could Ada's mother added, "I don't know why I'm telling you this. I'm sure you couldn't care less." Then she turned toward the hallway. "They're here!" she yelled up the stairs before turning back to Bernie. "She'll be down in a moment," she announced, after which she added, "You're going to have to move your van. It can't stay in the driveway. Not with everyone coming." Then she closed the door in Bernie's face. The thud echoed in the night.

Maybe Dad wasn't wrong after all, Bernie thought as she turned to Libby and made a palms-up gesture. A moment later, the door swung open again and Ada stood in the entranceway. She was wearing Hello Kitty pajama bottoms, a black hoodie, and her hair was gelled into spikes—not a good look in Bernie's humble opinion, although it seemed to be a trend

47

these days, a trend Bernie hoped would disappear sooner rather than later.

"Sorry about that," Ada said to her. Bernie decided she looked about ten. "Linda is in the middle of a hissy fit, but she'll get over it."

"You call your mother by her first name?" Bernie asked as Libby joined her sister. She'd gotten tired of waiting in the van.

Ada nodded. "I've just always called her that," she explained even though Bernie hadn't asked for an explanation, although she had been curious. "That's weird, right?"

"Well, kinda," Bernie began, but Ada interrupted her.

"I guess I should have told her about this sooner," she said, hugging herself as the cold air nibbled at her fingers and toes.

"Probably would have been a good idea," Bernie allowed. "When did you tell her?"

Ada put up three fingers. "Three days ago. I don't see why she's so pissed, though," Ada went on. "I mean I'm doing her a favor. She doesn't have to do the cooking."

"I don't think that's what she's upset about," Bernie said.

Ada frowned and started fiddling with the zipper on her hoodie. "I mean who cares what happened umpteen million years ago."

Bernie didn't make the obvious comment about Ada having hired her and her sister because of something that had happened ten years ago. Instead she said, "Maybe you should have told her about us sooner."

Ada grimaced. "If I had, she would have told me not to do it."

"You operate under the better to ask forgiveness than permission rule?" Bernie asked. It was a motto she was familiar with.

Ada smiled. "Exactly," she said.

"Me too," Bernie said.

"Once Linda gets an idea in her head, that's it," Ada said.

"Sounds as if our moms have a lot in common," Libby observed, tucking her hands underneath her armpits to warm them up. "Ironic, isn't it," she said as Ada hugged herself tighter and stamped her feet.

"It's cold out there," she complained. Then she gestured to Bernie and Libby. "Come in." Ada had raised her voice. Bernie thought it was to make sure that her mom heard they were coming in the house. "I'll show you where the kitchen is."

"Great," Libby said, putting on her best business smile as Ada laid out the schedule for the evening. She wanted the big reveal, as she called it, to happen right after Libby and Bernie served dessert.

"And then I want you to stay in the room and watch everyone's reactions," Ada reminded them.

Libby and Bernie both nodded.

"We haven't forgotten," Libby said.

"Don't worry, we'll be there," Bernie told her.

"Especially my stepmother's," Ada said.

"What does she look like?" Bernie asked.

Ada rolled her eyes. "She's the young blonde with the big boobs and the tight dress. My dad's trophy wife."

"Who else will be here?" Bernie inquired, figuring it would be good to have names she could put faces and attach reactions to.

Ada gave the sisters thumbnail sketches of all the guests. "And especially keep an eye on my uncle. He's the fat one with the big nose," she added as she led Bernie and Libby through the house into the kitchen and then showed them how to go out through the garage. "That way," Ada explained, "you don't have to use the outside steps."

"It sounds as if Ada isn't a big fan of her family," Bernie observed after Ada had gone back into the house to get dressed and she and her sister were heading toward the van.

"It does, doesn't it," Libby noted as she reached Mathilda and opened the rear doors.

"Like Mom," Bernie observed.

For a moment, Libby saw herself baiting a fishing hook. "You shouldn't have made that bet with Dad."

"You agreed."

"Only because I thought you'd be pissed at me if I didn't."

"It's probably just a mother/daughter thing," Bernie reassured her sister as she watched a few snowflakes drift down to the ground. It looked as if the storm was about to arrive.

"Do you really believe that?" Libby asked Bernie.

"Absolutely," Bernie lied. Even though she wasn't going to admit it to Libby, Bernie was having second thoughts about the bet. She sighed. Oh well, it was too late now.

"I guess we'll find out," Libby said as she started lugging the first carton of supplies into the kitchen.

Chapter 5

An hour into the dinner Bernie could feel the tension she had been holding in her neck and shoulders flow out of her body. Contrary to what she had been expecting, everyone was behaving themselves. Between her dad and Ada, she'd half envisaged flying fists and overturned furniture. But that was ridiculous. It just showed what happened when you allowed people's ideas to get into your head.

Everyone had arrived on time, between eight and eight-thirty, brushing snowflakes off their coats as they hurried inside to get away from the wind. Everyone, to Bernie's and Libby's eyes, seemed polite if not warm to each other. Bernie was thinking about that as she got ready to serve another round of Kirs when Ada's aunt, Sheryl, stepped into the kitchen.

"I hope I'm not interrupting anything," she said, introducing herself, not that she needed to. Ada's description had been on point. Dowdy.

"Not at all," Libby said.

Sheryl smiled and walked into the room and looked around as she fingered the diamond pendant that was hanging around her neck. Looking at her, Bernie reflected that her long, prematurely gray hair fastened back with a large clip, her lack of makeup, and her ill-fitting dark brown dress made her look older than she was.

"Can we get you anything?" Bernie asked.

Sheryl shook her head. "I just wanted to tell both of you that I'm glad you're here."

"Linda certainly doesn't agree with that sentiment," Bernie observed, thinking back to the speech Ada's mother had made when she'd answered the door. "She'd be much happier if we weren't."

Sheryl gave a regretful shake of her head. "Some people can never let go of anything," she said, "and, unfortunately, my sister and some other members of my family fall into that camp."

Bernie stopped pouring the crème de cassis into the wine glasses and directed all her attention at Sheryl. "My mother was like that, too," she observed.

"Sometimes," Sheryl replied, "you just have to let things go. Forgive and forget. That's my motto. You can always replace money. You know I called Rose." Sheryl sighed and shook her head. "She wouldn't talk to me. She said that Linda had to apologize to her directly."

"Which she wouldn't do," Libby guessed.

"You got that right," Sheryl said. "Anyway, enough of this. I know you're both busy, so I'm going to clear out and let you two work. I just wanted to pop in and say hello and tell you how glad I am that you're here."

"Thanks. We appreciate it," Bernie told her.

"That was nice of her," Libby commented after Sheryl left.

"It was, wasn't it," Bernie agreed as she finished pouring the crème de cassis and began adding the white wine.

Five minutes later, Bernie and Libby carried the drinks into the living room and offered them to the guests. At nine, Bernie called everyone into the dining room. At five minutes after nine, Libby and Bernie began service. They filled everyone's wine glasses with a Riesling—Ada's choice—then served the first course, lentil soup, in small blue bowls. Everyone seemed to enjoy it and commented on the coconut and ginger seasoning. Ada Sinclair's mom even went so far as to volunteer that the lentil soup was the best lentil soup she'd ever eaten, although Libby wasn't sure if that was damning the soup with faint praise or not.

Next, the sisters refilled the wine glasses and served the second course, salads composed of little gem lettuces, glazed walnuts, and thin slices of ripe pear dressed in walnut oil and lemon juice, after which came the third course, chicken Kiev filled with chive butter, wild rice, and glazed baby carrots.

When everyone was done eating, Bernie and Libby cleared the table. Libby rinsed the dishes and packed them away—she liked to clean up as they went; it made leaving quicker—while Bernie made the coffee, both decaf and regular, and started plating the dessert, a chocolate sponge roll filled with a mocha ganache and frosted with chocolate icing. It was both light and rich and looked more complicated to make than it was.

The slices were sitting on top of crisscrossed salted caramel ribbons and Bernie thought the presentation looked festive, if she did say so herself. The recipe was their mom's, an oldie but goodie. In fact, Libby reflected, you could say that about the whole menu. But classics were classics for a reason. They endured because they worked on multiple levels.

"So far, so good," Bernie observed as she finished plating the last slice.

"Unless something happens when Ada reads whatever she's going to read," Libby pointed out as she began pouring the coffee. Three decafs and six fully leaded.

"Nothing is going to happen," Bernie assured her. "What do you think? Should we get a sectional? Something in leather?"

"Leather would be nice," Libby agreed. "But what about the cat?"

"We'll put a blanket over the cushions," Bernie told her. "Maybe something tobacco colored? We could get Dad a new chair while we're at it," she mused. "Something a little . . . nicer. A little more . . . contemporary. Something that takes up a little less space."

Libby snorted. "Good luck with that. If Dad had his way, he'd be buried in that chair."

"True," Bernie conceded, remembering the fights her parents had had about it. Her mother had hated that La-Z-Boy recliner from the moment her dad had bought it at a garage sale and lugged it up the stairs. "It doesn't even recline anymore!"

"Unfortunately, Dad doesn't seem to care." Libby nodded toward the dining room. It was time to take in the coffee and dessert.

Again, everything went as planned. Everyone at the table commented favorably on the chocolate roll and Ada's brother and sister asked for seconds, which, as it so happened, the sisters had. Bernie was in the process of refilling the coffee cups for the second time when Ada nodded to her and mouthed the word *now*. Bernie nodded back; served the last cup of coffee to Ada's uncle, Henry; put the coffeepot on top of the trivet sitting on the sideboard; and signaled to Libby that the time had come.

Chapter 6

Here we go, Libby thought as she made a thumbs-up gesture and leaned against the far dining room wall, crossing her arms over her chest. The show was about to begin. She noted that if anyone at the table thought it was odd that the sisters remained in the room, they didn't indicate it. Instead they ignored them and went on eating and drinking.

A moment later, Ada cleared her throat. No one paid any attention. Libby had a feeling that no one in the family usually paid attention to Ada. She cleared her throat again, pushed her chair back, and stood up.

"I have something to say," Ada announced.

This time everyone stopped eating and turned to her.

Ada leaned forward and looked everyone in the eye. Then she began to speak. "Ten years ago to the day my dad died."

Vicky Sinclair, Ada's stepmother, frowned and let out a loud groan. "Please, let's not do this again," she told Ada.

Ada's mom put down her fork and nodded. "Vicky, for once, I agree with you."

"Thank you, Linda." Vicky said. She gave her a wintry smile and started playing with her diamond ring.

"Do what?" Ada demanded.

"Say what you were going to say," Vicky said.

"How do you know what I was going to say?" Ada asked, a truculent tone in her voice.

Ada's stepmother stopped playing with her ring and touched her blond hair. Her frown deepened. "It's obvious, isn't it," she told her. "You always bring the same thing up."

Marty Grover, Joel Grover's son, put down his napkin. "Please, Ada. Remember, you promised not to bring this up again after the last time. You're not the only one that suffered a loss."

"We all have," Vicky said. She dabbed at her eyes. "But we have to go on with our lives instead of dwell in the past. It's what your father would have wanted."

"You don't know what my father would have wanted," Ada snapped.

This is where everything goes south, Bernie thought as Ada's aunt, Sheryl, patted Ada's hand and told her everyone was going to be fine.

Ada looked down at her, then looked back up and said, "I have new information."

Ada's mom groaned and shook her head in a gesture of disbelief. "After ten years? Come on."

"I'll tell you what would be new," Ada's stepmother, Vicky, chimed in. "What would be new, Ada, is you not talking about this."

"You're going to want to hear what I have to

say," Ada replied. Bernie and Libby noted that her voice was beginning to rise.

Ada's uncle, Henry, swallowed a sip of coffee, carefully rested his cup on his saucer, and jumped into the conversation. "Ada, please," he said, reaching out to her. "Let's not rehash this now. There's nothing to be gained. We all agree bad things happened. We all agree everyone said things they shouldn't have said, but that's in the past. Now, let's finish our dinner so we can watch the ball drop and celebrate what's going to be a truly great new year."

Ada stuck her jaw out. "Fine, after I make my announcement."

Sheryl put her hand on her husband's arm before he could reply. "Let her talk, Henry. She deserves her chance. Isn't that right, everyone?" Then she turned to Ada. "Go ahead, dear," Ada's aunt instructed. "Say what you wanted to say."

"Thank you," Ada replied, looking around at everyone sitting at the table. Then she cleared her throat and began. "As I was saying, my dad died ten years ago today." She paused for a moment. This time no one interrupted. "As you all know, back then I didn't think my dad died from a pill overdose. I thought he had been poisoned."

Ada's stepsister, Erin, groaned. "Oh, God," she said. "Here we go again. Ada, tell me you haven't contacted the police."

Marty put down the spoon he'd been fiddling

with and said, "It wouldn't matter if she had, Erin. After all, they didn't pay any attention to her trying to drag my dad's name through the mud the last time. Why would they this time?"

Ada's mother tsk-tsked. "Ada, you have to let this go," Linda told her daughter. "This obsession of yours isn't healthy. You know what happened the last time."

Ada's brother and sister didn't say anything. They exchanged glances and rolled their eyes.

"I found something new," Ada declared as she reached into her skirt pocket, pulled out a small black and white notebook like the kind you buy in a drugstore, and waved it in front of everyone. "I found this in a box in the attic. Evidently, my dad kept a journal."

"Hardly a journal," Ada's mother corrected her. "More like a bunch of notes to help him remember stuff. An aide-mémoire, if you will."

"There are some interesting things in this book," Ada said, ignoring her mother's comment. "Things you all need to hear."

"Such as?" Ada's sister Rachel challenged.

Ada's brother, Rick, moved his plate back and began tapping out a rhythm on the dining room table with his fingers. "You always have to be the center of attention, don't you," he remarked. "You are beyond predictable."

Ada glared at him and kept on talking. "Things that confirm what I was saying about what happened to my dad and possibly Marty's dad not being an accident."

"Leave my dad out of this," Marty Grover growled as he threw his napkin on the table and started to get up. "If you don't, I'm out of here."

Ada turned to face him. "Listen, I'm sorry for what I did," Ada told him. "I was wrong."

"That's a new one," Ada's brother muttered as Ada pointed to the black and white notebook.

"I think your dad was a victim, too, Marty."

Marty sat back down. "Go on. I'm listening."

"Don't encourage her," Ada's stepbrother, Lance, told Marty.

Marty turned to face him. "Do you mind? I want to hear what she has to say."

"Why?" Rick replied. "It's all going to be nonsense. A total time suck."

Marty crossed his arms over his chest. "That may be, but I still want to hear it anyway."

"Don't you get it, Marty?" Ada's brother said. "My sister is nuts. Everything she says is nuts."

"Yeah," Ada's sister said. "She needs to get back on her meds big-time."

Ada glowered at Rachel and Rick. "I find it interesting that you don't want to hear what I have to say."

"That," Rick replied, "is because I've heard it all before."

"Multiple times," Rachel added.

Ada's mother pushed her plate away and looked

61

at Ada with distaste. "Why do you always have to do this?" she asked her.

"Do what?" Ada demanded. "I'm trying to . . ."

"You're trying to make a scene," Ada's mom said. "You're trying to cause trouble. As per usual."

Bernie sighed. She was thinking that maybe they wouldn't be getting that sofa after all when Peggy Graceson, Ada's neighbor, leaned over and patted Ada's arm.

"It's okay," she told her. "Anniversaries are hard. We understand."

Ada glared at her, but Peggy continued anyway. "This is hard for all of us. But meeting here like this . . . well, it's like a memorial to the fallen."

"That's funny coming from her," Vicky muttered as Ada shook off Peggy's hand and began to talk again.

"I thought everyone would want to hear. . . ."

"Ada, I know I don't and I'm sure I'm speaking for everyone else when I say that," Vicky snapped. "For heaven's sake, think about someone other than yourself for a change. Think about what this endless rehashing does to us. To me. Finding your dad . . ." Vicky choked back a sob and ostentatiously wiped away a tear that was trickling down her cheek with the back of her hand.

"You need to listen to me!" Ada yelled, her face growing red with frustration. "All of you need to shut up and listen to me!"

An uneasy silence settled over the room. Everyone exchanged glances. After a moment, Ada's uncle spoke.

"Read it then," he told Ada, "and get it over with so we can get on with the celebration."

"Happy to," Ada said, biting off each word as she opened the notebook to one of the passages she'd previously marked and began to read out loud. "You see what I mean?" Ada asked five minutes later when she had finished.

Bernie and Libby watched everyone at the table exchange more looks with each other. Ada's stepmother shook her head.

"No. I'm sorry, but I don't. I think that as per usual you're making something out of nothing. Those are my late husband's notes, nothing more." Vicky pushed a strand of blond hair behind her ear with a perfectly manicured finger. "I think that perhaps your siblings are right. Perhaps it's time for you to go back to your therapist."

Ada's mother turned to Ada's stepmother. "Frankly, I think that's for me to say, not you," Linda retorted.

Ada's stepmother shrugged. "Have it your way, Linda, but I don't think that ignoring Ada's . . . shall we say . . . disruptive tendencies . . . is doing her any good. Remember what happened the last time."

Bernie was wondering what *had* happened the

last time when Linda glowered at Vicky and said, "That was a fluke. . . ."

Vicky smiled sweetly. "If that's what we're calling it."

Linda shook a finger at Vicky. "Don't you dare blame my daughter. Without you it wouldn't have happened. And as for disruptive," Linda continued without pausing for a breath, "highly imaginative, yes, but disruptive, no. After all, she isn't the one who broke our family up."

Henry jumped into the conversation. "This again, Linda?" he cried.

Linda waved her hand in the air. "I'm sorry, Henry. You're right. What's the point? What's done is done. Name-calling doesn't help. Sorry, Vicky." And she looked at her watch. "It's almost midnight," she announced. "Time to go into the other room and greet the new year."

"Yes, let's," Ada's stepmother agreed. "I'm sorry if I overstepped," she told Ada's mother, although at the time Bernie and Libby didn't think she looked one bit contrite.

Chairs scraped against the floor as everyone followed Linda's request. The guests filed into the living room as Bernie and Libby began clearing the table.

"That was an interesting conversation," Bernie noted as she began picking up the plates.

"Wasn't it, though," Libby agreed. "I wonder what all that business with Ada was about?"

Bernie shook her head. She didn't know and at this moment she didn't care. All they had to do was serve the champagne and strawberries and they were out of there.

"We're almost home free," Libby noted as she gathered up the rest of the plates. Then she and Bernie began walking down the hallway into the kitchen. After all, she reasoned, the most combustible part of the evening was behind them.

"I don't know why dad likes fishing so much," Bernie said, entering the kitchen and depositing the pile of dishes by the sink. The whole baiting the hook thing was too gross, she reflected. Now fly fishing, on the other hand, was a whole different story. You used lures for one thing, the clothes were pretty snazzy, and since casting required real skill, the odds of her catching anything were zero to none. Unfortunately, her dad wasn't into that.

"Me either," Libby agreed. "For a moment there, I thought Vicky and Linda were going to come to blows," she observed as she put her plates next to Bernie's—they still had to wash them, dry them, and put them back in their covers.

Bernie laughed. "They weren't even close."

"They were getting there," Libby said.

"Getting there doesn't count," Bernie told her.

"Count for what?" Ada asked. She was standing at the entrance to the kitchen.

Both Bernie and Libby jumped and whirled around. Libby dropped the sponge she'd been holding.

"You startled me," Libby told Ada as she retrieved it.

"What were you two talking about?" Ada asked again. "What doesn't count?"

Good question, Bernie thought as she uttered the first thing that popped into her head. "Not doing something." Then she made up a story to go with what she'd just said. "We're catering an event for the summer solstice, but the group we're catering it for hasn't given us their menu yet. I know it's six months away and six months seems like a long time, but it's not." Bernie frowned. "They keep on telling us they're going to get to it, but getting to it doesn't count because we still don't know what we're doing."

"I've always wanted to go to a summer solstice party," Ada said wistfully.

"Then I'll make sure you're invited," Libby said, feeling guilty about the lie she was telling. But she noted as she said it that Ada seemed to have calmed down since the scene in the dining room. Her face had lost its flush and her body was no longer rigid with anger. So maybe there wouldn't be any fireworks after all. Now, there was a happy thought.

Chapter 7

Bernie and Libby could hear the low hum of conversation coming from the living room as Ada stepped into the kitchen. Bernie noticed she was still clutching the notebook she'd read out of.

"I can't believe how neat this place is," she commented, looking around the room.

Bernie laughed. "We try to keep on top of things," she told Ada as she put the dessert plates in the sink and began to run the water. She intended to soak them for a few minutes before she washed and dried them. "Makes cleanup a lot faster."

"And easier," Libby added.

"I can't seem to do that," Ada lamented. She sighed. "Linda says I'm a slob." Just mentioning her mother's name brought a flush back to Ada's cheeks and she started talking about the scene in the dining room.

"See what I mean about the way everyone acts?" Ada said to Bernie and Libby, turning to face one sister and then the other as she gripped the notebook tighter. "If that isn't a tip-off, I don't know what is. What? You don't think so?" she demanded when neither sister immediately answered.

"Well . . ." Bernie replied, taking three bottles

of California champagne out of the fridge and handing them to her sister while she tried to frame a tactful response to Ada's question. She didn't want to tell Ada what she was really thinking—that this was a case of Ada crying wolf—if she could avoid it, because she was sure Ada wouldn't be happy when she heard what she had to say and Bernie wanted to calm the waters instead of roiling them.

Ada held the notebook up. "There's proof positive in here that someone killed my dad and his partner and no one cares! No one wants to listen. They don't want anyone to upset their stupid business deals."

"Maybe there's another explanation," Libby was suggesting in the face of her younger sister's silence when Peggy, Ada Sinclair's neighbor, waved to her from the hallway.

Peggy paused for a moment. "Lovely dinner," she told Libby.

Libby smiled her appreciation. "Thanks. Can I help you with anything?" she inquired.

Peggy shook her head. "No thanks. I'm just getting the bag with the Christmas crackers out of the hall closet."

Bernie wrinkled her forehead. "Christmas crackers?" she repeated, puzzled. She had no idea what Peggy was talking about.

"Sometimes known as Christmas poppers," Peggy replied, using the more common name.

"Oh, those." Bernie laughed. She knew what they were now. She'd seen them when she'd been in Britain for her junior year abroad. If she remembered rightly, they were small segmented cardboard tubes wrapped in decorative paper and filled with a little prize or a piece of candy or a handful of confetti, and they made a popping sound when you pulled the two ends apart, hence the name. "I thought that was a British Christmas Eve tradition along with a roasted goose and plum pudding."

Peggy smiled. "Not to mention the hard sauce and the Christmas crowns and Charles Dickens." She readjusted her bra strap, which was peeking out from under her peasant blouse. "You're right about Christmas crackers being a British tradition, but we open them here at midnight on New Year's Eve. I think it started with Linda, Ada's mom," Peggy explained before she continued down the hall.

"Peggy is wrong," Ada said as she and Libby heard the hall closet door open, the rustle of coats, then the thud of the closet door closing. "My dad was the one who started the tradition," Ada continued. Her voice wobbled a little when she mentioned her dad. "He said it reminded him of home."

"He was British?" Bernie asked.

"He came over when he was six," Ada replied. "We've kept the tradition going in his honor."

"Sounds like a nice thing to do," Libby told her.

"It is," Ada assured her. "New Year's Eve wouldn't be New Year's Eve without them."

A moment later, Peggy waved as she passed by them again, a small shopping bag in hand. Libby waved back. Then she turned to Ada. "Was Peggy here the night your dad died?" Libby asked out of curiosity.

Ada nodded. "I already told you," she said impatiently. "Everyone here was."

"But she's not family," Bernie said, seeking clarification.

"Neither is Marty. But Peggy has worked in the business for like forever," Ada explained, her voice rising a notch. She ran a finger around the edge of the notebook. "Anyway, for my dad, family and business were one and the same."

"That's certainly true for us," Libby noted. "Family businesses," she paused for a moment, "can have their own problems."

Ada nodded vigorously. "You can say that again. I liked our New Year's Eves when Dad was alive. But now, they're the same, only they're not."

"I would have thought no one would have wanted to do this again . . . considering," Bernie noted.

"Mom wanted to. And my uncle. They said it helped keep my dad's memory alive. So, sometimes my mom buys the poppers now, sometimes Uncle Henry does. My dad bought them when he was alive." Ada's voice cracked. She stopped talking for a moment until she regained her composure. "And my mom is still making a roast turkey with this sausage stuffing that no one eats and these lumpy mashed potatoes." Ada wrinkled her nose. "I wish she cooked like you." Then Ada switched subjects before Bernie could thank her for the compliment. "So, what do you think?" she asked.

"About what?" Bernie inquired, although she knew perfectly well what Ada was referring to.

Ada's jaw muscles tightened. "About the way everyone acted, of course."

"Well . . ." Libby began, but Ada cut her off before she could complete her sentence.

"You saw how they were when I was reading. I could have been reciting the weather report or talking about the wave patterns in the Atlantic Ocean for all the interest they showed!"

And I was right there with them, Libby wanted to say, before she thought of spending a day fishing and changed her mind. After all, she wanted to calm Ada down, not send her over the edge into tantrum city.

"About that," Bernie said, clearing her throat. "I didn't quite understand the correlation between what you read and the possible homicide of your father and his partner and I'm not sure your family did, either."

No, no, Bernie. Don't go there, Libby thought, making a drop-it gesture with her right hand as Ada snorted and drew herself up.

"It's perfectly obvious," she said.

"Not to me, it isn't," Bernie told Ada, ignoring Libby's signal, which was getting more frantic by the second. "Can you explain it?"

Libby clenched her fists. Sometimes she wanted to wring her sister's neck.

"I don't expect you to understand," Ada informed Bernie, waving the hand with the notebook in it in a dismissive fashion. "It's not your job to understand. All I asked you to do was watch everyone's reactions to what I read and tell me what you saw."

"Which is what I'm trying to do," Bernie said. She was getting more annoyed with Ada by the minute.

"So, why don't you?" Ada demanded, putting the notebook down on the table.

"Because you keep interrupting," Bernie snapped. "You want to know what I saw?"

Ada crossed her arms over her chest. "I just said I did, didn't I?"

"Yes, you did and I'm going to tell you," Bernie said. "From where I was standing, everyone at the table looked annoyed, or bored, or fed up, or any combination of the three."

"They were pretending to be all that stuff," Ada cried. "They were putting on an act."

"I'm sorry," Bernie said in a gentler tone, "but they weren't. Isn't that so, Libby?"

"Well," Libby hedged. "That seemed to be the case, but . . ."

Ada interrupted before Libby could get the last part of her sentence out. "What are you both? Blind or something?" She leaned back. "My stepmother looked guilty as hell and my stepbrother looked as if he was going to pee in his pants."

Bernie shook her head. "That's not what I saw. Your stepbrother looked as if he was about to take a nap, your stepmother was doing something with her cell phone, your stepsister was fiddling around with her napkin, and I'm not even going to comment on the rest of the people there."

"My stepmother got to you, didn't she?" Ada's voice rose another notch. "She paid you off."

"To do what?" Libby asked, genuinely puzzled.

"To lie, of course," Ada answered, astonished that Libby was asking a question to which the answer was so self-evident. "To try to drive me crazy." Ada narrowed her eyes. "But it's not going to work," she growled. "I'm not going to let anyone silence me again."

Bernie and Libby exchanged looks.

"And why would Vicky do that?" Bernie asked in as calm a tone as she could manage. *Oh boy,* she thought. *I should have lied and told Ada what she wanted to hear,* she decided as a bad feeling grew in the pit of her stomach. Maybe Ada *was* cuckoo. Maybe her dad was right after all about getting involved. Maybe there was no such thing as simply catering a meal, cleaning up, and walking away from this family.

"Because she's in on it."

Bernie shook her head. She wasn't sure what Ada was referring to. "In on what?"

"The murders." Ada waved her hand in the air. "Don't you see it's a conspiracy? People can't benefit from their crimes. That's the law. I know because I looked it up. So everyone wants to pin this on me. They do!"

Bernie and Libby exchanged another look.

"I know you think I'm crazy," Ada told them, correctly interpreting their glances. "I can see it in your faces. And I admit, it sounds nuts. But it isn't. There are millions of dollars at stake here and bad publicity would wreck the deal. I know what I read meant," Ada insisted, blinking her eyes to hold back the tears. "I saw how everyone at dinner reacted. I don't know why you didn't see it, too. Maybe you just weren't looking closely enough." Ada glanced from Bernie to Libby and back again. "You're wrong, you know," she told them, even though neither Libby nor Bernie had said anything. Her voice got louder. "You are. Everyone in the room was just pretending not to care. They were pretending to be bored. They were pretending. They were. I don't know what's wrong with you that you didn't see that."

Bernie and Libby exchanged a third look. This was heading in the wrong direction. The last thing either of them wanted was a scene. It was time to back it up.

"Maybe Libby and I are mistaken," Bernie admitted. She chose her next words with care. "Maybe you're right. Maybe my sister and I weren't watching carefully enough. Maybe we didn't pick up on the signs."

Ada dabbed at her eyes and nodded. "Okay. I'm sorry that I yelled. And interrupted. This is just so"—she waved her hand in the air—"distressing."

"Of course it is," Bernie cooed. "How could it not be? Tell you what. Let's talk about what we saw later. We'll go over everything comment by comment. How's that?"

Ada stuck out her chin and planted her feet on the rag rug on the kitchen floor. "Why can't we talk about it now?" she demanded.

She's acting like a five-year-old, Libby thought. "It's almost midnight and we need to serve the champagne," she told Ada in the tone of voice she would use to talk to one.

"It can wait," Ada declared.

"No it can't," Libby said. Then she had an inspiration. She held up her hand to forestall Ada's comment. "And I'll tell you why. We're re-creating the evening from ten years ago, right?"

Ada nodded.

"So, I bet you served champagne before midnight on that evening?"

Ada nodded again. "We did. And we pulled our poppers just like we always do."

"Exactly." Bernie smiled, encouragingly. "That's your ritual."

"Yes, it is," Ada agreed.

"So, by re-creating that evening and reading from your dad's diary you were hoping to stir up fear and guilt in the people who were present the day your dad died. I mean that was the plan, wasn't it?" Libby asked.

"Yes, it was," Ada said. Her shoulders slumped. "I guess I've been reading too many mysteries. It was a stupid idea, wasn't it?"

"No it wasn't," Bernie assured her. "In fact, it was genius."

Libby jumped in. "Indeed it was. So now that your nearest and dearest . . ."

"They're not my nearest and dearest," Ada objected.

"It's just a figure of speech," Bernie told her.

"Your enemies, then," Libby said.

Ada smiled for the first time. "Exactly."

Bernie cleared her throat. Ada turned back to her.

"As I was saying," Bernie continued, "now that

everyone has had time to think about what you read . . ."

"And everyone is a little more relaxed . . ." Libby added.

"Maybe someone will slip up and say something," Ada declared, finishing Bernie's sentence for her.

"Exactly," Bernie said, relieved that Ada had grasped the concept so quickly.

"And if you come in quietly . . ." Libby continued.

"And stand in the back of the room, so no one knows you're there . . ." Bernie went on.

Ada brightened. "I might overhear something."

Bernie and Libby nodded in unison.

"Good thinking," Bernie said.

"Great idea," Ada cried. Then she hugged Bernie and Libby and took off for the living room.

"It must be tough to be her," Libby commented as she watched Ada go.

"Agreed," Bernie said. "All that guilt. All that anger. I wonder how much money we're talking here?"

"You mean in the business?"

"Given the product . . ."

Libby scratched her chin with a fingernail. "If it works . . ."

"I don't think the Sinclair family would be taking the company public if it didn't."

"Not necessarily. Sometimes things work on a small scale, but not a larger one. But if it does work everyone will see more money than they'll know what to do with, that's for sure," Libby opined. "A lot of men would pay anything to keep from going bald."

"And that's even more true of women," Bernie noted as she checked the time on her watch. It was time to get going. "Let's serve the champagne, finish cleaning up, and get out of here while we're still winning."

"You really want that sofa, don't you?" Libby observed as she carefully wrapped up her knives and laid them in their box.

"And you don't?" Bernie asked.

"Of course I do." Libby pointed outside. The snow had begun to thicken and the tree branches of the box elder next to the house were whipping back and forth in the wind, making scratching noises as they hit the wall. "But right now, what I really want to do is get out of here before we can't," Libby remarked, saying what Bernie had been thinking a few minutes ago.

Bernie sighed. "Roger that."

The weather report had predicted at least another four to six inches of snow and it looked as if this time the report was going to be correct.

Chapter 8

While Libby placed the washed and dried dinner dishes in their quilted, nylon storage containers, then put the foam discs between them, zipped the containers up, and placed them into the cartons they'd brought them in, Bernie began uncorking the champagne bottles and pouring the champagne into the flutes she'd arranged on two trays.

"Nice glasses," Libby commented on the ornate crystal glasses.

Bernie looked up. "But not Baccarat," she said.

"I know. Why did Linda say that they are?" Libby asked, referring to the conversation she'd had with Ada's mother a few minutes ago.

Bernie shrugged her shoulders. "Someone probably told her that they are and she doesn't know enough to know the difference." Bernie ran her ring finger around the edge of one of the flutes. "Aside from everything else, real crystal sings. These don't."

"Remember how we used to do that with the water glasses at Sunday dinner?" Libby reminisced.

"And Mom would glare at us."

"And then Dad would join us."

Bernie laughed. "And that would make Mom

even madder. We actually managed to do 'Twinkle, Twinkle Little Star,'" she said, remembering.

"We should start using the crystal again," Libby said. "They're just sitting in the china cabinet."

"We should," Bernie agreed. "I just hate to think of breaking one."

"How much are they now, anyway?" Libby asked.

"The last time I looked, five hundred dollars, but that was a year ago. They may be worth even more now. They probably are. Luxury goods keep going up."

"For four?"

"No, each."

"Wow," Libby said. "I'm impressed. And we have a whole set." She bent down and retied her sneaker. "They certainly weren't that much when Mom and Dad got them as a wedding present," she observed when she straightened up. "I don't think anyone in our family had that kind of money. Ever had it, for that matter."

"They didn't, but everything has gone up since they got married," Bernie pointed out.

"You can say that again," Libby replied, thinking of their family Sunday dinners and how much she enjoyed them. "We'll just be careful," Libby said, having decided that they would use the crystal. "I think Dad would like it if we did."

"Very careful," Bernie said. "There's something

to be said for cheap," she observed. "At least you don't have to worry about breaking them, and if you do, you can always buy more."

Libby pointed to the flutes Linda had asked them to use. "How much do you think these cost?"

"No idea," Bernie promptly replied and then she got her phone and looked them up. "Not much," she told Libby as she showed her their image. Then she made a clicking sound with her tongue against her teeth.

"What are you thinking?" Libby asked her sister.

"That the glasses are emblematic of Sinclair family relations."

"Wow." Libby opened her eyes wide. "That's quite the stretch. How do you get that?"

"People trying to pretend that things are other than they are."

"All that from one dinner?" Libby asked. "I think you're in the wrong business. I think you should be a psychologist."

"I'm serious," Bernie said.

"I am too," Libby told her.

Bernie put her hands on her hips. "So why do you think that Ada didn't tell her mom she'd hired us to cater the event until the last minute?"

"Not that that has anything to do with the matter we're discussing, but I think she wanted to surprise her. Obviously."

"She certainly did that," Bernie said, thinking back to Ada's mom's remarks when she answered the door.

"To use your words, I'm guessing it's emblematic of Ada's relationship with her mom. She doesn't even call her 'Mom,' for heaven's sake. What does that say?"

"That they don't have a warm, fuzzy relationship."

"Seems to be the case," Libby said. "She probably knew her mom would say no and since Ada wanted us there this was her work-around."

"It certainly doesn't promote good family feelings," Bernie remarked.

"No, it doesn't," Libby said. "The Sinclairs don't seem like the pleasantest group of people," she added. "At least not when they're all together."

Bernie shifted her weight from her right to her left foot. "No, they don't, do they. So much for my vision of family picnics and Sunday dinners with newfound relatives," Bernie said as she put two bowls of the chocolate-covered strawberries they'd made this morning on the trays next to the glasses.

"I thought they would say something when they saw us, didn't you?" Libby asked Bernie.

"Like what?"

"Like something along the lines of 'It's been a long time since our families got together,' instead of 'I'd like a bit more wine' or 'How did you cook these carrots? They're delicious.' "

"Maybe they don't know," Bernie said.

"Of course they knew," Libby replied. "Ada's mom told them."

Bernie thought about it for a moment. "Maybe she didn't tell the younger ones."

"Doubtful," Libby replied. "Ada knows. Why shouldn't the others?"

Bernie frowned. "In that case, I think it's even weirder that nobody said anything to us about the family feud. I mean, wouldn't you have, if the positions had been reversed? Instead of pretending we're just here to serve the meal."

"They haven't said anything because they don't want to," Libby answered.

"So much for family reunions," Bernie repeated. She sighed. "Oh, well. It was a nice thought."

"What I want to know is, did someone in that family do what Ada is accusing them of doing?" Libby asked.

"If they did, that certainly takes whoever we're talking about out of the realm of the merely unpleasant and puts them in a whole different category."

"And if they didn't, that puts Ada in front of the pack in terms of nuttiness." Libby shook her head. "That whole conspiracy theory thing she was trotting out is a bit . . . much."

"Well, Ada certainly has a flair for the dramatic," Bernie observed. "I'll give you that. I wonder what her stepmom was referring to when she said to Ada's mom, 'Remember what happened the last time?'"

Libby frowned. "I'm guessing Ada had some kind of breakdown."

"That's what I'm figuring, too," Bernie agreed. "I wonder what Ada thinks is so revealing about what she read?" Bernie mused as she picked up one of the trays. "I didn't hear anything even vaguely suggestive of naming a murderer, let alone indicating a crime had been committed, did you?"

Libby shook her head. "All I heard were to-do lists, lists of places to try to sell Re-Grow! to, random observations about things like the weather and commuting on Metro-North, and possible product advertising slogans. Unless those entries were in some sort of code," Libby posited.

Bernie scoffed at the idea. "Now that's what you call grasping at straws," she said.

"Granted," Libby said. "Although," she reflected, "it wouldn't surprise me if Ada believed that to be the case. Why else would she say what she did?"

"You may have a point, Libby." Bernie moved one of the bowls with the strawberries a fraction of an inch so that it lined up with the glasses. "Given the way she's acting, Ada might indeed, although if that were the case I'd think she would have told us what the code was and translated it for us."

"Okay. You're right. So, let's retire the diary code thing for the moment."

"Works for me," Bernie told her sister.

"But what if she's right about the other thing?" Libby asked.

"You mean the conspiracy she was talking about?" Bernie asked.

Libby nodded.

"On what basis are you proposing this idea?"

"On the basis that two people died in question-able circumstances . . ."

Bernie raised an eyebrow.

Libby corrected herself. "Okay. Might have died in questionable circumstances . . ."

Bernie raised a second eyebrow.

"Granted, there's a very thin chance that they did die in questionable circumstances," Libby allowed. "But"—and she held up one of her fingers to emphasize the point she was about to make—"there evidently is a lot of money at stake here and money never brings out the best in people."

"No, it does not," Bernie agreed, thinking back to the cases she and Libby had solved. "But that said, you're proceeding on a pretty flimsy hypothesis."

"I know, but there's always the chance that

Ada is correct and we missed something," Libby continued. "What if everyone *is* in this together?"

Bernie snorted. "Seriously? A la Agatha Christie?"

"It could happen," Libby protested. "I mean it is a possibility. After all, just because someone is paranoid doesn't mean they're wrong."

"And Mathilda can go one hundred miles an hour and we're entering her in the Indy 500 tomorrow." Bernie glanced down at her watch. They had to get a move on. The magic hour was approaching. "And I wouldn't worry about the diary being in code if I were you."

"I'm not," Libby said. "I was just proposing it as a theory."

"Because whether the damned thing is or isn't in code—and I don't believe it is—I have an idea that Ada's going to tell us the meaning of each and every entry that she read whether we want to hear it or not."

"We probably won't be able to stop her," Libby reflected gloomily, thinking of the conversation to come. "You shouldn't have told her we'd talk about what we saw later."

"I know," Bernie agreed. "But I was trying to get her out of here."

Libby shook her head and tucked the hem of her shirt back into her pants. "I would like to get out of here, too. For that matter, I'm sure everyone here feels the same way."

Bernie nodded her head in agreement. "Nothing like having someone accuse you of murder to put a damper on the festivities."

"And according to her family this is nothing new. It's something she's done on a regular basis," Libby said as she looked out the kitchen window at the snow. It was blowing in sideways sheets, making the streetlights hard to see. The storm had arrived in all its majesty.

"Do you think that's true?" Bernie asked.

"Yeah. I kinda do, not that it makes any difference."

"I think it's better if we just agree with everything Ada says. . . ."

"I wasn't the one disagreeing with her, Bernie," Libby pointed out. "You were."

"I already said I made a mistake."

Libby looked out the window again and let out a long sigh. "I just hope that Mathilda starts."

"Me too," Bernie said. "But that's not what I'm worried about. What worries me is going up the hills. I just hope that the roads are plowed so we don't get stuck going up that hill on Piedmont and slide back down." They'd done that last winter. Fortunately, the road had been empty at the time.

Libby picked up one of the trays. "Come on. The new year awaits."

Bernie nodded. "Indeed it does."

Ada's mother was handing out the Christmas poppers as Bernie and Libby walked into the living room.

"We are going to be rich," Bernie heard Ada's uncle, Henry, say as she and Libby approached everyone with their trays.

"I'll drink to that," Ada's stepmother said, taking a glass from Bernie's tray.

"It's about time our work paid off," Peggy observed to the room at large as Libby proffered her the tray she was holding. Peggy took a flute and nodded her thanks.

"Ah," Ada's mom said to Bernie as Bernie offered her a glass of champagne. "Just in the nick of time."

Everyone else in the room took a glass as well and Libby and Bernie put the bowls of strawberries on the coffee table and left.

"To us," Libby and Bernie heard Ada's mom say as they returned to the kitchen.

"To making more money than we know what to do with," Ada's uncle added.

"To travel and good times," Peggy Graceson said.

Once they were back in the kitchen the sisters picked up the glasses filled with champagne that they'd set aside for themselves and raised them.

"To a good new year," Bernie said.

"To our family," Libby said. "And to getting home in one piece."

"To a new sofa and to not having Dad's prediction come true," Bernie added.

"To no fishing," Libby added.

"I'll drink to that," Bernie told her. Then she and her sister gently clinked glasses and downed their champagne.

A moment later, they were back at work. Bernie and Libby finished packing their supplies in the cartons they'd come in, after which they wiped down the counters and the kitchen table and swept the floor. Then they went back into the living room to collect the empty champagne flutes and tell Ada they were going to leave after they'd washed the crystal and put it away. To the sisters' relief, Ada just nodded and turned back to watching the television. Evidently she had nothing more to say about her father's diary.

"Make sure you're careful washing those glasses," Linda called out to them as they collected the flutes from the coffee and side tables. "They're Baccarat, you know."

"Yes, we know," Bernie said. "Don't look at me that way," Bernie told her sister as they walked back to the kitchen. "Crystal or glass? What difference does it make?"

"It evidently makes a difference to her," Libby observed.

"Exactly my point," Bernie told her.

The sisters spent the next five minutes carefully

washing Linda's glasses in warm soapy water and drying them. They were putting them back in the kitchen cabinet when they heard a crash followed by a scream followed by an "Oh no."

Libby looked at Bernie and Bernie looked at Libby.

"Maybe someone saw a mouse and dropped their glass," Libby said.

"I'll go with that," Bernie agreed.

"We could keep packing and pretend we didn't hear it," Libby suggested.

"We could," Bernie said, weighing the possibility. "We could wait for someone to come get us."

There was another scream. This one was shriller.

Bernie sighed. "Another fifteen minutes and we would have been out the door."

"Which would have been lovely. Unfortunately, we're here," Libby pointed out as she put down the carton she'd just picked up.

"Unfortunately," Bernie echoed.

"Dad would have found out anyway."

"Yes, he would have," Bernie agreed. She didn't know how, but their dad always knew everything.

"By now we should know better than to bet with him," Libby said. "He always wins."

The third scream was the scream that did it.

"I guess we should see what's going on," Bernie said as she and Libby started toward the living room.

"Nothing good," Libby predicted.

"That's for sure," Bernie replied.

Chapter 9

When Bernie and Libby ran in, Ada was backed up against the far wall gnawing on her fingernails and muttering to herself. Everyone else was standing near the end table on the left-hand side of the sofa looking down at something. At first, Bernie and Libby couldn't see what it was because they were blocking the view, but then Ada's uncle moved to the right and they spied Peggy through the space he'd left. She was foaming at the mouth while she thrashed about on the Oriental rug.

"Peggy, are you all right?" Ada's stepmother was saying when Bernie and Libby walked in.

"Of course, she's not all right," Linda snapped at Vicky. Then she half knelt and said, "Peggy, what's wrong? What's the matter? Tell us."

"She can't," Ada cried. Everyone turned to face her. "She's dying."

"No, she's having a seizure," Linda said.

Ada began to rock back and forth. "I knew something bad was going to happen," she moaned. "I just knew it. This day is cursed. Cursed. I should never have done it. This is all my fault. My fault." And she covered her face with her hands and began to sob.

"Someone shut her up," Ada's sister Rachel said, which made Ada cry harder.

"For heaven's sake, do something!" Ada's aunt yelled.

"About Ada?" Ada's mother asked.

"No. About Peggy," Ada's aunt retorted.

"What would you suggest?" Ada's mother snapped.

"CPR," Ada's aunt replied.

"She's not having a heart attack, she's having some kind of seizure," Ada's mother replied. "I already told you that."

"She could be having rabies," Ada's stepbrother suggested. "It's really contagious. I don't think anyone should go near her."

"What is the matter with you, Lance?" Marty demanded of Ada's stepbrother as Bernie and Libby elbowed their way through everyone.

"Nothing." Lance pointed at Peggy. "She's foaming at the mouth. Isn't that what happens when you have rabies?" he asked. "I saw it on the nature channel."

"That's not people, you moron," Marty snapped at him. "That's animals."

"No, they said it could happen to people, too. Anyway, look who's calling who a moron," Lance retorted as Bernie and Libby brushed by him to get to Peggy.

"What happened?" Bernie inquired as she squatted down on one side of Peggy while Libby knelt on the other side. Peggy didn't look good. Her body was twitching and a small amount of white froth was coming out of her mouth. Bernie looked up at the faces staring down. "Someone? Anyone?" she asked when no one answered immediately.

Ada's mom was the first to speak. "I don't know," she said. "One minute Peggy was fine and the next minute she fell down and started doing this."

"She's obviously having some sort of seizure, Linda," Ada's uncle, Henry, observed.

"I think we've already established that, Henry," Linda told him.

"Somebody should put a pillow under her head," Henry suggested.

"I'll get one," Ada's brother, Rick, volunteered.

"Not one of the good ones," Linda called after her son as he ran off.

"What's wrong with you?" Sheryl asked her.

"There's nothing wrong with me," Linda told her. "What a thing to say."

"Not one of the good pillows?" Sheryl repeated, mimicking Linda's tone. "Seriously."

"Excuse me if I just don't want Rick to get my two-hundred-dollar pillow. I need it for my neck. I don't see what's wrong with that."

"What's wrong with that is that you're thinking of yourself—as per usual," Sheryl replied.

"Like you're one to talk," Linda snapped.

"I'm just saying you'd have a lot more if you spent less on things you didn't need," Sheryl replied. "Like a two-hundred-dollar pillow. That's ridiculous."

"Not if you have neck problems, it's not," Linda said. "You have no idea what it's like to live with pain."

"Maybe I don't, but your husband certainly did."

"What's that supposed to mean, Sheryl?" Linda demanded.

"You know. His little habit. And he lived with you, didn't he?" Sheryl said. Then Henry dragged her away before she could say anything else.

Libby ignored the bickering raging around her as she bent over Peggy. "Peggy," she said, "can you hear me?"

Peggy moaned.

Bernie leaned closer. "Peggy, talk to us."

But instead of answering, Peggy's body stiffened, arched, and came back down. Libby reached over and placed two fingers on the side of Peggy's throat. Her pulse was weak and thready. "Has someone called nine-one-one?" Libby asked without looking up.

"I did. They're on their way," Marty replied.

"I don't understand," Vicky said, shaking her head in dismay. "Peggy was fine a minute ago."

"We'd just drank our champagne and pulled our Christmas poppers and then blammo," Ada's stepmother explained to Bernie and Libby as Ada's brother came into the room with a pillow in his hand, went over to Peggy, and slipped the pillow under her head. "This happened."

Bernie got up. "What happened?" she asked Vicky. "Exactly."

Vicky looked at the ceiling for a moment while she collected her thoughts and then she started talking. "Peggy had this funny look on her face—I don't know how to describe it—and she started swaying back and forth. I asked her if she was okay and she said no. Then she grabbed for the table—I think she wanted to steady herself—but she missed and grabbed the lamp instead. Then she fell and the lamp went with her. Next thing I know, she's doing that." Ada's stepmother pointed to Peggy. "I just screamed. She really scared me."

"At first I thought she was fooling around," Ada's mom said.

"You'd have to be an idiot to think that," Vicky snapped.

"She was always playing practical jokes," Linda protested.

"Yes," Vicky answered. "But little stuff. Mostly at work. You know, like taking your lunch and hiding it. But nothing like this." And she nodded toward Peggy to make her point. Then she looked at her watch. "I wish the EMTs would get here."

"Me too," Bernie said. She thought she heard the faint wail of a siren, but she wasn't sure. "Although," she observed, "between the snow

96

and it being New Year's Eve it might take a while."

"Let's hope not," Sheryl said as Bernie took the throw off the sofa and covered Peggy with it.

Bernie didn't know if that would help, but it was the only thing she could think of to do. As she draped the blanket over Peggy she noticed Peggy was still clutching a Christmas popper, her hand tightening and loosening around it as her body contracted and relaxed. On impulse, because it seemed the right thing to so, Bernie gently removed the tube and placed it on the coffee table. A sprinkling of confetti fell onto the floor.

"I hear sirens," Henry announced.

Everyone nodded. The siren was audible to everyone now.

"Thank God," Sheryl cried, pointing to Peggy. People looked and then looked away. They didn't want to see. "Her eyes are beginning to roll back in her head. I don't know much, but that can't be good."

Linda sent Rick to wait by the front door for the EMTs. Everyone else milled around not knowing what to do except listen to the sirens getting louder. A couple of minutes later, they could see an ambulance pull up in front of the house and stop. Two men jumped out and Ada's brother opened the door and cried, "In here," his voice carrying into the living room. A minute later, the EMTs burst into the room.

"Over here," Bernie said, indicating Peggy as everyone moved back to give the EMTs room.

They knelt next to her and took her pulse and listened to her heart.

"Anyone know what happened?" one of the EMTs asked.

Vicky told the EMTs the same thing she'd told Bernie.

"How long has she been like this?" the second EMT inquired.

"Maybe ten minutes. At the most," Sheryl answered.

"Does she have a history of seizures?" the same EMT asked.

"I think I remember her saying something to that effect a while ago," Marty Grover said.

"Are you family?" the taller EMT asked Marty.

Linda answered instead. She shook her head. "She doesn't have any. We're the closest thing she has."

The first EMT nodded. Then he and his coworker went out to get a stretcher. They came back a minute later, placed Peggy on it, and carried her out of Linda Sinclair's house. Five minutes after that, they were speeding to the hospital.

"I hope she's all right," Sheryl said as everyone watched the ambulance disappear into the night.

"Me too," Libby replied. "What's that?" Libby asked Bernie, pointing to the green foil tube

Bernie had taken off the coffee table and was holding in her hand.

"Peggy's Christmas popper," Bernie said.

"It looks sad," Libby said, "all squished in like that."

"That's the way it's supposed to look when you open it," Bernie noted. "I wonder what was in it?" she mused.

"I don't know," Linda said. "Peggy did her own. She never shared."

"Doesn't it take two to make these things pop?" Bernie asked.

"It's supposed to," Henry replied. Then he shrugged. "But Peggy was funny that way. After her divorce, she always wanted to do everything by herself."

"What happened to her husband?" Bernie asked.

"He died a couple of years ago," Henry replied. "Why do you ask?"

"No particular reason," Bernie responded. "Just nosy I guess." And Bernie leaned over and put the popper back on the table. As she did she saw a glint of something inside the tube. She held it up to the ceiling light to examine it better. She could see a tiny speck glinting in the center of the tube. What was it? Bernie wasn't sure so she got up and took the popper over to one of the lamps.

"What are you doing?" Libby asked as she followed Bernie over.

"I thought I saw something." And Bernie held the tube under the lamp shade so she could see better. But that didn't help—the bulb was too dim—so she got her cell phone out and used the flashlight.

"What?" Libby asked, looking over her sister's shoulder.

"That," Bernie said, pointing to a small needle embedded in a round piece of cardboard that was placed an inch away from the tube's closing. If you reached your hand in, it would be impossible not to get pricked by it. Bernie turned to Linda. "Quick question," she said.

Linda turned toward her. Bernie thought she looked what? A mix of things. Exhausted. Relieved. Frightened.

"Yes?" Linda said.

"These poppers are filled with something, right?"

"That's the whole point," Linda answered. "Why?"

Bernie nodded to the one she was holding in her hand. "Because this one has some sort of pin stuck in it on the inside."

"I don't know what to say," Linda replied, looking out the window at the falling snow. "It must be a manufacturer's error." She turned toward Bernie and Libby. "But I don't see how that had anything to do with what just happened to Peggy."

"I didn't say it did," Bernie pointed out.

"Of course it does," Ada cried. Her eyes were wild and she'd run her fingers through her hair so it was standing on end.

"Don't be ridiculous," Linda snapped.

Everyone in the room turned toward her.

"Someone put that pin in there," Ada insisted.

"Yes, the manufacturer, like your mom just said," Vicky replied.

"No," Ada cried, her voice growing shrill. "It wasn't the manufacturer. It wasn't an accident. Someone did this on purpose. Someone poisoned her. Someone poisoned Peggy."

Henry sucked in his cheeks then frowned. The gestures made his nose look even bigger than it was. "Jeez, Ada," he said. "Come on. Not now."

Ada pointed a trembling finger to the spot on the floor where Peggy had been lying. Everyone turned to look. "She's going to die."

"No she isn't," Linda said, talking to her daughter in the same tone of voice you'd talk to a child. "She's going to be fine. The nice doctors at the hospital will find out what's wrong and they'll fix her up. She'll be right as rain."

"No. She won't be," Ada cried. "She's been poisoned just like my dad was, only this time whoever did it used cyanide or ricin, just like that guy in Russia did."

Sheryl blinked, swallowed, and put her hand up

to her throat. "What guy? What are you talking about?" she demanded.

Ada licked her lips and swallowed. "The guy in Russia, the one that was killed in the U.K."

"That was a heavy metal," Sheryl told her.

"And how do you know that, Ada?" Vicky demanded as she pulled up her bra strap and put it back where it belonged.

"Because Peggy has the same signs!" Ada yelled. Her face was getting red. "That's how I know." Then she wrung her hands and started to sob again, louder this time.

"Oh, please," Ada's stepsister, Erin, said. "Enough is enough. The stuff that killed the guy in Russia was radioactive . . . whatever. I forget the name."

"Thallium," Sheryl said. "It was thallium."

Erin turned to Linda. "Don't you have something you can give her? Honestly, I don't think I can take much more. She just makes everything worse."

"You can't take much more!" Ada screamed at Erin, taking a step toward her while she threw her words back at her. "That's funny coming from you."

Erin took a step back. She held out her hands. "Hey, you have to calm down."

Ada stopped and gestured to everyone in the room. "I know what you're doing, don't think I don't."

"And what would that be?" Ada's mother asked, shaking her head in dismay.

It must be hard watching your daughter come unglued, Bernie thought. Then as she was trying to decide what, if anything, to say, Ada ran over to her and grabbed her hands.

"Promise me you won't let them get me," she cried.

"Get you?" Bernie asked, at a loss.

"Yes," Ada said. "Don't you see? They—"

" 'They'?" Libby said, interrupting.

"Yes, *they,*" Ada replied, not explaining who "they" were, "killed Peggy and now they're going to try to blame her murder on me. Promise," she cried, her voice getting louder. "You have to promise."

"Libby and I promise," Bernie said to calm Ada down even though she didn't know what it was that Ada wanted her to promise, at which point Ada turned and ran out of the living room.

"Wow," Vicky said as Bernie and Libby watched her leave. "That was intense."

"We should go after her," Bernie said to her sister.

"Definitely," Libby replied as Vicky reached into her shirt pocket, came out with a couple of pills, and handed them to her.

"Here," Vicky said. "Give her these."

"What are they?" Libby asked.

"Something to help calm her down," Vicky told her.

"Like what?" Bernie demanded.

"Xanax," Vicky told her. "I always carry a couple around. I mean you never know when you're going to need them, right?"

"Right." Libby put the pills in her pants pocket and hurried to catch up with Bernie, who was halfway out of the room already. Libby didn't know if Ada needed those, but if Ada didn't she did.

Bernie had just reached the living room entrance when she heard a scraping noise and felt a blast of cold air eddying around her feet.

"Did Ada just go out?" Libby asked. She'd heard the noise and felt the cold air as well.

Bernie nodded. The front door was wide open and snow was blowing into the hallway.

"Come on," Bernie muttered as Linda cried, "Oh my God, I bet Ada's taking my car."

A moment later, Bernie and Libby heard a car starting.

"Stop her!" Linda screamed.

But it was too late. By the time Libby and Bernie got outside, Ada had vanished into the night.

"I hope she doesn't get into an accident," Libby said to Bernie as she looked at the snow coming down in horizontal sheets.

Linda's mother was waiting for them when

they got back inside. "This is your fault!" she screamed at them. *Just like her daughter,* Bernie thought as she watched Linda shake with rage. *Put the blame on someone else.* "This is on your head," Linda continued. "None of this would have happened if it hadn't been for you. You're just like your mother—bad luck. I should never have let you in this house."

"Funny," Bernie said, "but my mother said the same thing about you and your family."

Chapter 10

Bernie and Libby had gotten the phone call at three in the afternoon but had put off informing their dad about it till eight that night. They'd been too busy they'd told themselves. They'd been baking the apple pies for Mrs. Schneider to pick up, making five pans of lasagna, getting the dough made for tomorrow's cinnamon rolls, dealing with a leak in one of the sinks, as well as waiting on customers. But now the shop was closed and they'd run out of things to do.

Of course, they didn't have to tell their dad—by mutual consent none of the three had mentioned the Sinclairs since the New Year's Eve debacle—but neither daughter liked lying, even if it was lying by omission. Plus, their dad would find out they'd been in contact with Ada eventually anyway and then he'd be even more pissed that they hadn't told him. And hurt. Which was worse.

But now Bernie wondered if she and Libby should have kept their mouths shut as Sean raised an eyebrow and said, "You're actually going to meet with Ada Sinclair?" in a tone of voice that said, "How stupid can you get?"—the same tone of voice he'd used when Bernie was ten and she'd tried to sneak out of the house in the middle of the night for the second time in as many days.

"Yup," Bernie said, trying for nonchalance. She knew her dad was going to be pissed, but what else could she do, especially with Linda Sinclair's words echoing in her head. "Obviously, you think we shouldn't."

Sean gave her his patented incredulous look. "After everything that's happened? Of course, I think you shouldn't."

It had been a week since Ada had driven off into the night and her call to Bernie was the first contact anyone had had with her. Bernie knew this for a fact because Ada's mother was calling twice a day to ask if they'd heard from her. Bernie just couldn't decide whether Linda was more concerned about her daughter or her car.

"Think of it this way," Bernie said. "What else could go wrong?"

Sean shook his head. "Sometimes, your logic baffles me." He turned to Libby. "And you're going along with this? You think this is okay?"

Libby straightened her shoulders in the face of her dad's obvious disapproval. "Yes, as a matter of fact I do." Sometimes, you had to back up your sister, right or wrong.

Sean scowled at his eldest daughter's reply. "And I always thought you were the more sensible one of my children."

"I am," Libby said, maintaining her air of certitude.

"Not in this case," Sean said. "The fact that

you're meeting with a possible murderer doesn't bother you?"

"It's not as if we haven't dealt with those before," Bernie replied. Which was true. Her dad couldn't argue about that.

"And you don't know that about Ada for a fact," Libby objected.

"I know the police think she's a suspect. I know that's why they want to talk to her," Sean pointed out.

"They talk to everyone," Bernie countered. "That's what they do."

"Except for Ada," Sean replied. "And they couldn't do that because she ran away. That's not a big red flag to you?"

Bernie bit her lip. "Well, I agree it doesn't make her look good."

Sean snorted. "Now, there's an understatement if I ever heard one," he told her.

"Anyway," Bernie continued, "even if she did do what the police want to question her about— and I'm not saying she did—it's not like she's going to kill us." Bernie pointed to herself and her sister. "The motive for this was strictly personal."

"Well, there's something we can both agree on," Sean told his youngest daughter. "Which is why, if you remember, I told you nothing good would come of getting tangled up with Ada and her family."

Libby waved her hands in front of her face. "I know. I know. And you were right for the twenty-fifth time."

"Yes, I was. I told you something bad was going to happen," Sean couldn't stop himself from saying even though he knew he should be quiet.

"Yes, you did," Bernie allowed as she shifted her weight from her right to her left foot to work out a cramp in the arch of her left foot. She wondered if she should stop wearing four-inch heels for a little while and give her feet a rest.

Sean opened his eyes wide in feigned astonishment. "And yet, you want to continue your involvement after what happened on New Year's Eve. I gotta say you two are gluttons for punishment," he said, hammering his point home.

Bernie sighed as she thought about what had transpired that evening. It turned out that Ada had been right. Peggy had been poisoned. She'd died in the hospital two days after she'd arrived. Now the police wanted to question Ada about some of the statements she'd made on New Year's Eve as well as the fact that not only had she given the Christmas popper to Peggy, but she'd had a fight with Peggy at work three weeks before the party. No one knew what it was about—or if they did they weren't saying—but the two hadn't been speaking to each other since then. Ada had won the trifecta.

"Okay," Bernie argued. "It's true Ada has motive, means, and opportunity, but we don't know that that doesn't apply to the other people there as well."

"Maybe it does, but they didn't run off," Sean observed.

"A negative doesn't prove a positive," Bernie replied.

"It doesn't disprove it, either," Sean noted.

"Her mother wasn't pleased," Bernie reflected, thinking of what Linda had said to her and Libby. Even though Bernie knew it wasn't true, a part of her couldn't help thinking that Ada's mother was correct, that what had happened was her and Libby's fault.

"I wouldn't be happy either, if you had stolen my car and taken off," Sean observed. "Not that you would," he added hastily.

"The reason she took off is because she thinks she's being framed for Peggy's murder," Bernie told her dad.

"So you said," Sean reminded her. "Do you think she really believes that?"

"Yes, I do," Bernie replied. "Whether it's true or not is an entirely different matter, but she seemed genuinely terrified, didn't she, Libby?"

Libby considered her reply for a moment before she said, "I don't know about terrified, but she was definitely hysterical."

"Anyway," Bernie continued, "I promised her . . ."

". . . that you'd look into it," Sean said, finishing Bernie's sentence for her.

"Yes, I did," Bernie answered.

"And a promise is a promise," Sean continued, giving his sentence a sarcastic twist.

Bernie crossed her arms over her chest. "It is to me."

"Me too," Libby said, choosing to ignore her dad's tone.

"That's what you taught us," Bernie reminded Sean. She couldn't help herself.

He grimaced. "That's a low blow throwing my words back at me."

"But it's true," Bernie answered. "It's what you've always said to us."

"The folly of good intentions," Sean murmured, shaking his head.

Bernie and Libby didn't respond because there was nothing to say. Their dad was correct. *What was the more popular phrase?* Bernie thought for a moment. *Ah, yes. Something along the lines of "No good deed goes unpunished."*

Their father continued. "You shouldn't have promised Ada, Bernie," he said, turning his gaze from the window. It was snowing again, he reflected gloomily. He felt as if he was living inside one of those paperweights, the kind that you shake and watch white flakes coming

111

down. "I told you that family was nothing but trouble and, yes, I know I'm repeating myself ad nauseum," he added. "But I don't care."

"And you were right," Bernie said yet again.

"No. Your mother was right," Sean said.

"She usually was," Bernie noted.

"And yet here we are," Sean said.

"Yes, here we are," Bernie said, repeating her father's phrase.

Libby looked from her sister to her father and back again and decided it was time to change the conversation. "It's late," Libby announced. "And dinner is ready. How about we call a 'time-out' and eat," she suggested. "I don't know about you, but I'm hungry."

Sean nodded. He realized he was hungry, too.

"Works for me," Bernie said, and she and Libby headed downstairs to bring up the dinner they'd prepared.

Sean brightened when he saw what his daughters came back with: roasted chicken with roasted potatoes, carrots, onions, and parsnips; a green salad; French bread; and apple pie for dessert. He rubbed his hands together in anticipation.

This was one of his favorite meals. He knew that the chicken skin would be crispy; the meat would be juicy and flavored with rosemary, garlic, and lemon; and the vegetables would be cooked in the same pan, which meant they would be caramelized on the outside, soft on the inside, and bathed in the chicken's juices. Then there was the French bread to tear apart and dip into the juices and the green salad and a juiced apple pie for dessert. It was the perfect winter meal, the ultimate comfort food.

"Thank you," he said.

"My pleasure," Libby replied.

"Tell me, did you make this meal before you got the phone call from Ada or after?" Sean asked his daughters.

They both laughed.

"We can neither confirm nor deny," Bernie said as she handed her dad his plate.

"That's what I thought," Sean said, taking the plate and sitting down in his chair. "This almost makes me glad Ada called," he said as Cindy climbed up on the arm of his chair and waited to get something to eat.

Chapter 11

For the next ten minutes, the only sounds in the Simmons's flat were the sounds of Bernie, Libby, and Sean chatting about the weather forecast for the next week, the clink of cutlery on bone china as they ate, and the hoot of a freight train as it went by the town. Then Sean started the conversation about Ada back up.

"So why did you say you'd help Ada out?" Sean asked in a milder tone as he got up and tore off a piece of French bread from the baguette Libby had placed on the coffee table.

Bernie speared a piece of potato and ate it. Perfect. "You really want to know?" she asked her dad as she hunted around for another one on her plate. She didn't know why people called potatoes lowly. Cooked properly they were one of the better things in life.

"Yes, I really do," Sean replied.

"I didn't know what else to do," Bernie admitted as she cut her next piece of potato with her fork. She'd used Idahoes. She still liked them best for pan roasting. They browned up nicely and remained somewhat floury inside. "Ada was hysterical. It was the only way I could think of to calm her down. She still is hysterical," she concluded gloomily, remembering her phone conversation with her.

Sean sat back down, took the bread, sopped up the juices on his plate with it, and bit into it after he'd fed a small piece of bread and chicken to the cat, who jumped off the chair and took her booty into Sean's bedroom to eat. "Did you tell Ada to go home?" Sean asked Bernie after he'd swallowed. "Did you tell her the police want to talk to her?"

"Of course I did," Bernie replied, offended. "I even told Ada I'd get a lawyer for her so she wouldn't have to go in and talk to the police by herself."

"So, what did she say?" Sean asked after he'd eaten the last piece of chicken on his plate.

"She said she was afraid that someone was going to kill her," Bernie replied. "She said she wasn't going to go back until this thing was solved."

"She's talking about her family, right?" Sean clarified.

"That's what I'm assuming," Bernie replied.

"The Sinclairs give the Medicis a run for their money," Sean observed as he finished off his bread. He thought about eating another piece but remembered the apple pie and decided he needed to leave room for dessert.

"That seems like a slight exaggeration," Bernie observed.

"Poetic license," Sean shot back. "By any chance did Ada tell you where she was?" he asked his daughters.

Libby shook her head. "She didn't say."

Sean cast an eye on his children. "Are you sure?"

"We're positive," Libby and Bernie said together.

"Anyway, why would we lie?" Libby asked.

"Simple," Sean said. "You'd lie because the Hollingsworth police like her for this and you don't think she did anything and you don't want to take a chance that I might call up one of my old acquaintances in the Hollingsworth Police Department and tip him off. Not that I would. I hope you know that. Unless, of course, you were in imminent danger. Then all bets are off."

"Good to know," Bernie told her dad.

"Ada thinks the police may be in on the frame," Libby said as she ate a parsnip. They were such an underused vegetable. She wondered why because they were delicious. She made a note to herself to talk to Bernie about serving them more often at A Taste of Heaven. They could start with Michael Field's recipe for parsnip pie.

Sean rolled his eyes. "She is off the reservation, isn't she?"

"Ada is pretty far out there," Bernie allowed. "I'll give you that. But what if what she's saying is true? What if even part of what she's saying is true and she's innocent?"

"And what if pigs learn to fly?" Sean retorted.

"They could with genetic engineering," Libby pointed out.

Sean shot her a dirty look. "Ha. Ha. Ha."

Libby ducked her head. "Well, it's true," she murmured and went back to finishing her dinner.

"Given what you told me she said, she practically confessed," Sean said.

"She was extremely upset," Bernie said. "I think seeing Peggy dredged up memories of her dad's death."

"I'm guessing she *felt* guilty since she was the one who arranged everything," Libby said. "Which is different from *being* guilty."

Sean snorted. "I know the difference, thank you very much. English is my native language." He paused to eat a piece of carrot. "Since when are carrots purple?" he asked, referring to the one he'd just consumed.

"They've been around for a while," Bernie informed him. "We just decided to start serving them," she explained. "They look pretty."

Sean speared another piece of purple carrot and ate that one, too. Then he sampled an orange one. "They both taste the same," he observed.

"Pretty much," Libby agreed. "The purple ones are a little sweeter."

"I thought that I'd at least have you on my side," he said to his eldest daughter after he'd finished everything on his plate.

"Okay, I admit you were right about getting involved," Libby said.

"At least for that," Sean said.

"And I'm sorry we lost the bet. . . ."

Sean grinned. "I'm not. You want to double down?"

Libby ignored the question and said, "But for better or worse . . ."

"Worse . . ." Sean responded.

Libby ignored her dad's comment again. "We're involved now and for what it's worth I stand with Bernie. I think there's a chance Ada isn't guilty, either."

"Really?" Sean asked.

Libby thought about the expression on Ada's face when she and Bernie had walked into the room. "Yes. Really."

Sean put down his fork and shook his head. "My daughters, the finders of lost causes."

"I wouldn't go that far," Bernie told him.

"I would," Sean replied, putting his plate on the end table. "So, then tell me how would you explain her conduct," Sean challenged.

Bernie finished her potatoes and answered. "Like Libby said, I think Ada feels guilty. I think Ada feels that if she hadn't set up this scenario then none of this would have happened."

Sean rubbed his chin. "You're referring to Peggy's death, I presume, when you said, 'then none of this would have happened.'"

Bernie nodded. "What else would I be talking about?"

"So, was what Ada read compelling evidence that her dad was murdered?" Sean asked, going on to another piece of the puzzle—because he was sure that's what this was. A very complicated jigsaw puzzle.

Libby and Bernie looked at each other for a moment. Finally, Libby spoke. "I didn't think so," she said reluctantly.

"Neither did I," Bernie agreed. "Neither did anyone there, for that matter," she added, "although Ada thought they were just pretending not to understand."

"And were they?" Sean asked.

"Bernie and I didn't think so," Libby said, summoning up the expressions on everyone's faces in her mind, "but Ada swore they were."

"Do you think Ada was, as they used to say, shining you on?" Sean asked.

Both Libby and Bernie shook their heads.

"I think she believed what she told us," Bernie said.

"Interesting," Sean murmured. He tapped his fingers together as he thought. "What happened to the notebook?" He was thinking that it would be interesting to look at it if possible.

"I don't know," Libby said. "We searched for it after the police left, and it was gone."

"So, we can assume that Ada took it," Sean commented.

"She said she didn't," Bernie said. "I asked when she called."

Sean lowered his hand and massaged his right thigh. For some reason, it was aching when he'd woken up this morning. "Do you believe her?"

"Yeah, I think I do," Bernie said.

"Why?" Sean asked as he continued to rub his thigh.

"Two reasons," Bernie replied, eating the last bit of chicken on her plate.

"Which are?" Sean prompted when Bernie didn't reply immediately.

"First, Ada's tone of voice when she answered me. She seemed genuinely surprised when I asked her where it was."

"And number two?" Sean asked.

"Ada brought it into the kitchen with her when she talked to us after she'd finished her reading," Libby said, chiming in.

Bernie nodded. "When Ada came in she put the notebook on the kitchen table. I remember because she set it right next to the bottle of olive oil and I almost knocked the notebook to the floor when I reached for the bottle to pack it up. And I don't think she picked the notebook back up again when she went back to the living room. At least, I don't remember her doing it if she did."

Sean leaned forward. "What about you, Libby?"

"I didn't see her pick the notebook up, either," Libby said, backing up Bernie's observation. "And she didn't go back into the kitchen again," she added. "She was in the living room, and then she ran outside, got into her mom's car, and took off."

"Ergo, someone else who was there came in the kitchen and took the notebook," Sean said.

"That's the logical inference," Bernie said. "Which is one of the reasons I think Ada is innocent. I mean why go to the trouble of taking the notebook if there wasn't something damaging in it?"

"You may have a point," Sean reluctantly conceded. "Although, there is another possibility. Maybe no one took it. Maybe the notebook got thrown out in all the confusion."

Bernie made a face. "I'm not saying it's not possible, but I don't think it's very likely. Almost everything was packed up when Ada came in the kitchen, which meant we'd already taken the trash out."

"Or," Libby hypothesized, "the notebook could have fallen on the floor and we didn't see it and someone picked it up."

"Which leaves us where we were before, which is nowhere," Sean said, embarking on a different train of thought. "Everyone there did New Year's

Eve together every year," he noted as Cindy came back into the living room, jumped up onto his lap, circled three times, and plopped herself down.

Bernie nodded. "That is correct."

"Do they all work at Sinclair Enterprises?" Sean asked.

"Yes," Libby said. "And everyone is coming into money when the company goes public."

Sean absentmindedly rubbed Cindy's ears. She started to purr. "And, they do this Christmas popper thing every year, right?" asked Sean, continuing down his list.

This time it was Libby's turn to nod. "According to Ada, it's part of their New Year's Eve tradition."

"So, it would be easy enough to set up Peggy's death beforehand," Sean mused.

"Yes, it would," Bernie agreed. "In fact, you'd have had to, given it was cyanide. Then all you'd have to do was make sure that the right person got the poisoned popper."

Libby laughed. "I must say that's quite the sentence. Can you say that fast, five times?"

"I have a better one," Bernie replied. "Can you say, 'the proper person purloined the poisoned popper', five times?"

"How about we get back to what we were talking about," Sean said.

Bernie and Libby thought for a moment, then

Bernie said, "I'm guessing Linda probably bought the same kind of poppers every year, so maybe everyone had a favorite. For example, Ada's mom always took the red one, while Peggy always chose green."

"Thin," Sean observed.

"Agreed," Bernie said, "but plausible. There may be another explanation, but I can't think of it at the moment."

"Who did Ada speak to about discovering her dad's notebook in the attic?" Sean asked, changing course.

Bernie frowned. "As far as I know just Libby and myself. The whole idea was to take everyone by surprise. That's why Bernie and I were watching. But her mother could have seen the notebook and told someone else. I mean maybe Ada left it lying on her bed before she knew what was in it."

"It's possible," Sean allowed. He scratched behind Cindy's ears.

"Plus, I don't believe in coincidence," Bernie said. "Ada's dad and Peggy both dying on New Year's Eve, both poisoned, what are the odds?"

"Not that high, if it's true," Sean admitted.

"That's what Ada is saying," Bernie said.

Sean lifted his arms above his head and stretched. He was getting sucked into this, despite himself. "I'll have salad now," he told Libby, pausing to gather his thoughts.

She nodded and served him some on a salad

plate; shaved a bit of parmesan cheese over the baby romaine, endive, arugula, and walnuts; and handed the plate to her dad.

He smiled appreciatively. His daughters' salads were always crafted with an eye toward balance and appearance instead of carelessly thrown together without any thought.

"Excellent," he said as he took a bite of an endive leaf coated in olive oil, lemon juice, and a small sprinkling of sea salt. Then he got back to Peggy's death. "Next, we come to the most puzzling question, the question of the poison. Where did that come from?"

"Maybe it's a by-product of the Sinclairs' manufacturing process?" Libby guessed.

"Cyanide?" Sean said incredulously. "They're manufacturing a hair restorer. How would cyanide come into that?"

"I don't know," Libby said. "But they do use mercury to smelt gold."

"What does that have to do with anything?" Sean demanded.

"Nothing, really," Libby allowed. "I was just pointing out that industrial processes have by-products."

Sean raised an eyebrow. "And?"

"Well, the cyanide had to come from some-where," Libby observed. "So maybe it is a by-product. After all, you can't order it on Amazon."

"Not yet, anyway," Bernie observed. "But you could order it on the dark web."

Sean nodded. "Or make it."

"Seriously? How?" Libby asked.

"Let's get into that later," Sean said. "I think the more germane question is why kill Peggy at that particular time and place?"

"Obviously, someone was trying to send a message," Libby posited.

Sean nodded. "Exactly. Otherwise whoever did this could have killed Peggy in a less splashy manner."

"Splashy," Bernie said. "Nice word."

Sean nodded his thanks.

"Or," Bernie hypothesized, "maybe we're over-thinking this. Maybe this was the only time and place the killer could be assured of getting to her."

Libby broke off a piece of the baguette, buttered it, shaved a little parmesan on top of it, and ate it. "Then the second question would be, who was the message intended for?" Libby asked after she'd swallowed.

"If Peggy's death was in fact intended as a message," Bernie said.

"Which we don't know," Sean told her. Then he went back to eating his salad. "So, where and when are you going to meet Ada?" he asked when he was done.

"Ada told me she'd call and let me know," Bernie said.

"Just be careful," Sean warned, picturing a secluded rendezvous out in the woods somewhere.

"I'm always careful," Bernie responded.

Sean snorted.

"Well, I am," she insisted. "More or less," she added in the name of full disclosure.

"Mostly less," Sean said.

"Okay, I might have a high-risk tolerance," Bernie admitted.

"What does that even mean?" Libby demanded.

"It means I didn't mind getting in risky situations, unlike some other people I could name," Bernie told her sister.

"Oh," Libby said. "You mean the ones with common sense?"

Sean rubbed his chin with the knuckles of his right hand. "High-risk tolerance," he mused, savoring the phrase. "I like it."

Bernie grinned as a thought occurred to her. "I'm glad you do, because in keeping with that, remember how you asked Libby if she wanted to double down on our bet?"

Sean nodded. "Indeed I do."

"Well, Libby and I will take that offer."

Libby's head shot up. "We will?"

"Yes," Bernie firmly declared. "We will."

Sean rubbed his hands together. "It will be my pleasure to accept," he said.

"Bernie, are you nuts?" Libby demanded.

"Not at all," Bernie said.

Libby threw her arms up in the air. "Tell me why we're doing this?"

Bernie pointed at the sofa. "Because I just really, really, really want to get rid of this sofa." She paused for a moment and added, "And get Dad a new chair."

"My chair?" Sean squawked. "Who said anything about my chair?"

Bernie smiled. "Having second thoughts, are we, about doubling down?"

Stung, Sean straightened his back and stuck out his chin. "I most certainly am not," he declared. Then it was his turn to smile as he thought of the possibilities. "Maybe we'll go out to Montauk and make a weekend out of it. I always liked deep-sea fishing off the charter boats out there." He cracked his knuckles. "I look forward to it."

"What are we betting on anyway?" Libby asked plaintively.

Bernie told her.

Chapter 12

It was snowing when Ada called Bernie at six the next morning and it was still snowing when she and Libby left to meet Ada at ten-thirty. As promised, the storm had arrived at three a.m. and settled itself in for a long visit, bringing with it swirling eddies of flakes that clung to the trees and the lampposts and blanketed the streets and the cars, turning everything clean and white.

Due to the weather, the sisters had expected a light morning turnout at the shop but that hadn't been the case. At seven o'clock the line had become a scrum as people grabbed their coffee, pastry, and/or breakfast sandwiches and headed for the train station to begin their commute to work. Judging by the number of customers in the store, it looked as if the holidays were officially over.

"I guess people have gotten used to the weather," Libby observed as she made more coffee. At one point, she and Bernie had considered serving pour-overs as an option, but the logistics didn't add up. People wanted to get their coffee and get out. Usually they wanted dark roast in the morning and afternoon and a light roast or decaf in the evening when they stopped in to get dinner to take home.

"Either that or they don't have any more days off," Bernie replied absentmindedly as she surveyed what was left in the display case, which wasn't much. They had sold out of most of their pastries and almost all of their muffins. They definitely needed to make double batches this evening. The only thing that hadn't sold were the bran muffins. As per usual. They had almost a full tray left. Bernie pointed to them and said, "Libby, either we need to play around with this recipe and see if we can come up with something sexier or we need to stop baking them."

"Mrs. Congel will be sad if we do that," Libby noted, which was her usual comment when the bran muffin subject was broached.

Bernie made a face. "Come on, you know that's just an excuse," she replied. She and her sister had this conversation at least once every two months. "You just don't want to retire them because they were Mom's recipe."

"That's partially true," Libby admitted. When she made her mom's recipes she felt as if Rose was in the kitchen with her.

"Libby, Mom would understand. She would know that there are fashions in food like everything else. Maybe in a couple of years, bran will be the new big thing, eclipsing gluten-free, and we'll bring the recipe back. With a few tweaks," Bernie said. "You have to admit the muffins are pretty bland. And heavy."

"And Mrs. Congel and Mrs. Han and Mr. Schimmer? What about them?" Libby protested. "Because they will not be happy. They've been eating those muffins since Mom opened the shop."

"We'll bake a special tin for them. How's that?"

"I'll think about it," Libby said grudgingly. She knew Bernie was right, she knew she was being too sentimental, but she just wasn't ready to stop making the bran muffins quite yet. "Maybe in the spring," she conceded.

Bernie nodded. *Progress,* she thought as she went into the back to get the tray of apricot scones to fill in the empty spot that had been occupied by the corn muffins. Now that was her mom's recipe, too, but the corn muffins hadn't gone out of fashion.

In fact, just the opposite. They had people calling up to reserve theirs if they were going to be late because they were always gone by eight-thirty. The only reason they had extra today was because Mrs. Randall had canceled her order. Funny how these things worked, Bernie reflected as she took out the empty corn muffin tray and slid in the tray with the scones.

"Maybe we should think about making some savory tarts for breakfast," Bernie said, straightening up. "You know, galettes." She'd seen a couple for sale at the coffee shop, The Roaster, two blocks over and been impressed by their looks, messy circles of dough folded around sautéed combinations of gleaming potatoes, carrots, and onions layered with ricotta and feta, and garnished with oil-burnished radicchio leaves. "We could make some with eggs and some without. I think they would be a hit with the vegetarian crowd. Something different."

"I think you're right," Libby said. "And they'd be a good way to use up our dough scraps."

"And our leftovers," Bernie noted.

"Waste not, want not," both sisters chanted together and laughed. The saying had been their mother's mantra. And it certainly applied in the food business. At least if you wanted to stay in business it did.

Bernie looked at her watch. It was eight-thirty. Given the weather conditions, she and Libby had an hour before they had to leave to meet Ada. Plenty of time to phone in their order to Scilia's Fruits and Vegetables; do some paperwork; start the barbecue brisket, tonight's special; make the dough for parsnip pie; and shovel the walk in front of the shop yet again.

Fifty minutes later, the sisters had just finished with their tasks and gone out front to tell Amber and Googie they were taking off when Ada's uncle, Henry, burst through the shop door and headed straight for Bernie and Libby, colliding with Mrs. Livingston, who was standing in front of the display case trying to decide between an

131

apple cranberry muffin and a cheese Danish. She and Mrs. Paxton and Mrs. Elderberry turned and stared at him.

Sinclair was wearing a jacket that was too light for the weather; a long, maroon wool scarf wrapped around his neck; khaki pants; and regular shoes, which he stamped as he walked, leaving little clots of snow behind him on the floor Googie had just mopped.

This can't be good, Libby thought, taking in the ugly expression on Henry Sinclair's face as she asked him if anything was wrong.

Ada's uncle grunted and disregarded her question. "Where is she?" he demanded.

"Where is who?" Bernie asked, genuinely at a loss.

"Ada, of course."

"I have no idea," Bernie replied. Which was true. She knew where Ada was going to be, but she didn't know where she was right now. "Why? What's going on?"

Ada's uncle looked from one sister to the other and tapped his nose. "You're lying!" he shouted. "I can smell it."

"Ah, 'the odor of mendacity,'" said Bernie, quoting a line from Tennessee Williams's *Cat on a Hot Tin Roof.* "I know it well."

Henry Sinclair took a step toward her. "Don't get smart with me," he growled. "It's imperative that I find my niece."

"Imperative," Bernie mocked. "Not important, but imperative. Wow. Do you mind telling me why?"

"Yeah, I do mind telling you why," Sinclair replied, mimicking Bernie's voice. "I mind because it's none of your damned business." And he took another step toward her, made his hands into fists, and brought them up to his sides.

Bernie was just thinking that sometimes it didn't pay to be a wiseass when Googie stepped out from behind the counter. "Boss, you want me to call the cops?" he asked her.

Bernie shook her head. "That won't be necessary," she told him. "Mr. Sinclair was just leaving." She turned to Ada's uncle. "Weren't you?"

Henry Sinclair moistened his lips. "I need to speak to her," he said in a more subdued tone of voice.

"We'll tell her if we see her," Libby told him.

"Aha." Sinclair shook a finger at her. His voice rose again. "So, you *are* seeing Ada," he exclaimed while Mrs. Paxton's, Mrs. Livingston's, and Mrs. Elderberry's eyes widened at the spectacle that was taking place in front of them.

"I said *if,* not when," Libby told him as she reflected that thanks to Mrs. Paxton the entire town of Longely would know about this exchange within an hour or less. "Now," she continued, "unless you want to buy something,

I suggest that you leave or Googie *will* call the cops."

Henry opened his mouth to say something, closed it, then opened it again and said, "I need to talk to her. You make sure and tell her that."

"And how is she going to do that?" Bernie asked as Ada's uncle spun around on his heel and marched out of A Little Taste of Heaven, slamming the door shut behind him.

"You two lead the most fascinating lives," Mrs. Paxton trilled once the front door had closed. She put her hand to her heart. "I was afraid that man was going to commit an act of violence against you. My heart is still racing."

"Mine too," Mrs. Elderberry said. "This is the most excitement since the washing machine overflowed at the Laundromat."

"And my shoulder is bruised," Mrs. Livingston said, pointing to it. "That man certainly doesn't seem very nice. He didn't even say excuse me!" she noted indignantly.

"He's upset," Bernie said. "Very upset. My apologies, ladies. Whatever you want is on the house."

"I couldn't," Mrs. Paxton twittered.

"That's unnecessary," Mrs. Elderberry said.

Mrs. Livingston didn't say anything.

"It will be our pleasure, won't it, Libby?" Bernie said.

"Definitely," Libby agreed.

"What is going on?" Mrs. Livingston asked.

"Truthfully, I have no idea," Bernie told her as she stared out of the shop's front window. She couldn't see Henry Sinclair. The moment he'd stepped out onto the street, he'd vanished into a curtain of white. Bernie turned and looked at the clock on the wall. It was time to get going.

"That was interesting," Bernie said to Libby on the way up the stairs to say good-bye to their dad.

"Well, the ladies loved it. Food and drama. What could be better? And for free too."

Bernie laughed because what her sister said was true. "They'll probably come back tomorrow to see what else is going to happen."

"They'll come back anyway. They're here every day." Then Libby fell silent. She didn't say any more because by that time they were going into their flat and she didn't want to talk about what had happened in the shop in front of her dad.

They said their good-byes to Sean and put on their parkas and boots and gloves and went outside. Libby brushed the snow off Mathilda while Bernie started the van up. Five minutes later they were on their way.

What they didn't do was pay any attention to the silver Camry that pulled in behind them after they'd gone half a block.

There was no reason to.

Not that they could have seen anything but the headlights anyway.

135

Chapter 13

"Isn't this ever going to stop?" Bernie groused as she drove down Prince Street. They were headed for the first service stop on the thruway going north from New York City. Hopefully, that road would be plowed because the side streets in Longely were pretty bad at the moment.

"Not till tomorrow evening," Libby informed her sister. "At least that's what the weatherman is saying. He's predicting a foot and a half of snow."

Bernie groaned. "Jeez. You'd think we were living in Upstate New York instead of Westchester," she complained as she fiddled with the heater, trying to coax a little more hot air out of it and failing. "On the bright side, at least Mathilda's windshield wipers are working," she noted as she turned them on to high.

"If they weren't, we wouldn't be driving," Libby replied. "Which might not be a bad thing," she reflected. "We could always turn around," she added.

"We will if it gets really bad," Bernie assured her.

"Define bad," Libby challenged. Over the years, she'd learned that it paid to specify parameters when dealing with her sister.

"Worse than it is now," Bernie replied, which, Libby reflected, really wasn't an answer at all.

Then Libby thought of something else. "Maybe Ada won't even be there," she said. "Maybe she started out and turned around."

Bernie leaned forward so she could see better out of the windshield. "Why don't you call her and find out." She certainly didn't want to be out on the road if she didn't have to. She nodded toward her bag. "My phone is in the outside pocket."

Libby leaned over and got it. Then she dialed. The call went straight to voicemail. She left a message telling Ada to call back and hung up.

"What do you think?" she said.

"She's probably on her way," Bernie replied, keeping her eyes glued to the road. A moment later she added, "We need to do this. We need to hear what Ada has to say, especially now."

"Because of her uncle?"

"Because of him and other reasons," Bernie told Libby. "I wonder what got into him all of a sudden?"

"Peggy Graceson's death? The notebook?"

"He didn't seem to react to it when Ada was standing up there reading her excerpt," Bernie pointed out.

"Maybe he's a good actor. Maybe there really is something damaging in the notebook. Or maybe he's upset about something that has nothing to do with what I just said." Libby frowned. "I can hardly wait till Dad hears about his visit. I can see the smile on his face now."

"Having second thoughts about the bet?"

"And third and fourth ones," Libby noted.

Bernie looked at her sister, then turned her eyes back to the road. "You could have said no, but you didn't."

"You took me by surprise."

Bernie made a rude noise.

"I'm sorry, but you should have discussed it with me first."

"I thought we had," Bernie said.

"Maybe I changed my mind."

"Then you should have told me. I'm not a mind reader."

Libby bit back her retort and changed the subject. "Why did Ada pick a service area to meet anyway?" she asked Bernie. "Why not meet at the mall? Or a diner?"

"My best guess?"

"Well, Bernie, certainly not your worst one."

"Possibly because this service area is closer than the mall," Bernie replied after a moment's thought. "More convenient for her." The mall was half an hour away.

"Which means Ada's staying around here," Libby hypothesized.

Bernie nodded. "And the service area has some of the same advantages a mall has. Lots of vehicles. Lots of people around. Easy to get in. Easy to get out of."

"I get it, but so what?" Libby asked. "What does Ada expect to happen? Does she think we're going to blow her in to the cops?"

Bernie stopped at a red light. "From her actions, I'd say she appears to be entertaining that possibility, but that's ridiculous." Her dad had spoken to Clyde, his friend at the Longely PD. According to him, there wasn't a warrant out for her arrest. The police just wanted to talk to her.

"There isn't a warrant out *yet*." Libby took a sip of hot chocolate and was setting her cup back down in the cup holder when an idea occurred to her. "Unless her mom reported her car stolen. Then there would be."

"Do you think Linda would do that?" Bernie asked as she took a sip of the coffee she'd brought along. Although she envied Libby her hot chocolate, she was trying to lose the three pounds she'd gained over the holidays and somehow hot chocolate made with heavy cream, milk, and good-quality chocolate didn't seem the way to go.

Libby shook her head. "Honestly, I don't have a clue."

"I think Linda would have mentioned it to us if she had," Bernie noted. "God only knows she's told us everything else."

"Don't remind me," Libby said, looking out the window at a woman standing on the front steps of her house watching her kids and dog run zigzags in the front yard. She remembered when she and her sister used to build snowmen on the sidewalk in front of the shop. Back then snowstorms had been the best things ever. "At least someone is enjoying this weather," she observed.

Bernie sighed. "I just wish Ada would come home so we didn't have to speak to her mom twice a day. That lady never shuts up. Anyway, Linda's got another car."

"Well, she is worried."

"About her daughter or her vehicle?"

"Both, I would say." Libby turned from the window. "Do you think Dad would report us if we did something like that?" she asked.

"Ran off with his car?" Bernie clarified.

"Yes," Libby replied.

"No," Bernie said, slowing down. She had been following the red taillights of the vehicle in front of her, but he had turned off and now, without a guide, she was having trouble seeing the road. Everything was a blanket of white. "He'd wait till we came home and then he'd ground us for the rest of our lives—metaphorically speaking." Bernie stopped talking as she slowed down to fifteen miles an hour because the last thing she wanted to do was hit the curb and pop a wheel. Then she spotted another pair of taillights in front of Mathilda and picked up speed. Luckily the thruway entrance wasn't that far away and from there things would hopefully get better. "Anyway," she continued, "why would Ada call us and ask us to meet if she thinks we'd do something like that in the first place? That makes no sense."

"Nothing about this makes sense," Libby reflected gloomily as she finished up her almond croissant, which was excellent, if she had to say so herself. Usually she didn't like baking with marzipan. Most of the commercial brands she'd tried over the years were too sweet, but this one was quite wonderful. You could taste the almonds.

"Of course," Bernie reflected, "if Ada is paranoid in the clinical sense of the word, then nothing about her actions has to make sense."

"Except to her," Libby pointed out.

"But is she paranoid?" Bernie mused. "That's the question. Let's not forget that Peggy was poisoned ten years to the day after Ada's father was, so maybe her assumption is correct."

"If he was," Libby said. "We don't know that for a fact."

Bernie sighed. "At least the thruway will be plowed," she noted, trying to stay positive.

"And there probably won't be any traffic on the road," Libby commented. "After all, it's Monday and Mondays are never that busy. Not to mention the storm," she added. "Anyone with any sense is staying home."

"Yeah, we're the only morons out here," Bernie noted.

"You said it, I didn't," Libby said.

"You always have to have the last word, don't you?" Bernie snapped.

"No. Sometimes I have to have the first word," Libby snapped back.

"It was a rhetorical question!"

"I know what it was," Libby said.

"Don't be so pissy," Bernie countered.

"You're right. I'm sorry," Libby said as she reflected that bad weather, like bad food, never brought out the best in people.

Bernie grunted her acceptance and went back to concentrating on the road.

As it turned out, Libby's assessment was correct—traffic was nonexistent. Nevertheless, they got to the rest stop eight minutes late due to the weather conditions. In the summer, the parking lot would have been jammed with vehicles full of people going up to their summer camps, but this was a winter weekday on a bad weather day and the parking lot was empty except for a spattering of cars clustered around the entrance.

"Look," Libby said, pointing to the light blue Chevy near the door. "That's Linda's car."

"I guess Ada got here after all," Bernie said

as she pulled in next to it. Then she flipped up her parka hood, got out of Mathilda, closed the van door, jammed her hands in her pockets, and hurried inside with Libby following close behind her.

Chapter 14

"When was the last time you ate fast food?" Bernie asked her sister as she surveyed the vastness of the food court. Even with the bright overhead lights the place looked dim and it took Bernie a moment to realize that was because the snow was covering the skylights and blocking out the daylight.

"Garlic pizza. Last week," Libby promptly answered.

Bernie brushed a couple of snowflakes off her shoulder. "Pizza is a staple. No. I mean like Mickey Dee's or Burger King."

Libby considered her answer for a moment. It had definitely been a while. "Probably a couple of years. The last time I remember was when we ended up in that small town in Pennsylvania when the van broke down."

"Not since?"

"No. You?"

Bernie shook her head. "The same. Does that make us food snobs?"

"Bernie, I have news for you, we are food snobs," Libby said.

"You're right, we are. So, does that make us bad people?"

"No. It makes us foodies. Although," Libby

reflected, "I do like Mickey Dee's fries and I loved their apple pies when they fried them."

"Anything fried tastes good," Bernie noted. "And I like Popeye's chicken, so I guess that counts for something," she said.

"And their biscuits," Libby added. "I don't know why, but I do."

"Kind of like the way I feel about Hershey's Kisses," Bernie confessed as she looked around some more. "This place is practically deserted," she observed, gesturing at the pastel-colored plastic seats and tables lined up in rows, standing at attention under fluorescent lamps, as they waited for people to sit at them. "I can't imagine what the heat bill is in this place." She turned to Libby. "Do you think the franchises pay it?"

"Absolutely," her sister replied. "They pay a percentage in the mall. I'm sure it works the same here. And let's not forget the salaries the franchises are paying out," she said, nodding toward the servers standing behind their counters and chatting with each other or checking their cell phones as they waited to dish out hamburgers and tacos and fried chicken to people who weren't there. Along the far wall, a man slowly dragged a mop across the floor. He reminded Bernie of a snail moving across the sidewalk, leaving a gleaming trail behind him.

Bernie shook her head. "A Little Taste of

Heaven is so small time compared to something like this."

"Yes, it is," Libby agreed, "and that's the way I like it."

"Me too," Bernie said. She gestured to the food concessions. "This would make me nuts."

"I wonder what their net is," Libby mused.

"A lot when they're busy," Bernie said, looking around. She counted a total of seven customers in the food court. Ada wasn't one of them. "Do you see her?" she asked Libby.

Libby shook her head. "Maybe she's gone to the bathroom," she suggested.

"Or she's buying something in the convenience store," Bernie guessed, nodding to the shop that was tucked into a corner over on the right-hand side of the building. But when Bernie walked over and took a quick peek inside she didn't see anyone in there except for two bored-looking clerks who were communing with their cell phones.

Bernie walked back slowly scanning every available inch of space, making sure she hadn't missed anyone. She hadn't. She was just about to suggest that Libby stay where she was while she checked out the ladies' room when someone sitting across the room, in front of the Starbucks concession, put down their phone and waved at them.

"Over here," the person cried, standing up.

146

Bernie blinked. It took her a moment to realize who it was.

"Oh my God," Libby exclaimed, putting her hand to her mouth. "That's Ada."

"Yes, it is," Bernie said as she scrutinized the person walking toward them.

Life on the run hadn't been kind to Ada, Bernie decided. In the short time she'd been out of the house she'd lost weight and not in a good way. Her face was gaunt, she'd developed dark circles under her eyes, her skin was breaking out around her nose, and she'd acquired the pallor that people on the East Coast get in the winter. She'd cut and dyed her hair, having gone from a shoulder-length brunette to a pixie-cut blonde. But she must have done it herself, Bernie reflected, because her hair looked like straw and the cut had a hacked-off quality to it. That made Bernie wonder how she would look if she didn't have a decent haircut, or makeup, or she couldn't afford to go to the woman in Rye, New York, who shaped her eyebrows, or the seamstress in Longely who altered her clothes. She'd look a mess. Absolutely. No doubt about that.

Ada had also dispensed with her jewelry and makeup. Gone were the hoop earrings, bangles, and tangles of chains along with the glitter eyeshadow and bright red lipstick. Now, she was wearing a nondescript pair of skinny jeans; a gray T-shirt under an oversized, unzipped black hoodie; and a pair of dirty tan suede Uggs. She looked like your typical teenager, Bernie thought. She'd made herself look entirely unmemorable. You'd pass her on the street and not give her a second glance.

"I didn't recognize you," Bernie told Ada as Ada got nearer to them.

"That's the general idea," Ada said.

"You look about twelve," Libby told her. "But in a good way," she quickly added, hoping her comment wasn't misconstrued.

"So, where are you staying?" Bernie asked, using her casual, no-big-deal, just-between-us-girls tone of voice. "Is it nice?"

"Why won't you tell us? Don't you trust us?" Libby asked Ada when she didn't answer.

"It's not that I don't trust you, it's just that you can never be too careful," Ada told Libby as she led the sisters back to the table she'd been sitting at. Once there, she sat down, reached for her half-eaten breakfast sandwich, took a bite, chewed, and swallowed.

"Your uncle was in the store looking for you," Bernie told Ada as she took a seat across from her. "And he didn't seem very happy."

Ada stiffened. She put her sandwich down. "You didn't tell him about our meeting, did you?"

"Of course not," Bernie reassured her as she loosened her scarf. "What does he want?"

"I don't know," Ada responded.

"I find that hard to believe," Libby said.

"Well, it's true," Ada protested.

"I see," Bernie said.

Ada studied her hands.

"Let me guess," Bernie said as she looked at Ada. "Does it have something to do with the notebook?"

Ada bit her lip. "Maybe," she muttered. "I'm not sure."

"Really?" Watching Ada gave Libby an idea. The idea was farfetched but she decided to try it out anyway. "Was the whole New Year's Eve thing a setup?" Libby asked.

Ada squirmed around in her seat and looked everywhere but at Bernie and Libby.

"It was, wasn't it?" Libby said.

"Kinda," Ada admitted.

Bernie took a deep breath and let it out. She wanted to throttle Ada. Instead she managed to keep her composure and asked Ada to explain.

"I think you owe us that much," Libby said.

Ada swallowed. Bernie reflected she looked on the verge of tears. "I'm so sorry," she said. "I never meant anything like this to happen."

"We know," Bernie reassured her.

"I just . . ." Ada stopped, took a deep breath, and started again. "When I found Dad's notebook, it made me stop and think about when he died and that it was ten years ago and how the police never caught his killer and I was looking at the notebook and it's got all this stuff in it and I thought if I read it aloud and pretended all that stuff meant something . . ."

"Maybe it would flush out your dad's killer?" Libby said softly.

"Because you still believe he was killed," Bernie said.

Ada nodded. "But that's not what happened," she said. She started to say something else and then stopped. Her mouth fell open and the color left her face.

Bernie and Libby turned to see what she was looking at.

"Damn," Bernie cursed.

Henry Sinclair was standing in the entrance to the food court, shaking the snow off his jacket, and looking around.

Ada slid down in her seat and leaned over so she could grab her backpack, which was on the floor next to her chair. "You said you didn't tell him," she said to Bernie and Libby.

"We didn't," Libby said. "I swear."

"Then what's he doing here?" Ada hissed, slinking even lower in her chair than Bernie thought possible and pointing at Sinclair.

"He must have followed us," Libby told her. It was the only explanation she could think of that made sense. "He must have waited for us to leave."

"He was the taillights behind us," Bernie

realized, thinking back. At the time, she hadn't given them any thought. She'd just thought it was another vehicle. "I am so sorry."

"Maybe there's something in that notebook after all," Libby observed. "Or at least your uncle thinks there is."

"Unless he wants something else," Bernie said.

"I have to go," Ada declared. "I have to go now."

"Don't go, stay," Bernie pleaded. "You're safe with us."

Ada shook her head. "Really? I don't think so."

"You haven't even told us what you wanted to say," Bernie said.

"It's too late," Ada answered as Henry Sinclair started walking in their direction.

Ada stood up abruptly, accidentally knocking her coffee cup over with her hand. Bernie watched the brown liquid pool onto the table, then drip onto the floor as her uncle barreled toward them. In another moment, he was standing in front of them. The odor of alcohol wafted off of him.

"Your mother and your aunt are worried sick," Sinclair told Ada as he rubbed the top of his nose with his knuckle. His nose, Bernie noted, was even redder than usual. Probably due to a combination of the cold and booze, she surmised. "You need to come home."

"No," Ada replied, her voice rising.

"We have things to discuss," Henry declared.

151

"No we don't," Ada told him.

"It's time for you to grow up and take responsibility for your actions," Henry told her.

"That's a laugh coming from you," Ada retorted.

Bernie and Libby both stood up. They wanted to be ready for whatever happened. Also, Bernie didn't want to get any coffee on her new coat, the one she'd just gotten on sale at Barney's.

"You're the one that's causing all the problems with your running around," Ada told Henry as she grabbed her jacket and turned to go.

"No," Henry Sinclair said, reaching over, taking Ada's upper arm in his hand, and twisting her back around so that she faced him. "You're not going anywhere. You and I are going to have a little chat," he told her, as Bernie and Libby moved closer to him.

"Calm down, Henry," Libby told him.

"Don't you tell me what to do," Henry snarled at her.

"Let go of me, Uncle Henry," Ada demanded. "I have nothing to say to you."

Sinclair squeezed Ada's arm more tightly. "I think you do. No, I know you do. Don't play the innocent with me. You and I are going to have a nice, long talk."

"Let her go," Bernie ordered.

Sinclair ignored her. All his attention was focused on Ada.

"I'm not talking to you, Uncle Henry!" Ada

screamed. "I'm never going to talk to you again. You can go to hell."

"I'm telling you to let her go," Bernie repeated, plucking at the sleeve of Sinclair's jacket as she tried to insinuate herself between him and Ada.

Sinclair glared at Bernie. "Don't involve yourself in this," he growled. "You'll be sorry if you do."

"I already am," Bernie told him as she moved closer.

"I mean it, Simmons," Henry Sinclair said.

"So do I," Bernie replied as she half turned to her sister. "Hey, anytime you want to jump in here be my guest."

"Why can't we all just get along," Libby said, not being a big fan of physical confrontation.

"I don't know. Ask him," Bernie retorted, nodding toward Ada's uncle.

Libby was moving toward Sinclair's left side when Ada kicked her uncle in his right knee.

"That's my bad knee!" he screamed, gasping in pain. He loosened his grip just enough for Ada to slip out of his grasp and run for the door. "You're going to pay for this, Ada!" he screamed after her as he shook off Bernie and Libby and began hobbling after her. "Your mother should never have let you come home in the first place."

Sinclair hadn't gotten very far when Bernie grabbed the back of his jacket and pulled. Sinclair whirled around. Bernie was taking a step back

153

as Sinclair was raising his fist when she heard someone behind her say, "Is there a problem here?"

Bernie turned around. It was the security guard. His hand was on his Taser.

Henry Sinclair dropped his hand to his side and pasted a smile on his face. Then he said, "No, officer, no problem at all," the lie falling out his mouth effortlessly. "My niece and I were just having a little family disagreement." He chuckled. "You know how teenagers can get."

"No. I wouldn't know," replied the security guard, who looked as if he wasn't too far out of that age range himself. *Callow* was the word that sprung to Bernie's mind. He swallowed, his Adam's apple bobbing up and down. "We don't tolerate that kind of behavior here," he intoned, standing up as tall as his five feet six inches would allow and puffing out his spindly chest.

Henry Sinclair nodded. "And I respect that. As I said, this was just a little family spat that got out of hand." Henry raised his hand. "I promise it won't happen again."

Boy, is Henry Sinclair a good liar. Smooth as silk, as Mom used to say, thought Bernie as the security guard pointed to her and her sister with his free hand. "I suppose these are family members, too?"

"No," Sinclair answered. "Just friends of my niece. I know they're just trying to help, but they're really making the situation worse." And he gave the guard a big, disarming smile. "I'm sure you see this kind of thing all the time." Then he paused for a moment and added, "Now, if you don't mind, I'll go and see how my niece is doing. My vehicle is locked and I wouldn't want her standing out in a blizzard on a morning like this."

Double smooth, Bernie thought as the security guard nodded and told Sinclair to get out of there. Sinclair got. Bernie could tell the guard was relieved to see him go.

"And you two," the guard said, turning to Bernie and Libby.

"Yes, officer," Libby replied.

"Don't get involved in things that are none of your business."

"A sentiment my dad frequently expresses," Bernie noted.

The guard didn't crack a smile. "We don't tolerate disruption. If you continue to engage in this kind of behavior you'll get yourself banned from the food court," he warned.

"Oh, no. Say it isn't so," Bernie quipped, putting her hand to her heart.

The security guard frowned. His eyes narrowed.

"She's kidding, officer," Libby quickly said. "This won't happen again, officer. I swear."

"It'd better not," the security guard growled. He was resting both hands on his belt now, which Libby was happy to see.

"Are we free to go?" she asked.

The guard nodded. "Yeah." He made a move-it-along motion with his hand. "Get out of here."

Which they did. With alacrity. But by the time Bernie and Libby were out the door, both Ada and Henry Sinclair were nowhere to be seen. Not that the sisters had expected either of them to hang around and wait for them.

"I wonder what that was about?" Libby asked as she cleaned off Mathilda's passenger-side windows for the second time that morning.

"Me too," Bernie remarked after she'd cleaned off the side windows on the driver's side and gotten into the van. She started her up. Mathilda's engine coughed and sputtered and finally caught as Libby climbed into the van and shut the door behind her. It didn't close and Libby slammed it shut while Bernie turned on the windshield wipers. An inch of snow flew off the window. Libby fastened her seat belt.

"I can't believe what Ada said about the notebook," Libby said.

"Well, Ada's creative," Bernie observed. "I'll give her that."

"Those are not the words I would use," Libby noted. "This is like one of those puzzles where there's a box within a box."

Bernie just grunted. She was thinking about the drive home.

Chapter 15

Two days later, Sean was watching the early morning local news on the television when he called to his daughters. "Get in here," he cried. "You have to listen to this." After which he turned the volume up on the television.

"What?" Bernie asked as she came out of the bathroom drying her hair with a towel. Somehow, she'd managed to get butter in it—how, she wasn't sure.

"Everything okay?" Libby inquired as she joined her sister in the living room.

Both had come up from downstairs a half hour ago, where they'd finished baking banana chocolate chip muffins, cinnamon raisin buns, and ricotta, feta cheese, and spinach galettes for the morning rush; making coffee; restocking coolers; and starting the prep work for the lunch salads.

Sean pointed to the television. "Just listen." And he made the sound even louder.

An announcer was sitting behind the desk, hands folded in front of him, brow furrowed, every hair shellacked in place, a professionally serious expression on his face, reading off the teleprompter.

He said, "This just in. The body that was found

early yesterday morning on Hudson Street by a man out walking his dog has just been officially identified. It appears that Henry Sinclair, a prominent local citizen, was the victim of a hit-and-run accident. The police are looking for any information having to do with this incident. If you have any please call the tip line," and a number flashed across the screen. "Your information will remain confidential." When the number finished running, the announcer started on the next story: the missing money from the PTA fund-raiser for resodding the Hollingsworth baseball field.

"Holy cow," Libby said as Sean turned the sound down.

Bernie shook her head. "Holy cow is right."

"That's one way of putting it," Sean said, "although I can think of several others that would apply." He took a sip of the coffee Libby had brought him earlier in the morning. It was French roast with a touch of cream and two sugars. Just the way he liked it. He sighed in satisfaction and put the mug down on the side table. Then he grinned and said, "Suckers. You shouldn't have doubled down. Always walk away from the table when you're ahead," he added, a smug expression on his face. "Not that you ever were ahead in this case. I told you getting involved with the Sinclairs would be a mistake, and boy was I right."

"Henry Sinclair's death could be an accident," Libby protested.

Sean raised an eyebrow expressing his opinion of Libby's comment.

"It could be," Bernie said, taking Libby's side. She figured it was the least she could do given the circumstances. "It's possible. Maybe someone didn't see him walking on the road. It was still snowing yesterday morning and it's dark out. Maybe whoever hit him didn't realize what he or she had done. It's happened before," she insisted in the face of her dad's expression of disbelief. Then she conjured a different scenario. "Or maybe the person who did it was drunk or high or was on parole and fled the scene."

"Or maybe Ada ran him down," Sean said, thinking about the story his daughters had told him.

"That's a big leap," Bernie declared.

"Not to me," Sean said. "To me it's the obvious choice given what you guys witnessed."

"Obvious isn't always the correct choice," Bernie told him.

"Most of the time it is," Sean countered. "In my experience, A usually leads to B, which leads to C, etcetera, etcetera, and so forth and so on."

"I just don't see it," Bernie said, clicking her tongue against her teeth as she considered her dad's suggestion.

"Why not?" Sean said. "You said Ada and her uncle had a fight. You said she was terrified. It occurs to me that maybe she decided to finish her uncle off before he did her in."

Libby jumped into the discussion. "Now, that's assuming a lot. Just because the uncle was angry doesn't mean he was going to kill Ada."

"I didn't say he was. I said maybe Ada thought he was, with the emphasis on the word *thought*. People make bad decisions when they're scared," Sean told Libby. "They do things they shouldn't. It happens all the time. Especially when they feel alone and cornered, which describes Ada." Sean picked up his mug, took another sip of coffee, and lowered it again. "On another subject, I'm surprised the police aren't knocking on our door wanting to talk to you guys."

"Why should they?" Libby asked her dad.

Bernie answered for him. "Because of the fight in the service area. We were witnesses."

Sean nodded. "That's exactly right."

"How are the police going to know?" Libby asked. "They don't know we were there."

"I have one word for you," Sean said. "Video cams."

Libby turned to Bernie. "You can never leave anything well enough alone, can you?"

"No risk, no reward," Bernie shot back.

"What reward?" Libby demanded.

"Doing the right thing. Family unity," Bernie answered.

"Please," Libby said, thinking of being on a

fishing boat. Just the thought made her nauseous.

Bernie went over and gave her sister a quick hug. "Hey. It'll be fine. Don't worry about it. And anyway, there's another way to look at this," Bernie said after a moment had elapsed.

Sean cocked his head to one side. "I'm listening," he said.

"Yes," Libby added. "Do tell. I'm all ears."

"Okay then, ye of little faith, how about that this is proof of what Ada said?"

Sean snorted. "How do you get that, Bernie?"

"Simple," Bernie continued. "You can't say that the similarities between the crimes that happened ten years ago and the ones that just happened now aren't striking," she noted. "Two people hit by cars, two people poisoned."

"Possibly," Sean put in. "But we don't know if Ada's dad's death was deliberate or if he took too many painkillers and drank too much. And as for Grover's death, that could have been an accident. Sometimes, as Freud said, 'a cigar is just a cigar.'"

"True," Libby argued. "But the timing is very suggestive."

"However," Sean said, "following that line of reasoning could make Ada responsible for all four deaths. I thought your object was to prove her innocence."

"Give me a break," Bernie objected. "She was twelve when the first two murders—"

161

"If that's what they were," Sean pointed out.

"Were committed," Bernie said, finishing her sentence.

"Ever heard of *The Bad Seed*?" Sean shot back.

Bernie rolled her eyes. "That was a movie."

"Some movies are based on fact."

"And this is not one of them."

Sean grinned. "Just playing devil's advocate," he said. "I agree. It sounds implausible. The whole thing sounds implausible. What's the motive for someone killing four people in pairs ten years apart?"

"Something to do with the business?" Libby hypothesized. "They're about to go public now, which means everyone involved is going to get lots and lots of money."

"And ten years ago?" Sean prodded. "What happened then?"

Libby stifled a sneeze. She hoped she wasn't coming down with a cold. "I think the business was on the verge of going under at that point in time," she told him.

Bernie shifted her weight from her right to her left foot and started unwrapping her towel turban. "Or Peggy's and Jeff Sinclair's deaths could be a copycat killing," Bernie suggested.

Sean nodded his approval. "So, what are you going to do now?" Sean asked.

Bernie draped the towel over her arm and began combing her hair out with her fingers.

"Let me think about it," she said and went back into the bathroom to finish putting her makeup on.

She came back fifteen minutes later holding up her cell phone.

"What?" Libby said. "Why are you showing me that?"

Bernie tapped the cell phone's face. "Read the text," she said, handing the phone to her sister.

Libby did. The message read: I didn't do it. Help me. It was from Ada.

"Great," Libby said as she handed the phone back to Bernie.

"We owe her," Bernie said as she slipped the phone into the pocket of her vintage 1950s poodle applique felt skirt. For some reason, wearing it cheered her up. "She's family."

"She isn't and we don't," Libby replied.

"Yes we do," Bernie argued.

"Owe whom what?" Sean asked even though he had a pretty good idea what his younger daughter was talking about.

"Ada, of course," Bernie said.

Sean gave her a look of disgust. "I was afraid that's what you were saying." He finished the last of his coffee. "Does the phrase 'There's a sucker born every minute' mean anything to you?"

"Not really," Bernie told him.

"Then it should. See," Sean said and he waved his finger in the air for emphasis, "this is exactly the type of thing your mother was talking about. This is what I warned you against."

"And you were right," Bernie told him.

"That doesn't help," Sean replied.

"If we can't shed some light on this in a couple of days we'll back off," Bernie promised, hoping to placate her dad. "How's that?"

"Don't lie," Sean reproved.

"I wasn't," Bernie protested.

"Then what were you doing?" he asked.

"Being optimistic," Bernie answered.

Sean frowned. "Ha. So you say. Because I've never known you to back off anything once you get started."

"Gee, Dad," Bernie replied. "I wonder where I got that trait from?"

"Your mother," Sean answered promptly.

"I was thinking more of you," Bernie said.

"She was way more stubborn than I am," Sean said.

Libby snorted.

"Well, she was," Sean insisted.

"You know what you should do," Libby said, changing the subject.

"Take up golf," Sean suggested. "Learn bridge. Buy another car. Yes, I'll do that."

"I'm not even touching that one," Libby said, continuing on with what she'd been about to say. "Maybe you could speak to that friend of yours who headed the Hollingsworth PD. Maybe he can tell us what happened the first time around."

"Are you talking about Bill McCready?" Sean asked as Cindy the cat came out of Sean's bedroom, where she'd been asleep on his pillow; stretched; and jumped on his lap.

Libby nodded.

Sean corrected her. "He wasn't my friend."

"He was your colleague," Libby said.

Sean began to pet Cindy, his fingers ruffling her fur. "If I recall, he wasn't a particularly chatty person," Sean said. "Not to mention the fact that we didn't always see eye to eye. At all," he added, remembering the credit union robbery and how McCready had done something totally different than he said he was going to do—he'd called it improvising; Sean had called it screwing up—which had resulted in the robbers getting away.

"He still would be more likely to talk to you than us," Bernie said, pointing to herself and Libby. "Even if we are more charming."

"Ha." Sean put his palms in the air. "Then answer me this. Why would I call him when I don't think you should be doing this? Tell me that," he challenged.

Libby smiled and gave the only answer possible. "Because you're the best dad ever and you've always told us that justice counts."

"I'll think about it," Sean grumbled.

"Please, Dad," Bernie begged.

"I said I'll see," Sean told Bernie, playing hard to get.

But he knew that he would. He could never resist his girls.

And Bernie and Libby knew it, too.

Five minutes later, he gave it up, called, and set up a meeting with McCready.

Chapter 16

Libby's boyfriend, Marvin, pulled the hearse up in front of A Little Taste of Heaven and kept the engine running as he waited for Sean Simmons to come downstairs. It had warmed up since yesterday, the temperature was now a balmy twenty-five degrees, the sun was shining, and it wasn't snowing out. Thank God for that since the hearse didn't do well in the snow, Marvin reflected. Snow tires would probably help but his dad was too cheap to buy them.

"Who's going to get hurt anyway?" he always cackled when Marvin brought the topic up. Marvin was thinking about the implications of his father's remark when Sean stepped outside.

Marvin watched Sean frown as he carefully picked his way across the sidewalk to the hearse with the aid of a cane. He knew Libby's dad wouldn't be happy riding in the hearse; he never was. "I'll ride in one of these soon enough," he always said. Marvin had planned on picking up Libby's dad in his car, but, unfortunately, it wouldn't start. He'd called and told Libby, but Libby had told him to pick up her dad anyway, so here Marvin was, faced with an even more irritable than usual Mr. Simmons.

"What happened to your car?" Sean demanded

as he opened the door to the hearse and got in.

"It's in the shop." Marvin nodded toward the cane. "That's new."

"Tripped over the damned cat," Sean growled as he settled himself in his seat, laid his cane beside him, leaned over, and closed the door. It shut with a solid thunk. "Don't know why we have the rotten animal anyway," he muttered as he fished his pack of cigarettes out of his coat pocket and took one out. "I hate cats."

"Well, that may be, but you love this one," Marvin told him.

Sean glared at Marvin. "Did Libby tell you that?" he snapped.

Marvin didn't reply, having decided no good could come from answering.

Sean lit his cigarette and thought about what was coming. He could hear McCready now. Bad enough to have to be driven around like some old codger, but to show up in this? Sean shook his head. Maybe spending six thousand dollars to get his old car up and running wasn't such a bad deal after all despite what his daughters thought. So what if it didn't make financial sense? So what if he could use Uber? Screw that. He was tired of being carted around like a sack of potatoes.

"We can wait till tomorrow if you want," Marvin offered. "My car will be done by then." The starter needed to be replaced.

"No," Sean said after considering the possibility

for a moment. "We'll go now. I could be dead by then."

"Why do you say things like that?" Marvin asked.

"Because we're driving in a death mobile," Sean answered. Then he took a puff of his cigarette and gave Marvin directions.

"I thought this guy lived in Hollingsworth," Marvin said as he put the hearse in drive.

"He did," Sean replied, cracking the window and blowing smoke into the cold air. Marvin's dad complained if the hearse smelled of tobacco, not that the passengers would care. "Evidently he moved."

Marvin sighed. It was going to take him a lot longer to get to McCready than he'd planned for. Hollingsworth took twenty minutes, Frog Hollow would take at least forty, and he had things to do back out at the funeral home. Actually, it took Marvin a little over an hour. Even though the roads had been plowed, there were still icy spots and Marvin drove below the speed limit, ignoring the vehicles zooming by him, because the last thing he wanted to do was slide into a tree; they'd already passed two fender benders. If he did, his father would never let him hear the end of it.

Frog Hollow was a new development that had been built around a pond that up until a couple of years ago had been in the middle of a cow pasture. A New York City developer had bought the property and now the cows and the pasture were gone, replaced by rows of fourteen-hundred-square-foot two-bedroom, one-bathroom cottages, painted in varying shades of gray. Plopped down in the middle of a bulldozed field that looked a lot better with a layer of snow covering it than it did without it, they were intended for people ready to downsize.

"I wonder if there are any frogs left in the pond?" Sean mused as they stopped at the gate.

"Doubtful," Marvin replied after he told the guard who they were there to see. The guard shut his window and called it in. A moment later, he opened the window, told them how to get where they were going, and went back to texting.

"I think I'd slit my throat if I had to live here," Sean commented, taking in the gray houses and the gray sky.

Marvin just grunted. He was too busy trying to figure out where he was going. It took him ten minutes to find 1928. He'd gotten lost because he'd forgotten what the guard had told him and the houses and the roads were mirror images of one another and, to make things worse, some of the street signs hadn't been installed yet.

McCready was waiting for them on the stoop when they arrived. When Sean had known him, he'd been a dapper dresser who'd worked out at the gym three times a week, worn Hickey Freeman suits, silk ties, and had a buzz cut.

Now he had a gut that made him look as if he were into his seventh month and was wearing paint-splattered jeans, a grungy parka over a black stretched-out T-shirt, and needed a shave and a haircut. Retirement had not been kind to McCready, Sean decided, but then he considered how he must look to McCready. It was a depressing thought that he decided not to pursue.

"Jeez," McCready said as Sean got out of the hearse, "it took you long enough." Then he nodded at the hearse. "You always did like to prepare ahead."

"Well, it's better than not preparing at all," Sean shot back.

McCready shrugged. "Improvisation is a skill."

"No, it's a lack of forethought."

McCready nodded at Sean's cane. "What happened to you?"

"Tripped over my cat."

"Does that thing have a sword in it?"

"They're illegal in New York State."

McCready shrugged. "Still the Boy Scout, I see."

"No. I just like to stay inside the lines." And Sean jerked his chin in the direction of the house McCready was standing in front of. "What happened to your house?" This one was definitely a comedown from the large Victorian Painted Lady two miles outside of the town of Hollingsworth that McCready had owned.

McCready shrugged again. "Divorce and then my daughter-in-law convinced me to buy one of these things. Biggest damned mistake I ever made."

"Maybe she can get you your money back," Sean suggested.

"Naw. She and my son got divorced and she took off for Vegas to make some other sucker miserable. So, are we going to stand here or are you coming in?"

"Coming in," Sean answered.

McCready nodded toward the hearse. "And is your chauffer coming in or staying out?"

"Staying out," Sean answered for Marvin. Marvin was a nice kid, but sometimes he didn't know when to keep his mouth shut and Sean didn't want to take the chance and have Marvin derail the conversation right when Sean might be about to worm some nugget of information out of McCready.

"This won't take very long," McCready told Sean as Sean stepped inside the house. "I already told you everything I know on the phone last night. You could have saved yourself the trip."

"And miss the chance to see your lovely face? Never."

McCready laughed as he took Sean's jacket. "You don't change, do you?"

"Why change something that's perfection?"

172

Sean said as he glanced around McCready's house.

The place looked like one of those extended-living hotels salesmen stay at when they're on the road. The walls were painted a beigey white, the prints on the wall were from one of those stores in the mall that specialize in reproductions, and the furniture in the living room consisted of a brown leather sectional, a coffee table, two end tables, and three chairs. An oversized TV hung on the far wall.

"It came furnished," McCready explained, correctly interpreting Sean's expression. "It was the demo model."

"Convenient," Sean said, taking a seat on the sofa.

"I thought so at the time." McCready sat down on the armchair facing Sean. "To tell you the truth I miss the old days. I never thought I'd say that, but it's true." He gestured out the window. "I'm dyin' here. It's like living in the middle of nowhere."

"Maybe you should move back," Sean suggested.

McCready nodded. "I'm thinking about it. Anything would be better than this. Even living on Rivington Street." Rivington Street was Hollingsworth's drug central.

"Well, at least Rivington wouldn't be boring," Sean observed. "Sinclair and Gover," he prompted.

McCready interlaced his fingers and cracked his knuckles. Sean winced at the sound.

"And you're revisiting this why?" McCready asked.

"I already told you last night," Sean replied.

"Tell me again," McCready ordered.

Sean did since McCready was in the catbird seat, as his wife had liked to say—not that he'd ever asked what the catbird seat was.

"You honestly think these two incidents are linked," McCready said.

"My daughters do," Sean explained. "Ada Sinclair certainly does."

McCready shook his head. "You have my condolences. Ada really is a piece of work."

"That's what I told my daughters."

McCready cracked his knuckles again. "She comes off like butter wouldn't melt in her mouth."

"True," Sean agreed. He hesitated for a moment, then said, "But in this case Peggy was poisoned. That's clear. Maybe Ada's dad was, too, given the circumstances."

McCready leaned back. "I know what Ada Sinclair said about her dad, I know that she believes it, but I didn't think it was true then and I don't think it's true now. Don't you think we conducted interviews with the family?"

"I assumed," Sean said. "And?"

"Ada's dad had a prescription for what he took.

Ada said he didn't but he did. Evidently he was having back problems and the problems were getting worse. A lot worse. Plus, he was drinking the hard stuff and we're not talking just one or two a day. And he was depressed about the business. His wife said he was blaming himself for Sinclair Enterprises going under."

"Sounds like suicide to me," Sean reflected.

"Or an unintentional death. You know, forgetting what you've taken."

Sean nodded. He did know. He'd seen enough of it in his day. "Where did Ada's father keep his pills?"

"In one of the kitchen cabinets."

"Convenient," Sean noted.

"Lots of people do that. I do that."

"So, anyone could have gotten to Sinclair's meds?"

McCready shrugged. "Well, it wasn't like there was a combination lock on the kitchen cabinet or anything like that, if you get my meaning. But that said, pills are hard to grind up and hide in something. And these tasted nasty. I asked."

"So then why do you think Ada said what she did?"

McCready sighed. "I don't know what put a bee in her bonnet. Evidently she has issues, as they like to say these days. In our day"—McCready gestured to himself and Sean—"they would have said she was nutso."

"What kind of issues?"

McCready took a minute to collect his thoughts, then said, "Family stuff. New wife, stepkids, lots of bad feelings. But that just amped everything up. From what I could gather, she was always the odd one out. And most importantly, she'd just had a fight with her dad earlier that day. I think she blamed herself and this was her way of . . . ," McCready paused to summon the word he wanted, "deflecting."

"I see," Sean said. And he did. "But you know, just because you're paranoid doesn't mean you're wrong," Sean said, quoting an old saying.

"Doesn't mean you're right, either," McCready countered. "Personally, I think Ada just made the whole thing up. She heard her dad and his partner fighting and it all went from there."

"So they did fight?" Sean asked.

McCready nodded. "Evidently it wasn't unusual. They fought all the time." McCready scratched his chin. "It was the running joke. If one said something was black the other would say it was white." He contemplated the view outside his window for a second before turning back to Sean. "Ada's accusation was all speculation. There was no creditable threat. At least none that I could see. There was no way to prove anything one way or another. The only thing that was conclusive was that Ada's father died from a combination of pain pills and alcohol."

"You talked to the wives?"

"Of course I talked to the wives. They were both there."

Sean shook his head. Two wives. He'd had his hands full with one.

"Neither was what I'd call broken up," McCready recalled. "Just the opposite. In fact, I got the impression that the second one was talking about getting a divorce because she'd found out her husband was having an affair."

"With whom?"

McCready frowned. "One of the secretaries. What else is new?"

"You had a motive right there."

"The wife, the second wife, the partner. Yeah, we had lots of motives. But they turned out to be nothing. Most do, as you know."

Sean nodded, because he did. "And you talked to everyone else?" Sean asked.

McCready made an impatient gesture with his hand. "How many times do I have to repeat myself? For the last time, I did, and everyone was just as informative as the wife. Which was not informative at all."

"Just covering the bases," Sean said, making a show of apologizing.

"Like I just said, no one in the family had much to say," McCready went on. "They were shocked, appalled, blah, blah, blah. I got the distinct impression that no one could have cared less about what happened to Ada's dad. Poor guy. I can see why he did what he did. I'll tell you one thing, he had lousy taste in women. That was for sure." McCready's face darkened. "Then Ada Sinclair starts in. Makes this huge fuss. Gets everyone going."

"That must have been annoying," Sean commented.

"I would have liked to have strangled her," McCready admitted. "She even called the papers. The mayor called me in to reinvestigate."

"And?"

McCready threw up his hands. "Total waste of money and manpower. The department came to the same conclusion as before."

Sean leaned forward. "What did Ada do when you told her that?"

"She started screaming and crying and carrying on. They had to call someone in to give her a shot to calm her down."

"And do you think there was anything in what Ada was saying? Anything at all?"

"Honestly?" McCready asked.

"Yes, honestly," Sean replied.

"No, I don't," McCready told him. "Sinclair's death could have been an accidental OD, it could have been suicide, it could have been murder, but the first two seem like the likeliest scenarios to me. I thought that then and I think that now."

"So, you don't go with Ada's version of Joel

Grover poisoning her dad and then killing himself in a fit of remorse? I mean you do have to admit the two deaths happening so close together does raise some questions."

McCready snorted. "Agreed. However, Grover had a pistol for which he had a permit in the glove compartment of his vehicle. If he was going to kill himself why not use that? That's what I would have done. Wouldn't you?"

"Definitely," Sean answered. "Why indeed?" he murmured to himself. Killing yourself by smashing into a tree was notoriously unreliable. A gun, on the other hand, was extremely effective. This was something everyone knew.

"Sometimes coincidences do exist," McCready continued. "The weather was bad the night that Grover died and I'm thinking he was upset about his partner's death and he had had a few too many drinks. Maybe he wasn't paying attention. Maybe his reflexes were slower than they should have been." McCready took a deep breath.

Sean leaned forward and rubbed his left calf. He could feel his muscles begin to knot up. "Anything else?"

"Like what?"

"I don't know. General stuff. Stuff about the business."

"Well, like I said—or maybe I didn't—the business was on the verge of going under. That never puts anyone in a good mood."

"Do you know why?"

"Something about the formula to their star product not working the way it should," McCready answered. "Some test results. I heard rumors that a couple of the guys that tested it lost all their hair instead of the other way around." McCready snickered at the thought. "But those were just rumors."

"Evidently, they fixed whatever needed fixing," Sean said. "Because they're about to take the company public."

"That's what I heard, too. Do you realize how much money they're going to make if this formula works?" McCready asked. "Some men will pay anything to get their hair back," he reflected. He touched the top of his head. "Fortunately, that's not my problem." McCready glanced down at his watch. "And now it's time for you to go because I gotta be out of here in five."

Sean nodded and thanked McCready for talking to him. Then Sean got up, picked up his cane, and headed for the door. When he got there, he stopped and turned. "McCready, I don't suppose you remember the names of those guys?" he asked.

"Which guys?"

"The ones who lost all their hair," Sean said.

McCready grinned. "Yeah. As a matter of fact, I do. Well, one of them anyway. He worked at the plant. Guess that taught him to volunteer."

"Yeah. I learned that in the navy," Sean observed.

"Me, I learned it in the army," McCready said as he got up. Then he tore an edge off the newspaper sitting on the cabinet underneath the TV set, wrote the name down, and handed the scrap of paper to Sean. "Here. Go knock yourself out. Why do you want to know anyway?"

"Just dotting the i's and crossing the t's," Sean told him. As Sean left McCready's home, he'd pretty much decided that barring something startling, Sinclair's and Grover's deaths were as represented. But . . . He turned and knocked on the door. McCready answered.

"What now?" he barked.

"What percentage sure are you?" Sean asked him.

"Ninety-eight percent sure," McCready replied before he slammed the door in his face.

Still, Sean thought as he limped over to the hearse, *2 percent is 2 percent.*

Three days later in the name of thoroughness, Sean got hold of Jim Briggs and asked him about what had happened.

Nothing, as it turned out. The rumors McCready had heard were just that: rumors. According to Briggs, while the product hadn't made his bald spot go away, it hadn't made it any worse, either.

Chapter 17

Bernie and Libby didn't leave A Little Taste of Heaven for the offices of the *Sunset Gazette* until a little after two in the afternoon. First, Googie had been late because he'd locked his keys in his car; then the credit card machine had gone down for the third time in a week and Bernie had to get on the phone and scream at her service provider for half an hour before they promised they'd send a technician out by the close of the day; then Mrs. Conteras had phoned in with an emergency order for ten dozen cookies for her gallery opening—evidently her assistant had forgotten to order them; and last, but certainly not least, Vicky Sinclair had shown up at the shop.

Libby had been wiping off the five small four-tops they'd installed a year ago when Vicky Sinclair had made her grand entrance. She'd strode in, pushing the door open with enough force to make it bang against the wall. The four customers waiting to be served had turned to look as Vicky Sinclair marched toward the counter, her diamond rings glinting in the light.

Then she'd caught sight of Libby and stopped. Libby hadn't been surprised. Given Vicky's narrowed eyes and clenched jaw and the fact

182

that she'd never set foot in A Little Taste of Heaven heretofore, Libby hadn't thought Ada's stepmother was there for coffee and a muffin.

"I want to speak to you," she'd exclaimed, pointing a finger at Libby.

"In the back," Libby had said, going to close the door as a current of cold air snaked its way through the shop. Heaven only knows their heat bill was high enough as it was. And then there was the fact that they'd had one scene out front this week. They didn't need another. "Now what's this about?" Libby asked once they were in the prep room.

"What do you think?" Vicky asked impatiently, opening her sheepskin coat. It was warm in the back because both ovens were going. Her perfume, a floral scent, filled the air, making Libby sneeze.

Libby wadded up the paper towels she'd been using on the tables and threw them into the trash. "I haven't the foggiest," she said, annoyance spilling out in her voice.

"Foggiest? What does that mean?" Vicky demanded.

"It means I don't have a clue what the hell you're talking about," Libby told her.

Vicky tapped her long red fingernails on her thighs as she looked Libby up and down. "Don't play games with me," she snapped.

"I'm not," Libby protested. "Either tell me

what you came here to say or leave. I have work to do."

Vicky took a deep breath and let it out. "I'm talking about my stepdaughter. Not that you don't know."

"What about Ada?" Libby asked.

Vicky tucked a strand of blond hair behind her ear, then folded her hands over her chest while her right foot tapped out a rhythm on the floor. "I want to know where she is."

"So does everyone else," Libby replied.

"You met with her," Vicky said.

"And she ran off," Libby answered, wondering how she'd found out. Henry must have told her before he died. Otherwise, how would Vicky have known? The police hadn't come by so that meant that they didn't know. If they had, they would have wanted to talk to her and Bernie."

"But you know where she went to," Vicky insisted.

"I don't know who you're getting your information from, but you should find a new source," Libby told her.

"Henry said you knew," Vicky Sinclair informed her, proving to Libby that her guess had been correct. "He was quite clear on that."

"Well, he was wrong," Libby stated.

"I don't think so."

"Too bad we can't ask him."

"Isn't it, though," Vicky replied.

"I don't suppose you had anything to do with what happened to him?"

Vicky Sinclair drew herself up. "That's a dreadful thing to say."

"You can always leave if you're insulted."

Vicky Sinclair sniffed and ignored Libby's suggestion. "I'll tell you what I told the police. You want to find out who ran over Henry find the little chippie he was seeing."

Interesting, Libby thought.

"And no, I have no idea who that is," Vicky Sinclair went on, answering Libby's unasked question, "and I don't care." Then Vicky said, stated really, Libby thought, "I bet your sister knows where Ada is."

"No, Bernie doesn't," Libby told her.

"What don't I know?" Bernie inquired, as she put a carton filled with takeout containers on one of the prep tables, having just come back from a quick trip to BJ's for paper goods.

"Vicky was saying that you knew where Ada Sinclair was and I was telling her that you didn't," Libby answered, recapping the conversation. "She seems pretty intent on finding her," Libby added.

Bernie turned toward Vicky. "My sister is right. I have no idea where she took off to," she told her.

"That's not what I heard," Vicky said.

"Who did you hear it from?" Bernie asked.

185

"Because whoever you heard it from doesn't know what they're talking about."

"She heard it from Henry Sinclair," Libby told Bernie.

Vicky shook a finger at Libby. "I can talk for myself."

Libby held her hands up in front of her and took a step back. "Sorry."

"He probably wasn't the most reliable source of information," Bernie observed, "considering he was the one that spooked Ada in the first place. When did you talk to him?"

Vicky fiddled with her gold chain instead of answering.

"Obviously, it had to be before he died." Bernie slipped out of her black-and-tan-checked cloth coat and hung it on a hook attached to the wall near the door. "Did he come to your house looking for Ada?" she asked, as she took off her hat and stuffed it in the coat's pocket.

"None of your business," Vicky told her.

"Why would he do that?" Bernie asked Vicky, smiling at her. "I'm just curious. It seems like such an odd thing to do, considering."

"Considering what?" Vicky demanded.

Bernie answered slowly. "Well, it's just that I didn't get the impression that you and Ada got along. In fact, I think that's the last place she'd show up. It's certainly the last place I'd go if I were looking for her."

Vicky touched the base of her throat. "Is there a point to this?"

"Yeah," Bernie replied, "there is. I think you're making the thing with Henry up."

A dot of color appeared on Vicky's cheeks. "You're making a mistake," she told Bernie.

"How's that?" Bernie inquired.

"Taking Ada's side. Not telling me where I can find her."

"Why do you want to find her so badly anyway?" Bernie asked. "Tell me and maybe we can help."

Vicky's mouth twisted into a semblance of a smile. "I think you've done enough already."

"If you feel that way, why are you here?" Bernie asked.

"You're right, I shouldn't have come," Vicky Sinclair told the sisters.

"Then why did you?" Libby asked.

Vicky shrugged. "It was a bad idea."

Bernie took a step forward. "Maybe you're looking for Ada's dad's notebook."

Vicky snorted. "Don't be ridiculous."

"I'm not," Bernie told her.

Vicky shifted her coat to her other arm. "Ada didn't like Peggy, you know," Vicky told her. "They had a big fight."

"I heard," Bernie replied.

"Which is why the police are looking for her."

"How did they find out about the fight?" Bernie asked Vicky.

"Someone told them. Obviously."

"Obviously," Libby said. "I think my sister is asking who it was."

"What difference does it make?" Vicky replied.

"It could make quite a bit of difference if what Ada says is true. If someone is trying to frame her," Bernie said.

Vicky glared at Bernie and Libby. "She's a congenital liar and troublemaker and if our sale gets derailed because of you and your sister," she said, "well, I won't be responsible for the consequences."

"Good to know," Libby chimed in.

Bernie shook her head. She wasn't following Vicky Sinclair's logic. "What do we have to do with your IPO?"

"Think about it," Vicky answered.

Bernie did. "Bad publicity could derail the sale?"

Vicky Sinclair clapped. "Very good. Now you're getting it. Ada needs help. She needs to go somewhere she can get it."

Bernie studied Vicky for a moment, then shook her head. "You want to commit Ada? Is that why you want to find her?"

"That's none of your business," Vicky Sinclair replied, her voice rising.

Bernie put her hands on her hips. "I think maybe it is."

"I'm serious," Vicky told her.

"So am I," Bernie replied.

Vicky Sinclair looked from one sister to the other, pivoted on her high-heeled boot, and stalked toward the prep room door without saying anything else.

"That was rather rude," Libby observed. "You think Vicky Sinclair wants what she said she wants?" Libby asked her sister.

"Yeah, I do," Bernie replied. "I think she wants Ada out of the way. I think she's afraid Ada's going to create some sort of scene, like she did the last time. Investors don't like to invest in companies with lots of drama."

"Or maybe Vicky wants that notebook and she thinks Ada has it," Libby hypothesized.

"The notebook Ada is using for bait?" Bernie said.

"It certainly is effective," Libby observed. "A little too effective."

Another thought struck Bernie. "Do you think Ada is lying about that?" she asked her sister. "Do you think the notebook has something in it? Something that proves what Ada's been saying?"

"I don't know what to believe anymore," Libby commented as she reached in her pants pocket, took out two squares of chocolate, unwrapped them, and handed a square to Bernie. Then she popped the other one in her mouth while she considered what had happened since New Year's Eve. "I can definitely understand why Mom severed her ties with the Sinclairs. They really are crazy making."

Bernie picked a cat hair off her black turtleneck sweater. "What can I say, Dad was right."

"For sure," Libby agreed.

"What interests me is the notebook. If there's nothing in it, why is it of such interest to everyone?"

"Because people think there is something in it, even if there isn't," Libby said. "Unless, of course, there is. This whole thing is giving me a headache."

"I think we're overthinking this," Bernie replied.

"Maybe," Libby replied. "But where is it?"

Bernie clicked her tongue against the front of her teeth while she tried to picture what had happened on the evening that Peggy had died. It was difficult. Everything was muddled. Bernie spoke slowly. "Ada left it on the kitchen table when she went into the living room and it was there when we served the champagne. I remember that."

"But then afterward, after Peggy was killed and we came back in . . . ." Libby said, her voice fading away as she tried to put together a coherent timeline.

Bernie scrunched up her face as she continued willing her memories up. "I don't remember the notebook being on the table at that point, but it certainly could have been and I didn't notice it. There was too much going on."

"Yeah," Libby said, thinking back to the scene that evening. "Our attention was definitely elsewhere."

"And by that point Ada had left the house," Bernie recalled as she spied another cat hair on her other sleeve. She picked it off and deposited it in the trash. The last thing A Little Taste of Heaven needed was for someone to find a cat hair in their chocolate chip cookie. "She didn't go back in the kitchen. She left through the front door."

"But she could have doubled back later to get it," Libby posited.

"That's true. She could have come in through the garage or the side door. But everyone was there. It would be hard to get in and out without being seen. Not impossible, but definitely difficult. Or," Bernie raised a hand for emphasis, "another family member could have snuck in and filched the notebook. That seems more reasonable."

Libby shook her head. "Too many possibilities and none of them seem to be leading anywhere." And she pointed to the clock on the wall. "The *Sunset Gazette* closes at four today. We should go now before something else happens. Who knows? Maybe getting some background information will help us whittle things down."

191

"Well, it certainly can't hurt," Bernie observed although she wasn't sure it was going to help that much, either. She'd spoken to the *Gazette*'s editor last night and the woman had said that offhand she didn't think they'd run large stories about the events Bernie was asking about, but that she'd pull the relevant issues for them and they were welcome to come and read them if they wanted to.

We're grasping at straws here, Bernie had thought when she'd hung up. She still thought the same thing now.

Chapter 18

The office of the *Sunset Gazette* was located on the outskirts of Hollingsworth. Launched twenty-five years ago, the paper was the brainchild of a former ad exec who'd gotten tired of the commute into the city, cashed in his stocks, and taken a chance on his boyhood dream. The *Gazette* came out twice a month and contained all the local news that was fit to print and some that wasn't, as the motto on top of the *Gazette*'s front page proclaimed.

The single-story building the newspaper was housed in had been constructed in 1952, and whenever Bernie passed it on one of her errands she always thought the structure belonged down in Florida. Originally intended as a storage facility for a paper mill, the building had been repurposed when the company had moved down to South Carolina. Now, the flamingo pink cement block structure contained four small businesses, none of which—except for the *Sunset Gazette*—seemed to stick around for more than six months.

The unplowed parking lot was almost empty when Bernie and Libby drove up, the gray skies making the pink blocks appear forlorn, as if they were pining for sunny skies and warmer temperatures. Bernie carefully maneuvered the van around the mounds of snow, driving in the tracks of previous vehicles, and parked Mathilda next to the entrance.

"It's gotten colder again," Libby observed as they got out of the van. She stopped to zip up her jacket.

"It's the wind," Bernie answered as she hurried toward the entrance. The door let out a loud creak when Bernie opened it. The linoleum on the four steps down to the hallway, colorless after years of use, was curling up at the steps' edges, and Bernie and Libby had to be careful not to trip on it as they walked down them. The *Gazette*'s office was at the end of the hallway.

"I think this would be a perfect setting for a horror movie," Bernie commented, indicating the flickering fluorescent overhead lights.

Libby didn't say anything. She just walked faster, picturing a zombie jumping out at her.

Lori Scheu, the woman Bernie had spoken to on the phone yesterday, opened the door when Bernie and Libby were a couple of feet away. Bernie put her at about sixty, which surprised her because Lori Scheu had sounded around forty on the phone. She had a pleasant face framed with curly gray hair. Her glasses were perched on the top of her head and she was wearing her coat and a blue and white scarf wound tightly around her neck.

"I have an electric heater going and it helps, but

194

not enough," she explained as Libby and Bernie followed her inside the *Gazette*'s office. While it wasn't as cold in there as it was outside, it was cold enough. Bernie was surprised her breath wasn't showing in the air. Maybe it would in another couple of minutes.

"What happened to the heat?" Bernie asked.

"Funny, that's what I've been asking the landlord," Lori Scheu answered as she led them away from the reception area toward her office. "He keeps telling me he's going to fix it and doesn't. Fortunately, we're moving to the strip mall near the new medical center next week." She rubbed her hands together to get the circulation going. "They're demoing this place next month to build a housing complex, so he doesn't really care."

She stopped in front of her office. "I guess we stayed too long at the party," she observed as she led them inside. "Excuse the mess," she apologized, gesturing to the stacks of books and papers that filled every spare nook and cranny of the small room. "We should have been out of here months ago. Frankly, I don't come back here at night anymore to finish things up. Too creepy."

"I can imagine," Libby said. "I certainly wouldn't."

"Thank God for file sharing," Lori said as she indicated two seats on the other side of the heater. "Sit."

When Bernie and Libby did, Lori moved the heater closer to them. It was one of those tall columns that blow hot air out and Libby thought it was fighting a valiant fight, but not valiant enough for her to take off her coat and gloves.

"Now then," Lori said as she reached into her coat pocket, took out a pair of fingerless gloves, and put them on. "After you called last night I tried to remember the incidents you asked about."

Bernie leaned forward. "And?"

"I'll be happy to share what I recall, but it isn't that much," Lori replied. "You know at the time the deaths occurred they were considered unfortunate, nothing more, and I was having health issues then so I really wasn't paying close attention." She pushed the two editions of the *Sunset Gazette* sitting on her desk toward Bernie and Libby with the tips of her fingers. "Here. Read these first and then we'll talk."

"This is it?" Bernie asked, looking at the newspapers. Somehow, she'd expected more.

Lori smiled apologetically. "I told you I didn't think there'd be all that much," she said to Bernie. "It's our publishing cycle," she explained. "Since we come out every two weeks we tend to focus on the most recent events, and these deaths happened seven and five days before we went to press."

"So, right in the middle and the beginning," Libby said.

Lori nodded. "Things that happened earlier tend to get short shrift, unless they're something major, of course. Like the town librarian running away with the high school coach."

"That happened?" Bernie asked.

"Nine years ago," Lori told her. "And to be fair, the news is a small part of the paper. We mostly do a calendar, social events, birth and death announcements, and ads, of course. We're what you call a throwaway. Did you check the other local papers?"

Bernie nodded. "I did indeed and I didn't find anything. Evidently, except for you no one else picked the story up." Then Bernie pulled the paper toward her and began to read.

There was nothing there she didn't already know. Jeff Sinclair's and Joel Grover's deaths hadn't even made the front page. The article dealing with them was located on the top right-hand side of page five, sandwiched in between a review of the high school production of *The Wizard of Oz* and a story about the local elementary school chess club.

The story was headlined TRAGEDY STRIKES, the first paragraph of which detailed Ada's dad's death and the subsequent fatal auto accident of his partner; the second and third paragraphs went on to mention the roots both men had in the community, talk about the business they'd founded, and mention the charitable organizations they'd been involved in; while the last paragraph featured a number of quotes from surviving family members talking about how much the deceased would be missed.

The article Libby was reading was even shorter and less informative. Published a couple of weeks later and written by Lori, who had also written the first one, it was buried on page fifteen and captioned ACCUSATIONS FOUND BASELESS. The two-paragraph story went on to state that due to an anonymous source the police had opened an investigation into the deaths of Jeff Sinclair and Joel Grover and after a number of interviews they had concluded that the tip they'd received was baseless and that no charges were being filed.

"Can you tell us anything more?" Libby asked as she pushed the paper back in Lori's direction. "Anything that's not in the article."

Lori sighed. "As I said, not too much. I can tell you that Ada Sinclair came running in here after she read the second article and screamed at me that the article was a lie and that the police chief was covering things up because he was having an affair with her mother."

Libby raised an eyebrow. "McCready with Linda Sinclair?"

Lori nodded. "That's what she said."

"And did you believe her?" Bernie asked.

"No. Linda and McCready went out after college for a little while," Lori replied. "They remained friends but they weren't involved after that."

"How can you be so sure?" Libby asked.

"It's a small town; it's hard to keep secrets here. Anyway, I knew the person he was having an affair with."

"So, you didn't believe Ada?" Bernie asked, double checking.

"No, I didn't," Lori said. "I thought the deaths were the result, as they would say in a Victorian novel, of a confluence of unfortunate events. It's what everyone believed."

"And now?" Libby asked.

"I still don't think so."

Bernie leaned forward. "Even with Peggy's and Henry's deaths?"

"Even with those," Lori said as she absent-mindedly began rolling the pencil that was sitting on her desk back and forth on the wood with the palm of her hand. It made a rattling noise. That, the ping of the space heater, and the ticking of the clock on the wall were the only sounds in the room. "Despite what Ada said I didn't think McCready covered anything up back then and I don't think so now. Why would he? Especially if what Ada said was true about Grover murdering Sinclair. Which, in light of recent events, makes even less sense than it did before."

"Do you think Ada could have been involved?" Libby asked.

Lori stopped rolling her pencil and started neatening up the stack of papers on her desk. "You mean in Peggy's and Henry's deaths?" she asked. "Or her dad's? Or Joel Grover's?"

"Either," Libby said. "Or both. Take your pick."

"So, let me get this straight," Lori said slowly. "You're asking me if Ada, a twelve-year-old girl at the time, killed her dad and then blamed it on his partner, after she caused his death."

"I agree, it is far-fetched," Libby allowed. Certainly, her dad thought it was. "I'm just covering all my bases.

"It's like something straight out of a horror movie," Lori declared. "Although, I suppose just for the sake of argument Ada could have put her dad's pain pills in his drink. Anyone in the house could have done that. But arranging for Joel Grover's death? How would she have done that?" Lori sat back in her chair. "And even if Ada had done that, why would she then go to McCready and insist he investigate when the deaths had already both been ruled accidental? Why open up that particular can of worms? She was home free."

"True," Libby allowed.

Lori continued. "I'm sorry, but I just don't see her doing something like that. In a horror movie, yes. In real life, no. In real life, twelve-year-olds tend to run away to their friends' houses and drink too much and get really, really sick."

"True," Bernie said, remembering the really sick part as she buttoned up the top button of her camel's hair coat and turned up the collar to thwart the stream of cold air blowing on her neck. "I'll tell you one thing," she said. "If I were the Sinclair family, I think I'd be doing something else on New Year's Eve from now on. Like going to sleep at ten and calling it a day."

"That's what I do," Lori volunteered. "The older I get the less I like New Year's Eve and I haven't had a New Year's Eve like the Sinclairs' have had, let alone two. Thank God."

"Two deaths on two New Year's Eves," Bernie reflected. "Definitely not the Sinclairs' good luck holiday. I don't think eating lentils or black beans for prosperity is going to change that."

"Maybe they should switch to celebrating Chinese New Year," Libby suggested.

"Or the solstice," Lori said as she leaned forward, started fiddling with the papers on her desk again, stopped, and leaned back in her chair again. "Now, Peggy's death was clearly a homicide," she continued, returning to parsing the topic at hand.

Libby nodded. "As was Henry Sinclair's."

"That could have been a hit-and-run," Lori pointed out.

Libby leaned forward. "Do you really believe that?" she asked.

"I'm not sure," Lori admitted. "The circum-

201

stances suggest otherwise from what you've said, but it *was* dark, the weather *was* bad, and there are no streetlights or sidewalks where Henry was walking. Add the fact that he was walking with the traffic and dressed all in black and you have . . ."

"A recipe for disaster," Libby said, finishing Lori's sentence for her.

The three women shifted in their seats and listened to the sound of a truck going by on the road near the mall.

"On the other hand," Lori observed after a minute, "I have to say that Ada disappearing the way she did doesn't look very good. People from around here are saying that she did it, that she killed Peggy and ran over her uncle."

"And do you believe that?" Libby asked.

Lori frowned. "I mean, it's possible."

"But you don't believe it," Libby intuited from the expression on Lori's face.

"No, I don't," Lori allowed.

"She's running because she's scared," Bernie told Lori, remembering what Ada had said and how she'd acted.

Lori leaned forward, picked up her pencil again, and began tapping it on the stack of papers in front of her. "I understand how one could see her disappearance as an admission of guilt. Still, it is a stretch. Her killing Peggy . . . and maybe her uncle." Lori's frown turned into a grimace. "It's true she wasn't getting along with them . . .

but killing someone . . . that's quite a leap. It's amazing how the people here always jump to the worst possible conclusions." Lori shook her head and followed up with, "Ah, the joy of living in a small town."

"You know the family, right?" Bernie asked when Lori didn't say anything else.

"Not intimately," Lori replied. "We don't run in the same social circles, but, yes, I know them. We chat when we run into each other at the grocery or hardware store or the movies. As I just said, it's a small town. People know people. Or if you don't know them, you know their relatives. You hear things. Plus, doing what I do"—she indicated her office with a sweep of her hand—"I hear more than most."

"And . . . ," Bernie prodded when Lori didn't continue.

"I don't like to say bad things about people," Lori confided. "Repeat rumors and gossip. There's enough of that going around."

Bernie sat back, clasped her hands together, rested them in her lap, and waited. In her experience that first sentence was always the prelude to someone doing exactly the opposite.

"But," Lori said, "I guess this case is different."

"Anything you could tell us would be very helpful," Libby told her. Then she, too, sat back; folded her hands in her lap, as her sister had done; and waited.

Chapter 19

Lori reached over and turned the heater a notch higher. After a moment, she began. "I've lived in this town for the last forty years and been editor of the *Sunset Gazette* for the last fifteen and the one thing I can say about the Sinclairs is that there's always been drama. Lots of drama."

Bernie asked the obvious question. "What kind of drama?"

"Not comedy, that's for sure," Lori replied. "My husband used to say the Sinclairs put the *d* in *dysfunctional*." She went on to give examples. "Like when Ada's mom, Linda, found out that her husband was having an affair with Vicky— this when Vicky was working for him as an assistant—Linda locked him out of the house."

"Doesn't seem unreasonable," Libby observed.

Lori raised a finger. "That's where most people would walk away. Does Jeff walk away? Or bang on the door? Or call a locksmith? No, he does not. He gets in his SUV and bashes the front door in."

"Messy, but effective," Bernie commented.

"And then," Lori continued, "to put the finishing touch on everything, Linda goes into the garage, gets a five-gallon container of gasoline, throws the gasoline on the SUV, and lights it up. Fortunately, the firemen arrived in time to save the house from going up in flames as well."

"Obviously, Linda was unclear on the concept," Bernie remarked.

Lori went on. "Yes. It was quite the story—not that I wrote about it in the paper."

Libby cocked her head. "Why not?"

"The publisher is a family friend of the Sinclairs," Lori told her. "I also couldn't write about the time Ada got into trouble for shoplifting and for doing E." Lori extended her hands palms upward. "Mickey Mouse stuff, right?"

Bernie and Libby nodded.

"Most people," Lori said, continuing her narrative, "would have grounded their kid and left it at that or sent them to a therapist, but Linda hired some people to come and kidnap Ada and take her to some camp or other out west in the middle of nowhere. One of these outdoor, living in the wilderness kind of deals."

"Like boot camp," Libby said.

Bernie wrinkled her nose. "Lucky our dad didn't believe in that," she commented, thinking about all the stuff she'd pulled in her adolescence.

"Anyway," Lori went on, "Ada was there for three weeks before she ran away and hitchhiked back."

"I'm impressed," Bernie said. "Shows determination."

"Then she went and had a mini nervous breakdown—or at least that's what her mother said."

"And judging from your tone of voice you didn't believe it?" Bernie asked.

Lori shrugged. "Some people said it was drugs and she was in a rehab facility. The other story I heard was that Ada had tried to stab Vicky, her new stepmom-to-be, and Linda had worked out a deal and put her daughter in a psychiatric facility so she wouldn't get arrested."

Libby thought about the crack someone made at the Sinclairs' New Year's Eve dinner about Ada needing to go back on her meds and wondered if that's what the person who'd made the remark was referring to. "How about the rest of the family?" Libby asked.

Lori rubbed her forehead. "Pretty much the same kind of stuff. Lots of fighting, saying bad things about each other, borrowing money and not returning it. And let's not forget Henry."

"What about him?" Bernie asked.

"He was a real hound dog, if you get my meaning. Always sniffing around."

"And his wife put up with it?" Libby asked.

Lori shrugged again. "She didn't throw him out, if that's what you mean. Too nice for her own good if you ask me. And," she continued, "Ada's brother and sister weren't exactly stellar in the behavior department, either. I think the brother or maybe it was the sister, I can't remember now, stole their neighbor's car . . ."

"Would that be Peggy's?" Bernie asked.

Lori nodded. ". . . and cracked it up."

"What happened to the kid?" Bernie asked.

"Nothing from what I heard," Lori replied in answer to Bernie's raised eyebrow.

"Peggy worked for the company, too, didn't she?" Libby asked, rechecking her facts.

Lori nodded. "From the beginning. She's in charge of shipping." Lori corrected herself. "*Was* in charge of shipping."

Bernie flexed her fingers, trying to get some feeling back in them. "So, the Sinclair kid got away with stealing the car because she or he was the boss's kid?"

Lori made her hand into a gun and pulled the trigger. "Bingo. Bernie gets it in one. And, I have to add, Vicky's kids weren't too much better than Linda's. In fact, they were even a little bit worse, if memory serves. Lots of parties, lots of drinking, lots of missing school. They both got thrown out of the community college they were going to for cheating."

"The usual stuff," Bernie said.

"Maybe for you," Libby observed.

"Hey, it's not my fault that you always got caught," Bernie told her. "Sorry," she said, turning to Lori. "Go on."

Lori nodded. "And things got even worse

behavior-wise after Jeff and Joel died. By that time, Jeff had divorced Linda and married Vicky, who was claiming that Jeff had left his part of the business to her, while Linda was claiming that Vicky had forged a new will. Linda challenged the will in court, but the two women ended up settling instead. Then Marty and Peggy threw their hats into the proverbial ring."

"You're kidding," Libby exclaimed.

"Nope," Lori told her. "The whole thing was a bonanza for the lawyers. Finally, everyone came to their senses and settled."

"I can see that. Do you know the settlement terms?" Libby asked.

Lori jammed her hands underneath her armpits. "Not officially. But I heard that Vicky and Linda got shares, as did the other people who worked there, on the condition that everyone take a salary reduction."

"Why would they agree to that?" Libby asked. "I don't think I would."

Lori answered, "Because the business was on the brink of going under."

Bernie shook her head. She didn't get it. "Then why did they stay? It seems like a bad deal to me."

"My guess?" Lori asked.

Bernie nodded and rubbed her thighs to get the circulation going. Her legs were beginning to feel like Popsicles.

"Because everyone saw the potential of the

hair growth product they were developing and no one wanted to give up on it. And they were right. They stayed the course and now everyone is going to get millions. I mean, growing back your hair? That's golden."

"But what happened before?" Bernie asked. "Why was Sinclair Enterprises going downhill?"

"A lot of infighting. Distribution problems. Not enough advertising. They had problems with some of their products. Their shampoo left a film on your hair and their conditioners were hard to rinse out. But they've improved their products and lowered their prices. And then their formula for their hair regrowing product, Hair for All, didn't always work. Evidently there were a few glitches."

"That's what my dad said," Bernie noted.

"But new products take a while to develop," Lori said. "Of course, there was this guy Mason who claimed their product made his hairline recede."

"Did it?" Bernie asked.

"He was losing hair pretty fast at that point anyway, so it's hard to tell. But Mason was convinced. In fact, he was so upset he even tried to shoot Joel Grover. I still remember Joel running down Main Street and this guy Mason running after him yelling, 'Stop, stop. I want to kill you,' and waving a gun in the air." Lori couldn't help it. She laughed at the memory. "Fortunately for

Joel, Mason was using his father's gun and didn't know how to release the safety."

"What happened to Mason?" Bernie asked.

"Nothing, really," Lori told her. "He plea-bargained the charge down to two years' probation and when that was done he moved away."

"Unlike the Sinclairs," Libby noted.

"Well, they certainly don't seem to bring out the best in each other," Bernie observed. "It doesn't sound as if the Sinclair family is big on talking things out. Little things become big things. So, you get this pressure cooker. And the pressure builds and builds and then blammo. Someone goes nuts."

"The question is who," Lori said.

"I wish I knew," Libby told her.

Bernie nodded and pulled the neck of her turtleneck sweater up to her chin. She sighed. Was that her breath she was seeing? "Last question." If she didn't get out of there soon, she'd be frozen to her chair. A slight exaggeration, but not by much. "Do you know if Ada had any friends?"

"Not many, from what I understand," Lori replied. "She pretty much kept to herself. But there was one."

Bernie and Libby leaned forward and waited while Lori looked up Ada's friend's name and her last known address.

"She used to be friends with my daughter," Lori explained.

Chapter 20

It was late by the time Bernie and Libby left the office of the *Sunset Gazette*. In the interval, the clouds had gathered, the wind had picked up, and the air smelled of the snow that the weatherman had promised was on its way.

"I need a hot drink," Libby announced to Bernie as her sister drove out of the parking lot.

"And a hot bath," Bernie added. She couldn't feel her feet anymore. "I don't know how Lori Scheu works there," she added. "It's like being in the tundra."

"There's no 'like' about it. It *is* the tundra." Libby stuck her hands under her armpits to try to warm them up. The tips of her fingers hurt from the cold. "I hope I didn't get frostbite."

Bernie snorted. "Be serious," she said.

"I am," her sister replied. "She's got to be wearing at least three sweaters under her jacket, as well as a couple of pairs of tights, and wool socks," Libby said, referring to Lori, "and I'm just wearing one layer."

"I don't think all those layers would have helped," Bernie observed. "I don't know what would."

"I'm not sure our conversation helped, either," Libby said as Bernie turned onto the main road.

Libby squinted. Was that white thing she saw drifting down from the sky a snowflake? She wasn't sure, but she certainly hoped not.

"Of course it did," Bernie said, turning her head to look at her sister. "We got the name and address of a friend of Ada's, didn't we?"

"If the address is valid."

"Why shouldn't it be?"

"Maybe she's moved."

"And maybe she hasn't. Maybe Ada's staying there. And even if she isn't, maybe this Kate Silverman can tell us something. Maybe she can point us in the right direction."

"Possible," Libby admitted. "I suggest we go home, warm up, get ready for the evening rush, and check it out tomorrow."

"We should go now," Bernie countered.

Libby frowned. "Why? If Kate Silverman is there now, she'll be there tomorrow."

A car behind Mathilda honked and Bernie realized she'd been sitting at an all-way stop sign. She waved an apology and made a right onto Avondale.

"Highbridge Court is on the way home," she told Libby.

"No it's not," Libby protested.

"It's not that far out of the way," Bernie replied.

"How can you say that?" Libby demanded. "It's in the opposite direction."

"Just a couple of miles."

212

"I need to warm up," Libby said.

"The heat will come on in the van soon."

Libby made a rude noise. "I'd get warmer holding my hands over a candle."

"Don't whine."

"I'm not whining."

"Really?" Bernie said.

"Yes, really."

"Then what are you doing?"

"How about taking my best interests to heart."

"I don't even know what that means."

"You could call."

"I know I could call, but it's not the same, and if by chance Ada is there she'll take off on us."

"Why would she do that?"

"Duh. Because she probably thinks we let her uncle know where she was."

Libby checked her watch. "We need to get back to the shop."

"We still have some time."

Libby half turned toward her sister. "No we don't," she snapped. "Mrs. Hare is coming in for her order."

"Which is already boxed and waiting for her. Don't you care about Ada?" Bernie asked, careful to keep her eyes on the road.

"Frankly, at this moment, I care about not getting pneumonia," Libby retorted.

"You're not getting pneumonia and we're going," Bernie told her.

"Sez you," Libby shot back.

"Yes, sez me," Bernie answered.

"Why does it always have to be your way?" Libby demanded.

"Because I'm driving," Bernie replied, "and our deal is that the driver gets to choose. If you want to drive, just say so and I'll pull over and then we can go where you want."

Libby didn't say so. She didn't like driving in this kind of weather. Which her sister knew. Ever since Libby slid off the road into the path of an oncoming minivan five years ago this coming February she'd had a "thing" about driving in the winter. Especially when there was a possibility of black ice on the roadways.

"Good," Bernie said in the face of Libby's silence. She turned onto Croyden Street. "This shouldn't take too long."

"She's probably at work," Libby groused, putting her hands over the vent to capture the anemic stream of warm air the heater was now throwing out. "This is going to be a complete waste of time."

Bernie sighed. "You know what? You need to eat," she told Libby. "That's why you're so grouchy."

"I'm not grouchy," Libby protested.

"Really?" Bernie said. "What would you call it?"

"Cold. I'm just cold," Libby responded even

as she admitted to herself that what Bernie said was true. She did have a tendency to get grouchy when she was hungry.

"You're probably cold because you're hungry." Bernie pointed to her bag. "I have some dates in there."

"I don't like dates," Libby complained, even though she did like them. They weren't chocolate, but they'd do in a pinch.

"And I don't care!" Bernie yelled, losing her last shred of patience. "Eat them anyway."

"Fine," Libby replied as she began looking through Bernie's bag. "You don't have to yell."

Bernie suppressed the urge to strangle her sister, choosing to remain silent and grit her teeth instead.

Libby ate the dates. "These aren't so bad," she allowed when she'd eaten them all.

Bernie grunted. She wasn't ready to talk to her sister yet. At least not in a polite way.

The sisters rode in silence for the next five minutes. Libby was the one who broke it.

"I can see why Mom did what she did with the Sinclairs," Libby said, offering Bernie a conversational olive branch as she looked out the window. The sky, the streets, the piles of dirty snow on the ground all looked bleak. It seemed like a long time before spring would come around.

Bernie caved. "So can I," she said as she pulled

215

over to let a semi that was riding her tail go by her. Mathilda shook as the truck zoomed by. "You think it was just the money?"

"I think the twenty-five grand was probably the proverbial last straw," Libby answered. "According to what Lori said, there was a lot of stuff going on. Knowing Mom, she was probably involved in it one way or another. Trying to help."

"And losing that amount of money . . ." Bernie's voice trailed off. "That was a lot in those days."

"Yes, it was," Libby said as she thought about the amount of work it had taken to get it. "Hell, it's a fair chunk of change these days."

Chapter 21

The apartment building complex Kate Silverman lived in was located on the edge of Hollingsworth. A developer had built five three-story brick buildings in anticipation of the town growing toward the thruway. But it hadn't. Instead, it had expanded in the opposite direction, leaving Highbridge Court marooned without nearby services or decent access roads.

As Bernie drove into the development, she noted that time and deferred maintenance had taken their toll on the buildings. The mortar between the bricks needed pointing, the parking lot was full of potholes, and the paint on the doors and window frames was chipped.

Instead of catering to the young, single commuters going into the city, Highbridge Court had become home to large herds of deer as well as a miscellaneous blend of students from the local community college, low-income families, and people who needed to rent by the month, although rumor said that was changing. Bernie had heard that a multinational company was negotiating buying the property, tearing it down, and building a large warehouse in its place.

But that hadn't happened yet, so hopefully Kate Silverman still lived in an apartment on the second floor of the middle building. As Bernie steered around a pothole, Libby had gone back to grousing about what a waste of time this was probably going to be and listing all the things back in the shop they needed to be doing.

"I guess we'll find out if this was a bad idea or not soon enough," Bernie said as she parked Mathilda as close to the building as she could get. Then she got out and started trudging toward the entrance. Libby followed, trying—and failing—to step around the piles of snow in her path.

"Whoever plowed this parking lot needs to do a better job," Libby observed, stopping to brush some snow off the cuffs of her jeans.

"That's an understatement," Bernie replied as she opened the door to the building and stepped inside. There was no intercom system or lobby so she had walked directly into the hallway. The building smelled of disinfectant and fried foods. A couple of lights in the hallway needed new bulbs and the floor needed to be washed. It was white with the salt people had tracked in on the bottom of their shoes. A bulletin board on the far wall was covered with notices and below the bulletin board sat a stack of flyers for the local grocery store. Two strollers and a bike were stored in the alcove by the stairs where the mailboxes were located.

"At least it's warm in here," Bernie commented as she began to climb the stairs.

"Warmer," Libby corrected, unwilling to let Bernie have the last word.

A child started to cry as Bernie reached the second floor, its shrieks rising and falling as they pierced the building's quiet.

"Someone's having a rough day," Bernie commented as she searched for the apartment number Lori Scheu had given her. Some of the numbers had come off the doors, which made things more challenging.

"Not as bad as I'm having," Libby muttered.

Bernie ignored her sister and concentrated on the number sequence. Kate Silverman's apartment turned out to be the last one on the far right-hand side of the hallway. Bernie stopped in front of it and rang the bell. When it made no sound, she knocked.

"Yes?" someone responded a moment later.

"Kate Silverman?" Bernie asked, while she flashed Libby an I-told-you-so look.

"Who wants to know?"

Bernie told her. "Lori Scheu said you might be able to help us. We need to talk to you about Ada Sinclair."

The door opened a crack. Bernie could see the outline of a woman standing in the doorway. She was wearing sweatpants and a cami. Her hair was sticking out from her head and she looked as if she'd just gotten up.

"This isn't a good time," Kate Silverman said,

slamming the door shut. It closed with a thud that echoed down the hall.

Libby grinned. "Well, partner, I guess it's time to mosey on home."

Bernie ignored her sister and banged on the door with the palm of her hand. "We just need a few minutes of your time."

"Then I suggest you call and make an appointment," a raspy voice behind Bernie and Libby said.

Bernie and Libby spun around. Kate Silverman's next-door neighbor was standing in the hallway, glowering at them. "People have a right to a little peace and quiet," she spat out as she clutched the ragged, oversized cardigan she was wearing.

Bernie was about to reply when she heard Kate Silverman's door swing open. "I'm sorry, Mrs. Bitterman," Kate said, stepping out onto the carpet.

Mrs. Bitterman sniffed. Her nose was long and narrow and seemed to quiver with indignation. "I'm trying to watch my TV shows and your friends come banging on the door any time of the day and night."

"I think I explained that they weren't my friends," Kate Silverman told her in a tone Bernie could only describe as long suffering.

"Then why were they banging on your door asking for Ada?" Mrs. Bitterman demanded triumphantly. She pointed at Libby and Bernie. "Just like these two are doing now."

"As I told you, they made a mistake," Kate Silverman replied. "The same mistake these two are making now."

"So you say," Mrs. Bitterman told her.

Kate Silverman crossed her hands over her chest and planted both feet firmly on the floor. "Yes, I do."

Mrs. Bitterman stuck out her chin. "We'll see what Mr. Forsethy says."

"Who is Mr. Forsethy?" Libby asked.

"The landlord," Mrs. Bitterman replied, looking down her nose at Libby. "Your friend is about to get her third and final warning from him," she informed Libby and Bernie. "Then she's going to get kicked out of the building."

"I don't think that will be necessary, Mrs. Bitterman," Bernie said. "Kate was just letting us in, weren't you?" she said, turning to Kate.

"Definitely," Kate said. "Happy to," she added through clenched teeth, the expression on her face telling a very different story.

Chapter 22

Mrs. Bitterman watched through narrowed eyes as Bernie and Libby followed Kate Silverman into her apartment. "And see that this doesn't happen again," she admonished, shaking a finger at them as Kate Silverman closed the door behind her.

"Friggin' cow," Kate muttered. She folded her arms over her chest and turned toward Bernie and Libby. "Thanks a lot," she said.

Bernie smiled. "Always happy to oblige. Who is that woman anyway?"

"She's the landlord's aunt."

"Lucky you," Bernie observed.

"Tell me about it," Kate said. "Living next to her has turned into an absolute nightmare. The previous tenant moved to Delray Beach down in Florida." Kate sighed. "God, do I wish she were back."

Bernie continued. "So, I can assume from your neighbor's remarks that you know Ada?" she said.

Kate didn't say anything.

"Please," Bernie said. "Ada's in trouble and we're trying to help."

"So you say," Kate replied, sounding unconvinced.

"Yes, I do," Bernie told her. "Call and ask her."

"I can't. I don't have her number," Kate told her.

"Lori Scheu said you were her friend," Libby informed her as she looked around Silverman's apartment.

Libby's first impression was one of a meticulously kept large studio apartment with a sleeping alcove and a galley kitchen. The walls of the main room were a pale blue, while the kitchen and sleeping alcove were a slightly darker shade of the same color. The sofa and two armchairs were black leather, while a large, embossed, round metal tray sitting on a stand served as a coffee table.

Bernie pointed to it. "Nice," she said, referring to the intricate pattern.

"Thanks," Kate replied. "I got it in Morocco"—she nodded to the two rugs on the floor and the one tacked up on the far wall—"along with those."

"It must be hard to fit everything in," Libby observed, noting the unpacked cardboard boxes stacked underneath the window on the wall facing them.

Kate shook her head. "It really is. You know how it is. You have stuff you should throw away, but you can't part with it."

Bernie thought of some of the shoes living in her closet. "I certainly do." She undid her coat. It

223

was warm in the apartment. "But I don't believe you."

"About keeping stuff?" Kate asked.

"God, no." Bernie laughed. "About not having Ada's phone number," Bernie said.

Kate shrugged. "It's true. I did have it, but she's using a burner phone these days."

"I know," Bernie said. She'd found that out when she'd tried to call Ada back after her last phone call.

"And she never gave me the number," Kate said. "She's probably got a different phone by now anyway. Despite what Mrs. Scheu may have heard, we haven't been friends for quite some time."

"Then why were people knocking on your door looking for her?" Libby asked.

Kate shrugged again. "We used to be friends, that's true, but, like I said, that was a long time ago."

"How long?" Bernie asked.

Kate's face hardened. "Long enough."

"So who were the people knocking on your door?" Libby inquired.

"Salesmen," Kate replied. "Mormon missionaries."

Bernie took a deep breath and let it out. "Somehow, I doubt that." Bernie had a pretty good idea who had come knocking, but she wanted to hear what Kate Silverman was going to say.

"Then I guess it sucks to be you," Kate told her as she pointed to the clock hanging on the kitchen wall. "I have to get ready to go to work," she said. "So, if you don't mind . . ."

"Actually, I do," Bernie told her.

"Too bad," Kate threw back at her.

"You know," Bernie told her, "I can always ask Mrs. Bitterman if she can describe the people who were knocking on your door. I bet she'll be able to describe them down to the last detail."

A vein below Kate's eye began to pulse. She took a deep breath and let it out. "Fine," she spat out and she walked into the kitchen.

Bernie and Libby followed. They watched as Kate took a bottle of Diet Coke off the counter, twisted the top off, and began to drink. "Breakfast," she explained. "I have to be at work in three-quarters of an hour."

"What do you do?" Libby inquired.

"I waitress at the all-night diner on Pine Street."

"Michael still there?" Bernie asked.

Kate shook her head. "You know him?"

Bernie nodded. "From when I worked at Freddie's."

"He took off," Kate informed her, her face softening a little at the mention of Michael. "He's got a gig down in the city."

Bernie had heard he was in jail in Tucson, but she didn't feel this was the time to share. "We really do want to help Ada," Bernie said instead.

Kate rummaged around in her kitchen cabinet, came out with a bag of Oreo cookies, and ate one. Then she offered the bag to Bernie and Libby.

"Thanks," Libby said. She and Bernie both took a couple and Libby handed the bag back, even though she could have eaten a few more. Evidently the dates hadn't been enough.

"Even if I believed you . . ." Kate continued.

"Which you have no reason not to . . ." Bernie assured her. "I don't think Lori Scheu would have given us your address otherwise."

"Possibly," Kate said. "I'm sorry, but I can't help you. I really don't know where Ada is. And if I'm being honest, I'm just as glad."

"Why?" Libby asked as she unzipped her parka. It really was warm in here. Suffocatingly so.

"Because the truth is I'm tired," Kate replied.

"Tired of what?" Bernie inquired.

"Of being Grand Central Station. Of getting into trouble because of Ada. Of being her friend. You want to know who came looking for her, I'll tell you. First Ada's mother bangs on my door, then her aunt and her stepsister and stepbrother turn up, and now you. Frankly, I'm done with all the drama. I have better things to do than get involved in whatever particular brand of crap Ada's gotten herself into this time. I have bills to pay and a life to lead that doesn't revolve around Ada."

Bernie noted the phrase *this time,* tucking it

226

away for future reference. "So, was Ada here?" Bernie asked.

"Yes, she was," Kate admitted as she took another cookie. "I told everyone she wasn't because she asked me too, but I lied. She was here. Actually, she's been here on and off."

"When was that?" Libby asked.

"She was here New Year's Eve. Late. She stayed for a couple of days. Then she left and came back." And Kate named the day Ada had run out of the service plaza. "She banged on my door and woke me up. She was hysterical."

"What did she say?" Bernie asked.

"She was babbling something about her family trying to get rid of her any way they could, and then she said she had to hide," Kate answered.

"And you believed her?" Libby asked Kate Silverman.

"I believed she was really upset."

"And you let her in," Libby observed.

"Of course I let her in," Kate snapped. If someone came banging on your door with a story like that, wouldn't you?"

"Yes," both Libby and Bernie said together.

"Exactly. I mean Ada obviously needed help." Kate took a third cookie and nibbled on it while she thought. A moment later she said, "She gets really . . . worked up. Ada and I were neighbors before my mom and dad bought another house and moved off the block. We used to hang out

227

together, and while it's true that even then Ada tended to blow things up, as in dramatize, it's also true that her family isn't very nice."

"There's a difference between not being very nice and doing what Ada was accusing them of doing," Libby said, pointing out the obvious.

"Yes, there is," Kate agreed. "Her mom . . ."

Libby brushed an Oreo crumb off her parka. "What about Linda?"

"She was pretty mean to Ada . . . especially after Mr. Sinclair left her for Vicky. It was like she was taking her stuff out on Ada. She was always much nicer to Rick and Rachel," Kate said. "Of course, now that I'm older I can sorta see why she was." Then she stopped talking.

Bernie and Libby remained silent. They'd learned a long time ago that sometimes the best thing to say is nothing at all.

After a moment, Kate started speaking again. "She had a really bad temper."

"Linda?" Bernie asked.

"Ada too," Kate replied. "Both of them. Only Ada's mom was worse. She could get very scary when she got mad. It's like you flipped a switch and she became a whole other person. Like Bonnie and Clyde."

Bernie corrected her. "I think you mean Jekyll and Hyde."

"Whoever," Kate said, dismissing Bernie's correction with a wave of her hand. "Of course,

228

Mrs. Sinclair could be different now," Kate reflected. She studied her nails for a moment. Bernie noted that she needed a manicure. "She probably is. Maybe she was just going through the change or something like that."

"Maybe," Bernie replied, thinking back to Linda. She'd impressed her as cranky and put upon, but that was about it. Then again, you never really knew what went on in people's heads, did you?

Kate continued talking. "I remember she was pretty pissed when Ada took all the tropical fish out of Rachel's fish tank and let them go in the creek in Candle Park. Ada said she wanted them to be free. And then there was the time Ada dumped a whole container of flour on the kitchen counter because she was looking for something. Her mom was pretty pissed about that."

"I would be too," Bernie said. "Was there more stuff like that?"

"A lot more. Like turning on the water in the bathtub and forgetting about it."

"That would make me nuts," Bernie observed.

Kate glanced at the clock on the wall again. "I really have to get ready to go."

"One last question," Libby said.

"Make it a fast one," Kate told her.

Libby nodded. "Did Ada say anything when she was here about what happened the night Peggy Graceson died, or why she took off?"

"That's two questions," Kate pointed out. "But no. All she said was that she was hungry and that she needed to stay with me and that she'd made a big mistake."

"A mistake?" Libby asked. "What kind of mistake?"

"No idea," Kate answered. "I asked her but she said she didn't want to talk about it. Then she told me her family thought they were so smart and flopped down on the sofa and went to sleep. She was out in like two seconds."

"Do you know what Ada meant by that?" Libby asked.

"Your guess is as good as mine," Kate told Libby.

"How long did Ada stay with you that time?" Bernie asked, changing the subject.

"She was gone when I woke up the next morning," Kate said. "Hey, if you catch up with her, tell her I want the forty bucks she took from my wallet back."

"Well, there's one thing that's certain," Libby said after she and her sister left Kate Silverman's apartment and started down the stairs.

"What's that?" Bernie asked.

"Ada can't get far on forty dollars," Libby noted. "At least not these days."

"She's got credit cards."

"I bet they're maxed out. I mean why else would she have taken forty bucks?"

"True," Bernie allowed.

"So, what now?" Libby asked her sister as they walked outside.

"Same as before. We find Ada."

"And how are we going to do that?"

"The usual way," Bernie said.

"Which is?" Libby asked as she and Bernie climbed into Mathilda.

Bernie turned on Mathilda's engine.

Libby leaned over, grabbed the door handle, and pulled the door closed. "Ask the Magic 8 Ball?" she said when her sister didn't reply.

"I prefer a Ouija board myself," Bernie replied. "On the other hand, that might not be necessary." And she indicated the left side of the parking lot. Two people were getting out of a light gray Chevy SUV.

"Wow," Libby said when she realized who they were.

"Yes, indeed." Bernie grinned. "Maybe the gods are finally smiling."

"All I can say is it's about time," Libby declared.

Chapter 23

Libby and Bernie watched Ada's brother and sister as they hurried across the parking lot. They were both the same height, about five feet ten inches, and they were walking at the same pace, but neither one was talking to or looking at the other.

Ada's brother, Rick, had his hands jammed into the pockets of his parka, his parka zipped up to his chin, a watch cap on with a pair of large, silver headphones clamped over it, and he was looking down at the ground, trying, as Libby had, to avoid stepping into the piles of snow scattered over the ground.

Ada's sister, Rachel, was equally occupied. She was busy looking down at her cell as she walked. Her face was partially obscured by the fur-rimmed hood on her expensive down coat and Bernie couldn't help noticing that she was wearing fur-trimmed boots as well. Definitely not a PETA follower, that was for sure, Bernie reflected.

Bernie hadn't gotten a good read on them on New Year's Eve other than to think that they both thought that the world revolved around them. Watching them walk confirmed her opinion. In not looking where they were going, Rick and Rachel were assuming that everyone would watch out for them. Or was Bernie being unfair? Was this a generational thing, she wondered. She couldn't decide. She and Libby weren't that much older, but they hadn't grown up glued to their cell phones.

But one thing was clear: if either sibling had been paying attention to where they were going, they would have noticed Mathilda. The van was hard to miss, what with the shop's name painted on its side in turquoise and green. As it was, they both walked by the van on the way to the middle building's door, the same entrance Bernie and Libby had just come out of. They were still lost in their own thoughts when Bernie turned off Mathilda's engine.

"You think they're going to talk to Kate Silverman?" Libby asked Bernie.

"Well, I don't think they're here visiting an aging relative, do you?"

"No, I don't," Libby replied. "Let's find out, shall we?"

Bernie nodded and she and Libby slipped out of the van and quickly followed behind Ada's siblings. When they closed the distance, Bernie leaned over and tapped Ada's brother on the shoulder, while Libby did the same with Ada's sister.

The siblings jumped and spun around.

"Jeez," Rick said, having put his hand over his heart.

Libby smiled brightly. "Howdy," Libby said. "Sorry if we startled you."

"You didn't," Rachel told her, although they obviously had.

"Fancy seeing you two here," Bernie added.

Ada's sister's eyes narrowed. "I could say the same of you. Why are you here?"

"Oh, we're catering an event," Bernie lied. "Are you visiting Ada?" she asked, all innocence.

The brother and sister exchanged a glance.

"We would if we knew where she was," Rick said, removing his headphones and hanging them around his neck.

Rachel buttoned the top button on her coat and said nothing.

"We heard Ada came back," Libby said.

Rick gave a casual shrug. "If she has, she hasn't been in contact with me or my sister. As far as we know she's still in the wind."

"Ah," Bernie said. "That's too bad."

"Yes, it is," Rachel answered, even though her tone said otherwise. She pushed her hood back and ran her fingers through her hair. Bernie noticed that she'd gotten a new haircut, a shorter one that emphasized her cheekbones and the slight downward curve of her nose. "We're all concerned."

"Absolutely," Rick replied, echoing his sister's response.

"Funny, I got the opposite impression," Bernie observed.

"Naturally, we're all . . . annoyed . . . but we're

all concerned, too," Rick told her as his breath made designs in the night air.

"I just wish she hadn't taken my mom's car," Rachel added.

Interesting that Ada called her mother Linda, while Rachel called her mother mom, Bernie reflected. Ada really did seem to be estranged from her family.

"Yeah. Mom's really pissed about that," Rick confided.

"I imagine she would be," Bernie replied. "I know my dad would have been really pissed if I'd pulled a stunt like that. What happened to hers?"

"She drove it into a ditch," Rick responded. "She's a really bad driver. Even though she thinks she isn't."

"So, now my mom's using my car." Ada's sister gave a disgusted snort. "Which means we have to go to work together."

"That's terrible," Bernie said.

"Yes, it is," Rachel agreed, missing Bernie's sarcasm. "Now I have to get up at seven in the morning."

"Ada's always doing that kind of stuff," Rick noted.

"Causing problems?" Libby asked.

Rachel nodded. "Exactly."

"What kind of problems did she cause Peggy?" Bernie asked. She'd decided not to repeat the stories Kate Silverman had just told her.

Rachel shrugged her shoulders. "They had this big blowup about something or other."

"But you don't know what?" Bernie asked.

"The police asked us that and I'm telling you what I told them. I wasn't there. I had already left work."

"Me too," Rick said.

"So, who besides Ada and Peggy were there?" Libby inquired.

This time Rick was the one who replied. "Aunt Sheryl was. She was the one who told me they had the fight. Vicky could have been there, too. They were working on tax stuff that week." Rick frowned. "The worst part is that now we have to fill in for Ada at work."

"She's supposed to be doing office stuff. Not that she ever does," Rachel said, as she put her hood back up. "She has 'issues.' " She bracketed the word *issues* with her fingers. "She's always had issues. Even when we were kids, she never did what she was supposed to do. She made up stories about why she couldn't. Or blamed us. And my mom believed her."

"That must have been rough," Bernie observed.

"It was," Rachel agreed.

"It's nice that you still care about her and all," Libby added. "Is that why you're visiting Kate Silverman?"

Rick and Rachel exchanged another glance.

"Why would you say that?" Rick asked.

Bernie replied, "It's just that the rest of your family has been here looking for Ada so my sister and I assumed you guys were doing the same thing. You know, out of concern for your sister's safety."

Rick shook his head. "Ada and Kate were best friends in school, but they're not anymore."

"That's not what I heard," Libby lied.

Rachel sniffed. "Honestly," she said, "I think you two should stick to catering, because you're not very good at this private detective thing."

"At all," Rick added. "You guys don't have a clue."

"Then why don't you enlighten us?" Bernie asked.

"Yeah," Libby seconded as she looked from Rick to Bernie and back again. "We'd really like to hear what you have to say."

"We have nothing to say," Rachel replied.

"I'm not so sure of that. Why don't we go somewhere and talk," Libby suggested. "It's too cold to be standing outside like this. We could get a drink or a nice cup of hot chocolate."

"Thanks, but I'm fine," Rachel said.

"If you don't want to go someplace we could always go up to Kate Silverman's place and chat there," Bernie suggested.

"You really don't take no for an answer, do you?" Rick told her.

"My sister prides herself on it," Libby explained.

"We really need to speak to your sister," Bernie said to Rachel and Rick.

"And we already told you we don't know where she is," Rick told her.

"But you think Kate Silverman does," Libby said. "That's why you're here."

"Think whatever you like," Rick told her.

"Then what are you doing here?" Bernie demanded.

"Not that it's any of your business, but maybe," Rick replied, "my sister and I know someone else who lives here. Maybe I know a couple of people who live here. Or maybe Rachel and I are friends with Kate Silverman. After all, we all grew up together. Have you thought of that? Ada is not the only person in the universe—even though she likes to think she is."

"I would if I believed in coincidence," Bernie replied. "Which I don't. What do you think, Libby?"

"I have to agree with you, Bernie," Libby replied. "The odds of Rick and Rachel showing up here to not look for their sister are slim to none."

"I don't really care what you two believe," Rachel told the sisters. "Last I heard it's a free country and we can go where we want." She frowned. "Now, if you don't mind."

As Rachel started to take a step toward the building, Bernie put a hand on Rachel's arm. "Wait," Bernie said.

Rachel spun around and gestured to Bernie's hand with her chin. "Take your hand off of me."

"Sorry," Bernie said. She took a step back and was lifting her hand up when a thought occurred to her. "Or, maybe Libby and I are wrong," Bernie said slowly.

Rick clapped. "Finally."

Bernie ignored him. She thought about the cartons under Kate Silverman's windows and the fact that they had bothered her when she'd seen them. Kate Silverman didn't seem like the type of person to not unpack. So, maybe the cartons weren't Kate Silverman's. Maybe she was keeping them for Ada. And maybe that's where the notebook Ada had read from was.

"Maybe you and your sister are here for the notebook," Bernie said to Rick.

"What notebook?" Rachel asked.

"The one your sister read from on New Year's Eve. The one your sister claims contains proof that your father and Joel Grover were murdered," Bernie said.

Rick snorted. "Seriously? Was that ridiculous or what? You were there. You heard what Ada read. It was a bunch of junk."

Libby raised an eyebrow.

"And some old formulas. Things that didn't work," Rick explained. "My dad had a habit of doing that. He logged his mistakes. Frankly," Rick continued, "I'm surprised it was up there.

My mom did a massive clean out after my dad died. She gave everything to Goodwill."

"When was this?" Bernie asked.

"About a month after he died," Rick replied. "I helped load the car."

"If you ask me, the whole thing was another episode of the Ada Sinclair show," Rachel said. "This is the kind of thing she always does. She's a . . ."

"Disrupter?" Bernie asked.

Rachel smiled. "Yes. That's the word I'm looking for."

"Okay," Libby said, "moving along. Is there anyone besides Kate Silverman that your sister would stay with?"

"No one. My sister doesn't have any friends," Rick said. "She's always been a loner."

"Except for Kate Silverman," Bernie said.

"Not anymore. My sister is just exhausting."

"We really need to get in touch with Ada," Libby repeated.

Rick let out a strangled laugh. "You want my advice?" he said. "Let the police sort this out. Look at what happened on New Year's Eve."

"That's what we want to talk to her about," Bernie said.

"I wouldn't go near her. Look what she did," Rachel said.

"You really think your sister killed Peggy?" Libby asked.

"Why would she run if she wasn't guilty?" Rick demanded.

"Because she was scared," Bernie said.

Rick snorted. "That's ridiculous."

"People do stupid things when they're frightened," Bernie said, repeating what her dad told her. She stifled a sneeze. "And given the way your uncle acted later on . . . following us the way he did . . . I'd be freaked out, too."

"Maybe he was concerned about his niece," Rachel told her. "Have you thought of that?"

"That's what he said, but that wasn't the impression I got," Libby recalled.

Rick shrugged. "Believe what you want. We have to go."

"To do what?" Bernie asked.

"To save the world, of course," Rick said. "You know what?" he added.

"What?" Libby repeated.

"Do yourself a favor. Stay out of this."

"Is that a threat?" Bernie asked.

Rachel laughed. "Another drama addict. No. It's not a threat. It's a piece of good advice. And just for the record, don't continue to feed Ada's fantasies. You're not helping."

"We're not," Libby protested.

"What do you call what you're doing?" Rachel demanded, after which she turned and started walking toward the apartment building Bernie and Libby had just come out of. Rick followed.

"Do you think what Rachel said about us and Ada is true?" Libby asked her sister as she watched Rick and Rachel open the door and disappear inside.

"No, I don't," Bernie replied as she got into Mathilda. She put the key in Mathilda's ignition and turned it. The engine caught on the first try. A miracle.

"What about the notebook?"

"I'm out on that. However, one thing is clear. The notebook served as a catalyst to the New Year's Eve fiasco."

"I wonder if someone was counting on that," Libby mused as she slammed the van door shut. "Actually, we don't even know if they're going to talk to Kate Silverman. Maybe we're wrong. Maybe they really are going to talk to someone else."

"I think I have a way to find out," Bernie said as she drove over to the SUV Rick and Rachel had come in. She stopped the van in front of it and got out.

"What are you doing?" Libby asked.

"You'll see," Bernie told her. "This might not work," she added. "A lot of vehicles don't have car alarms anymore." On the other hand, a lot of them still did. And Kate Silverman's windows overlooked the parking lot. "Here goes nothing," Bernie said to herself and she drew her leg back and kicked the SUV's bumper with as much force as she could manage. The SUV's horn started blaring.

"I guess this one does," Bernie said as she watched Kate Silverman's window.

Lights came on. People started sticking their heads out of their windows. A moment later, Rick Sinclair stuck his head out of Kate Silverman's window and started looking around.

"What the hell!" he yelled as he spotted Bernie next to his vehicle. "Is that noise coming from my car?"

"Sorry!" Bernie shouted back. "I tapped it."

"Stay right there," Rick told her. "I'll be down in a second."

"There's your answer," she said to Libby once she'd jumped back into Mathilda. It was time to leave. She didn't want to be around when Rick came downstairs. Something told her he wasn't going to be in a good mood.

Chapter 24

Sean looked at the clock on the wall. It was nine at night and he was not happy. He was not happy because Ada's aunt, Sheryl, was sitting on the sofa between his daughters. Taking up quite a bit of room, he could have added had he been asked. Which he hadn't been.

"I know this is late," Sheryl was saying to him. "I know I should have called first, but I was afraid if I did you wouldn't see me."

Sean grunted. She was correct. He wouldn't have. Especially at this hour.

"So, I'm going to make this short."

Sean crossed his arms over his chest and waited.

Sheryl opened her coat and began. "I know we haven't been in touch for a long time."

Sean nodded. Also true. "Go on."

"And I know that that's my family's fault. They took advantage of Rose." Sheryl bit her lip. "And I'm really sorry about that."

"Is that why you're here?" Sean asked. "To apologize? Because a card would have sufficed."

"No," Sheryl replied. "I'm here to ask you to help find Ada . . . and help straighten out any . . . mess she's gotten herself into. She tends to be"— here Sheryl paused for a moment—"somewhat overreactive. She tends to make things worse for herself, and while I know your daughters are involved in this I was hoping that you could lend a hand as well." Sheryl swallowed. "I hope you don't think I'm out of line for saying this but I think Rose would have wanted you to. She always had a soft spot for Ada. Well, think about it," Sheryl said in the face of Sean's silence. Then she stood up and walked out the door, leaving before Bernie and Libby could ask her any questions.

For a moment, everyone was silent. The only sound in the room was the clink of the furnace in the basement and the crack of the house joists protesting against the cold. Then Sean spoke.

"That was interesting," he said, more a pronouncement than anything else.

"Well?" Libby said.

"Well what?" Sean asked her.

"Why didn't you tell her?"

"Tell Sheryl what?"

"That you are helping."

Sean shrugged. "I suppose I just wanted to see her eat a little humble pie. She was never that nice to your mom." Sean made room on his lap for the cat, who reclaimed her seat, having vacated it when Sheryl had walked in. "But what she said was true about your mom having a soft spot for Ada." He glanced down at the piece of sour cream chocolate cake sitting on a plate on the side table next to his armchair and rubbed his hands together. "Let's talk while we eat," he said.

Which they did. This was Bernie and Libby's go-to chocolate cake recipe. It was their mother's, but Bernie and Libby didn't love it just for that reason. They loved the recipe because it turned out a cake that was both moist and chocolatey and not overly sweet, and it didn't hurt that it was simple to make, basically fail-proof, and open to a host of variations.

This time Libby had flavored the buttercream icing with raspberry liqueur and used strawberry preserves between the layers, but the cake worked equally well with Grand Marnier or coffee or cinnamon or bananas, or plain with a dusting of powdered sugar and/or vanilla-flavored whipped cream.

While they were eating, Sean told his daughters about Clyde's call. According to his old friend the presence of a toxic substance—in this case cyanide—on the needle in the popper had been confirmed. Officially.

"So, I was right," Bernie said.

Sean nodded. "It was a good guess on your part."

"It certainly took them long enough," Libby grumbled.

Sean shrugged. He knew from his time as the Longely chief of police, the labs were always backlogged.

"Although I'm still having trouble believing that the amount on the needle would be enough to kill someone," Bernie observed.

"Evidently it is if you're taking antiseizure medication—which Peggy was," Sean told her "The two substances do not combine well."

"Who knew," Libby said.

Sean took a sip of milk. No matter what anyone said, he still liked milk and chocolate cake. "Evidently, the murderer did."

Libby licked a smidge of buttercream off her fork and rolled it around on her tongue, contemplating the marriage of chocolate and raspberries. The tart and the sweet. It always worked in the culinary world.

"So where did whoever killed Peggy get the cyanide from?" Bernie asked. "It used to be fairly common—exterminators used it all the time. You could buy it at the local hardware store—but not anymore."

"It's simple," Sean said. "Just grind together millions, maybe billons of apple seeds and peach pits and bitter almonds and there you go. Cyanide."

Bernie laughed. "I'm being serious, Dad."

"So am I," Sean replied.

"How do you know that?" Bernie demanded.

Sean chuckled. "I arrested someone who did that."

Bernie put her feet on the floor and leaned

forward. "Did you tell us that story, because if you did I don't remember it and I think I would have."

"I didn't," Sean told her. "Your mom was on one of her campaigns when it happened."

Bernie and Libby both leaned forward. They loved their dad's stories. Their mother, however, had not.

Sean took another sip of milk and began. "This guy—Ralph Edwards, if I recall his name correctly—was trying to make cyanide so he could poison his wife. He had a whole lab set up in the basement of his house because he'd read somewhere that crushed apple seeds are a good source of cyanide. Which is true."

"Did he succeed?" Libby asked.

Sean took another sip of milk and a bite of cake. "No, but not for want of trying. He did manage to extract the poison from the apple seeds. However, his wife figured out what was going on before he could slip the cyanide into her food." Sean took another bite of his steadily dwindling piece of cake.

"Lucky her," Bernie commented.

Sean nodded. "And how. At first, she couldn't figure out why her husband was buying all these apples and carting them down to the basement. When she asked him, he told her he was making vodka, which she believed. But she got suspicious when she was looking for something in the garage one day and found a book called *Nature's Poisons: How to Identify and Use Them* hidden in her husband's tool chest."

"That would have given me pause," Libby remarked.

"Me too," Bernie agreed.

"It definitely gave his wife pause, I can tell you that," Sean remarked. "Of course, there were other signs as well, like the huge life insurance policy her husband had just taken out on her, the affair he was having with his twenty-year-old assistant, and the fact that she'd almost been in a very bad accident because someone had tampered with the brakes on her car. P.S. Her husband was an automotive engineer."

"Why didn't he just hire someone to shoot her?" Bernie asked.

Sean laughed. "Funny thing, I asked him the same question when I arrested him. You know what he said?"

Libby and Bernie shook their heads.

"He said he didn't want to spend money on something he could do himself."

"Sometimes it doesn't pay to be cheap," Bernie observed.

"So, what you're saying is all we have to do is find someone who is cornering the apple seed market and we'll be all set," Libby said.

"Exactly," Sean allowed.

"Or," Bernie suggested, "maybe cyanide makes

your hair grow. Maybe it's the secret ingredient in Sinclair Enterprises' new product. So what if there are a few unfortunate side effects."

"That's ridiculous," Sean huffed.

"I was kidding, but people used things like that all the time. Like I said, until fairly recently, exterminators used cyanide to get rid of mice. Sometimes they got rid of the family instead. And back in the day they put arsenic in face powder because it made women's complexions paler," Bernie continued. "And they used belladonna in eye drops, because it made women's eyes shine. And let's not forget the people who put tapeworm larvae in capsules and sold them as diet pills until the FDA pulled them off the market. That happened fairly recently."

"Were they effective?" Libby asked.

Bernie nodded. "Very much so."

Sean shook his head. "Amazing what people will do."

"Isn't it, though. Women used to have their lower ribs removed to make their waists smaller." Bernie tapped her fingers on the edge of her mug while she thought. "Realistically speaking, whoever killed Peggy probably got the cyanide on the dark web."

Libby turned to Bernie. "Do you know how to access the dark web?" she asked her sister.

"No. Do you?"

"No."

Libby leaned forward. "Do you know anyone who does?" she inquired.

"I don't know. I never asked."

"But what do you think?"

"I think probably not."

"That's my point." Libby sat back up. "Most people don't."

"But that doesn't mean someone in the Sinclair family doesn't know how," Bernie countered. "A negative doesn't prove a positive."

"Then it would have to be one of the kids," Libby observed. "The adults are too old."

Sean laughed. "Talk about making assumptions."

"Libby, you don't know that for sure," Bernie was saying when her cell rang. She picked it up and looked at the displayed number. It wasn't anyone she knew so she didn't answer. It had been a long, frustrating day and she wasn't in the mood for a chat about insurance rates or some such thing. A moment later, the message icon came on and Bernie picked up her phone again and listened to the voicemail. Then she cursed.

"Damn," she said. "You have got to be kidding me."

Chapter 25

"What's wrong?" Libby asked her sister, although she wasn't sure she wanted to know the answer because judging from the expression on her sister's face whatever was going on wasn't good.

"That was Ada," Bernie told her.

Libby let out a groan. "What's the matter this time?"

"I have no idea, but evidently she's on her way over to Kate Silverman's apartment and she wants us to meet her there right away."

"Now?" Libby asked, her voice rising.

"Yes, now. Isn't that what I just said?"

Libby gestured to the clock on the wall. "It's almost ten, Bernie," she pointed out. "We have to be up at five."

"Believe me, Libby, I'm well aware of when we have to get up," Bernie told her sister.

"Did Ada happen to say why she wants us there?"

In answer, Bernie played Ada's voicemail message for Libby. No reason was stated.

"Great," Libby muttered, handing Bernie's phone back to her. "Can you call and ask her."

Bernie did, but Ada didn't answer. A moment later a text appeared on Bernie's phone. Can't talk. Come. Urgent. She showed it to Libby, who groaned louder.

"Just because Ada says it's urgent doesn't mean it can't wait until tomorrow, Bernie," Libby told her.

"Evidently Ada doesn't think it can."

"That's because she's paranoid," Libby replied.

"Even paranoids . . ."

". . . are right some of the time," Libby said, finishing her sister's sentence for her. "I know. I know. But what's the point of going? She's just going to run away again anyway," Libby said, recalling their last encounter at the service area.

Sean looked from one daughter to the other and back, following the conversation with interest.

"That wasn't her fault," Bernie retorted.

"Then whose fault was it?" Libby demanded.

Bernie stood up. "Ours for letting ourselves be followed. You have to admit, she did sound scared."

"She always sounds scared," Libby pointed out. Actually, if she were being honest, Ada had sounded terrified. Which, Libby decided, was probably why Ada was using a burner phone. No. It definitely was why she was. That way no one could track her. Something must have spooked her. Libby couldn't argue with that. She just wasn't sure that she wanted to know what that particular something was. Or maybe not. Maybe she was imagining it. Maybe Rachel was right.

Her sister was exhausting. "Why can't she call the police?"

"Good question," Sean commented. "Indeed, why can't she?"

"Because according to Lori Scheu she thinks the police are in cahoots with whoever wants to harm her," Bernie replied.

Sean rolled his eyes. "That's ridiculous."

"I'll tell her that when I see her," Bernie said to her dad. "I'm sure that will make her feel better." Then she turned to her sister. "Listen," she said to Libby, "you can stay here if you want, but I'm going."

"At least let me finish my cake," Libby replied.

"Then you're coming with me?" Bernie asked.

"I just said that, didn't I?" Libby answered.

"Okay. But eat fast," Bernie replied as Sean took another sip of his milk.

"Ah, the drama," he intoned after he swallowed. "I'm glad I'm not getting called out in the middle of the night anymore." He snapped his fingers. "Oh, wait. I remember. When I did it was because it was my job. Something I got paid for."

Bernie turned toward her father. "What do you always tell us about sarcasm being the refuge of a weak mind, Dad?"

"Number one, I didn't say that; number two, I wasn't being sarcastic," Sean told her. "I was being accurate."

Bernie flicked a cake crumb off the front of her

black cashmere turtleneck sweater. "Okay, Dad. I get it. You won the bet. You were right about the Sinclairs. They have a penchant for drama."

"If I'm right, then why are you going?" Sean challenged as Cindy bumped her head against his hand to signal she wanted him to keep rubbing her ears. "You know this is probably nothing." It was one thing for him to be out at night, but he wasn't keen on his daughters being out there. Especially in bad weather. Not that he'd say that. If he did that would just encourage them to do the opposite.

"The same reason you'd be going if you'd gotten the call," Bernie told her dad as she headed for the door.

"I wouldn't be going," Sean called after her.

Bernie stopped and pivoted. "Yes you would."

"No I wouldn't," Sean insisted.

"Yes you would," Bernie told him. "You want to know why?"

"I'm all ears," Sean told her.

"You'd go because Ada needs help and you'd go because you couldn't stand not knowing what was going on."

"So, you're telling me I'm a sucker?" Sean asked as Cindy began to purr.

"I think more like a hard candy with a soft center. A bonbon," Bernie replied.

Sean laughed and shook his head. "Somehow *bonbon* sounds worse than *sucker*," he told her.

Bernie walked over to her dad and kissed him on the forehead. "It does, doesn't it," she told him. Then she gave Cindy a quick scratch under the chin before turning and heading back toward the door.

Libby sighed as she finished her last bite of cake and cleaned the plate off with the tip of her finger. She'd been looking forward to an early bath and bed, not going on some wild goose chase, she thought as she licked the frosting off her finger. On the other hand, family was family and it was possible that Bernie would need some help. No. Not possible. Certain. Her sister always leaped before she looked.

"Stay safe," Sean told Libby as she put down her fork. "And look after your sister."

"Definitely," Libby replied. Then she stood up and kissed her dad on the forehead, after which she headed toward the door. "You're going to owe me for this big-time, Bernie," Libby called out as she followed her sister down the stairs.

"More cake for us," Sean told Cindy the cat as he listened to his daughters' footsteps on the stairs.

Cindy meowed her agreement and licked up the drop of milk that had spilled on Sean's shirt. He scratched around Cindy's ears. Her purring intensified, filling the room. He remembered seeing Ada when she was two years old when he'd gone over to her mother's house with Rose.

Which was the first and last time he'd been at Linda's place, the place in which she was still living.

Ada had pitched a fit then, and evidently from what he was hearing she'd been doing that ever since. He remembered getting the feeling that she was the designated "bad child" of the family. The one who was always in trouble.

Was that dynamic still in play? he wondered. After all, family dynamics didn't change all that much. Not really. Rose had thought Ada was the misunderstood one, the one who had gotten the short end of the straw, but then she was the one who thought all juvies were merely misunderstood. And they certainly weren't. But there was a middle ground. Now, he wasn't saying Ada was a saint, but he couldn't see her killing someone, either. Especially the way Peggy had died. That took foresight and organization— two characteristics he was pretty sure from what he'd observed that Ada didn't possess.

Sean took another sip of milk, cut himself another sliver of cake, and sat back in his chair and thought about the next step in shedding some light on this mess. That was easy. It entailed finding out about Peggy Graceson. Always start with the victim. That was his motto. And while Bernie and Libby were out on their wild goose chase, Sean decided he might as well do something constructive, which in this case meant picking up the phone and calling McCready and hearing what he had to say about Peggy Graceson. A question he should have asked when he was out there the last time.

"I'm definitely slipping, Cindy," Sean told the cat. "And that's the truth."

Cindy continued purring.

Chapter 26

While Sean was on the phone with McCready, Libby and Bernie were driving to Kate Silverman's apartment. It had started to snow again, the flakes drifting down like confetti, lightly coating the tree branches, buildings, and cars, brightening and softening their outlines.

"You have to admit, it is pretty out," Libby observed.

"It would be even prettier if we were inside looking at the scene through a window," Bernie replied as she pulled over to let an SUV pass them. "Go and be an idiot!" she yelled at the vehicle as it flew by and vanished into the night. "Your brakes don't work any better on ice than mine do."

"We *could* be inside," Libby pointed out, continuing with what she'd been saying. "We don't have to be on the road. In fact, we can still turn around. It's not too late."

"We could, but we we're not going to," Bernie told her.

Libby made a rude noise.

Bernie threw her a quick glance. "Hey, you don't have to be here. You could have stayed home."

Libby raised her hands in a gesture of surrender.

"You're right, you're right," she said to her sister. "Now, tell me again why we're doing this."

Bernie pulled over again to let another SUV zoom by. "Moron," she muttered before answering her sister's question. "We're doing this because what happens if something's really wrong and we aren't there to help?"

"I take it that's a rhetorical question?"

"No, Libby, it isn't. Then we'd feel guilty."

Libby snorted. "You might, but I won't," she told her.

"Really?" Bernie said after she'd got back on the road.

Libby held up her hand and measured out an inch with her thumb and her forefinger. "Okay. You're right. I'd feel this much guilty. But I'd survive. What do you think is going on with Ada anyway?" Libby said.

"Not something good," Bernie answered as she leaned forward to better see the road they were on. "That's for sure."

"That could be her anthem," Libby observed.

Bernie grunted. What could she say? Her sister was right. Neither she nor Libby said anything more for the rest of the trip. Bernie concentrated on her driving and Libby occupied herself by composing tomorrow's to-do list in her head.

They had three sweet potato pies to make for Mrs. Singer's book club, two apple pan dowdies for Mrs. Sloan's knitting circle, twenty-four French macaroons for Mrs. Hubbard, a coconut layer cake with chocolate-rum frosting for a dinner party Mr. Bertrum was giving, and a brisket with sweet potato pancakes and roasted vegetables for Mr. Leffert, as well as everything else they had to do, which included but was not limited to filing this quarter's sales tax. Always a fun couple of hours. If they were lucky. And they could find all the receipts.

Twenty minutes later, the sisters were a block away from Kate Silverman's apartment when Libby pointed to the dancing lights reflected in the cloudy night sky. They were coming from the direction of Kate Silverman's housing complex.

"That doesn't look good," Libby noted.

"No, it doesn't," Bernie agreed.

"Could be fire engines," Libby guessed.

"Or a zombie apocalypse."

"Are we still having them?"

"As far as I know, we are."

"Good to be aware of," Libby said.

A couple of moments later, Bernie pulled into the parking lot of the apartment complex and spied the three cop cars sitting in front of Kate Silverman's building. Their flashers were on, but the officers were absent.

"Do you think they have something to do with the text Ada sent us?" Libby asked.

"Does a duck quack?" Bernie answered as she

parked the van in the fire lane of the building on the far right.

"We're going to get a ticket," Libby protested.

"Somehow, I think the police are otherwise engaged at the moment, and if we do get one we'll just expense it to the business," Bernie replied as she pocketed the keys, jumped out of Mathilda, and hurried toward Kate Silverman's building.

"We most certainly will not," Libby said indignantly as she followed Bernie. Was it her imagination or had it gotten colder out since they'd left the house?

Two minutes later, the sisters were inside Kate Silverman's building. The hallway seemed the same as the last time they'd been here except for the smell of garlic that dominated the air and the strollers jammed into the stairwell.

Bernie and Libby were halfway up the stairs to the second floor when they heard voices. Men's voices. Then Ada's. A moment later, they saw three policemen coming down the stairs. Ada was between two of them with her wrists handcuffed behind her back, while the third policeman brought up the rear.

Bernie thought Ada looked as if she'd been sleeping when the police had come for her. Her hair was sticking out in clumps and she was wearing flannel pajama bottoms, a black long-sleeved T-shirt, a hoodie, and a pair of duck boots in addition to her parka.

But then, thinking back to when Ada had last communicated with her, Bernie realized she was wrong. Ada hadn't been sleeping. This was the way she'd been dressed when the police had arrived. Watching Ada coming down the stairs, Bernie couldn't help thinking how small and lost and young she looked sandwiched between the two beefy cops. All she wanted to do was grab Ada and spirit her away.

Chapter 27

And then there was the guilt. It was baseless. Bernie knew this. But it didn't help. She still couldn't help feeling that if she hadn't waited for Libby to finish eating her cake maybe she would have gotten to Ada before the police did and things would have gone differently.

"Officer, why are you arresting her?" Bernie asked the policeman closest to her. She was careful to use her most respectful voice, being a firm believer in the power of nice—at least to start with. Especially when you weren't holding any cards.

The policeman looked her up and down. "Who is she to you?" he inquired.

Good question. Bernie thought for a moment. *Family? Client? Pain in the butt?* She settled on family. "Family."

"Relation?" the policeman asked.

Ada spoke up. "She's my sister," she lied. Neither Bernie nor Libby contradicted her.

"Is she?" the cop asked Bernie. His tone was skeptical. "Because you two don't look alike. Not even a little bit."

Now it was Bernie's turn to lie. "Half sister. Same mother, different fathers."

"I see," the cop said. Bernie could tell that he

didn't believe her, but that he was letting it go. "In that case, you'd better go home and start thinking about who you want her lawyer to be because we're taking her in on suspicion of homicide," he told Bernie.

"I didn't do it," Ada cried out. "I told you that."

The second cop, the one on the left side of Ada, the one who wasn't talking to Bernie, turned to Ada and said, "Oh well, now that you've told us that that changes everything. We'll take you right back upstairs and take these cuffs off."

Ada turned to Bernie. "You have to believe me," she pleaded.

"I do believe you," Bernie said.

"So do I," Libby added quietly.

"Thank you. Someone is framing me," Ada said in a voice laden with tears. "Please help me. I'm begging you. You have to find out who is doing this to me."

"We will," Bernie assured her. She was reaching out to pat Ada's shoulder when the second cop shook his head.

"No physical contact with the prisoner," he said.

Ada shrank at the word *prisoner*.

"Ada, I promise we'll figure this out," Bernie said, wishing she could say something more reassuring as she put her hand back down by her side.

"Don't worry," Libby added as she flattened

herself against the wall so everyone could get by her. "Everything is going to be fine." But she could tell from the expression on Ada's face that Ada didn't believe it and, frankly, Libby wasn't sure she believed what she'd just said, either.

"Let's hope what you're saying is true," Bernie said to Libby in a low voice as she watched the three policemen convey Ada down the rest of the steps, into the hallway, and out the door into the cold winter night.

"I wonder what she wanted us to do?" Libby mused.

"Or what she wanted to tell us," Bernie said as she started climbing up the rest of the stairs. "Maybe Kate Silverman can tell us. Maybe she knows."

But Kate Silverman couldn't tell them because she wasn't in.

"She's at work," Mrs. Bitterman, Kate Silverman's next-door neighbor, snapped, having opened her door the moment she'd heard footsteps in the hallway.

She must have been waiting by the door, Bernie thought as Mrs. Bitterman started her rant.

"Go talk to her there, and when you do you can tell her for me, this is it. She's going to have to find another place to live. I'm sick and tired of her friends coming and going at all hours of the night. And this, this is just insupportable." Mrs. Bitterman's voice spluttered with indignation.

She rested her hand over her heart. "Having the police bang on the door like they did. I never in all my life expected to live someplace where that would happen. Ever. I was terrified. I thought I was going to have a heart attack and the police were going to have to call the EMTs." And she gave Bernie and Libby a pointed glare.

"Mrs. Bitterman, we're not Kate Silverman's friends," Libby explained. "We came to speak to Ada."

Mrs. Bitterman's eyes narrowed. "Is that the girl the police just carted away?"

Bernie groaned. *Oh no! Talk about making things worse! Why did you say that, Libby?* Bernie thought as she stepped in front of her sister and answered for her. "It's a case of mistaken identity," Bernie lied. She seemed to be doing a lot of that lately, she reflected. "They got the wrong person."

"I don't believe you."

"It's true, Mrs. Bitterman. I swear." *I'm going to hell for this one,* Bernie decided as she raised her right hand.

"It doesn't matter. In fact, that just makes my point," Mrs. Bitterman said, giving the belt on her dark blue terry cloth robe a vicious yank before shaking a finger under Bernie's nose. "If your friend wasn't sleeping in Kate Silverman's apartment, then the police wouldn't have come pounding on the door and none of this would have happened." Mrs. Bitterman put her hand to her heart again and repeated what she'd said before, a fact Bernie felt it wiser not to point out.

"They almost frightened me to death. All that noise and commotion. It's amazing they didn't have to call an ambulance to take me to the hospital. Giving out the keys so her friends can come over and do heaven knows what," she spat out.

"Ada wasn't partying, if that's what you're implying," Libby said from behind Bernie's back. "She just needed a place to sleep."

"Why wasn't she sleeping in her own bed?" Mrs. Bitterman demanded. "That's where every self-respecting person should be." She stifled a cough. "I tell you, there's absolutely no respect for the elderly anymore. None. Everyone around here thinks they can do whatever they want. Things have certainly gone downhill since I was a girl. My mother would be turning over in her grave if she saw what passed for manners these days." And with that pronouncement, Mrs. Bitterman turned and went back inside her apartment, slamming the door behind her.

"Good job, Libby," Bernie told her sister.

"Well, it definitely wasn't my finest hour," Libby agreed.

"You can say that again," Bernie replied.

"Well, it definitely wasn't my finest hour," Libby repeated.

"Ha. Ha."

"I wonder if she was the one who called the cops," Libby said as they started walking away.

"Doubtful," Bernie replied, "considering what she just said. I suspect that if she was going to call the cops, she'd do it in the morning or afternoon."

"Yeah," Libby conceded. "She did look as if she'd been asleep."

"Exactly." Bernie took the keys to the van out of her bag. "But here's another question. How did the cops know that Ada was here?" Bernie asked as she and Libby headed down the hallway.

"Obviously, someone must have told them," Libby opined.

"Obviously. But who?"

"I'm guessing most likely a family member," Libby said as she and Bernie started down the stairs.

"Like Rick or Rachel?" Bernie asked, remembering their meeting with Ada's brother and sister.

"Could be. They were both here."

"We should talk to them."

"Them and the rest of the Sinclairs," Libby said. "After all, everyone else in the family knows about Kate Silverman as well."

"And then there's Kate Silverman herself," Bernie said. "Let's not forget about her."

"What about her?" Libby asked.

"I don't know. Maybe she got tired of Ada crashing in her apartment and dropped a dime on her. Maybe she'd asked Ada to leave already—considering her situation with Mrs. Bitterman I can definitely see that happening—but Ada kept coming back despite Silverman's request."

Bernie paused, leaned down, and pulled her left boot up. It had slid down around her ankle. That was the trouble with suede, she reflected. It stretched out. She wondered if a shoemaker could put a zipper in the side as she finished what she'd been saying to her sister.

"After all," Bernie continued, "she did tell us she wasn't Ada's friend anymore. Or words to that effect. She certainly acted that way."

"Do you think she was telling the truth when she said that?" Libby asked. "Or was she trying to mislead us into believing Ada wasn't crashing there anymore?"

Bernie clicked her tongue against her teeth while she thought. "Well, she did let her stay there," she finally said. "It's not like she changed the lock or anything. If she really didn't want her coming there she certainly could have. It's simple enough to do."

"True," Libby said, mentally reviewing their conversation with Kate Silverman. "When we first spoke, I thought Kate Silverman was telling the truth about not being Ada's friend anymore, but now, thinking back, I'm not so certain.

Silverman certainly wanted to get us out of her place as fast as possible."

"Well, there's one way to find out," Bernie observed.

"Call her?"

"No. We should go to the diner and ask her."

"What's wrong with calling, Bernie?"

"Obviously, because then we won't be able to see the expression on her face when she answers our questions."

Libby grimaced. "Because you're so good at reading people," she muttered under her breath.

Bernie turned toward her sister. "Look who's talking. You did really well with Mrs. Bitterman. Talk about throwing gasoline on the fire."

Libby threw out her hands. "So sue me. This is what happens when you drag me out in the middle of the night."

"It's hardly the middle of the night and I didn't drag you anywhere. You agreed to go." By now Bernie and her sister had reached the bottom of the stairs.

"True," Libby admitted grudgingly because she had volunteered. She sighed her long-suffering sigh in case Bernie didn't realize the sacrifice she, Libby, was making. "She's not going to tell us the truth."

"Maybe she will."

"Why should she?"

"Because I'm going to make her want to."

271

"You're going to lie."

"Let's say I'm going to massage the truth."

"Well, I hope it's a good one," Libby told her sister. Then she sighed again. "Sure. What the hell. Of course. Besides, who needs sleep anyway?"

"It's only five minutes out of our way," Bernie pointed out as she put her jacket hood up in preparation for going outside. "Here's another question."

"Oh, goodie."

Bernie ignored her sister's response. "What turned Ada from a person the police wanted to talk to to a full-on murder suspect?"

"Obviously, the police know something we don't," Libby said as she followed her sister into the cold. "Which isn't hard," Libby observed. "Considering that we know nothing."

"We know a little," Bernie said, correcting her.

"Very little," Libby countered as she wiped a snowflake off her cheek.

The snow was coming down harder now, covering the tops, the windshields, and the hoods of the vehicles in the parking lot, which was why Bernie didn't see the note right away when she got into Mathilda.

Chapter 28

Libby closed the van door. She was putting on her seat belt when she spied the piece of paper pinned under the windshield wiper. "I told you, Bernie," she said, a victorious tone in her voice as she pointed to it. "I told you we'd get a ticket."

"Great," Bernie groused. *The perfect end to the perfect day,* she thought as she got back out of the van to get it.

But when she retrieved the piece of paper from under the windshield wiper blade, it was obvious Libby was wrong—unless they were giving out tickets written on pieces of paper ripped from lined, yellow legal pads these days, that is. Someone had left them a note. *Odd,* Bernie thought as she unfolded it and brushed the snow off. Then she held it up to the street lamp and read it.

"How much?" Libby asked when Bernie climbed back into the van a moment later. "Because the business isn't paying it. You are."

"It's not a ticket," Bernie informed her.

"Then what is it?" Libby asked. "An invitation to a party?"

"Not exactly."

"Then what?" Libby asked as Bernie handed the sodden piece of paper to her sister.

"Just read it," Bernie said and turned on the van's overhead light so Libby could see better.

"Okay," Libby said, squinting. The writer had used a gel pen and the ink had run but it was still possible to make out the words. "Stay out of this. You've been warned. But if you want answers you're looking in the wrong place," she read aloud. Libby took a deep breath and let it out. This was not what she'd been expecting.

"That's a weird note," Bernie said to Libby.

Libby turned to face her. "The content or its existence?" she asked.

"Both," Bernie said, wishing she'd brought something hot to drink along with her. "It seems schizophrenic to me."

Libby raised an eyebrow. "In what way?"

"Well, the note is telling us to walk away at the same time it's suggesting we're going down the wrong trail. Evidently the writer can't decide what he or she wants us to do—stay or go."

"What trail?" Libby asked rhetorically. "We don't have a trail."

"Evidently whoever wrote this thinks that we do." Bernie stifled a sneeze.

"At least it's not a death threat," Libby said, indicating the note with a nod of her head.

"Now there's a cheery thought," Bernie told her.

"They could have written, 'Stop or you die,' or words to that effect," Libby pointed out.

Bernie rolled her eyes. "They could have written lots of things. They could have written, 'Back off or we'll make you drink gas station coffee and eat Velveeta for the rest of your life.' But they didn't."

"Laugh all you want," Libby told her. "But it wouldn't surprise me if the person who left this note is the person who killed Peggy Graceson. Which makes it a death threat by extension."

"Talk about a leap of logic."

"The expression is a leap of faith," Libby said, correcting her sister.

Bernie frowned. She wasn't in the mood for a semantic discussion. "Whatever. What you said is ridiculous. We don't know that the person who wrote the note is the person who committed the murder," Bernie observed. "Or murders," she said, thinking of Ada's uncle, Henry.

"Why else would they be warning us away, Bernie?" Libby demanded.

"Maybe they have our best interests at heart."

"Doubtful.

"Not necessarily," Bernie replied. "For that matter, why leave us a note at all? Why say anything—especially since Ada is now in custody?"

"Why indeed?" Libby stuck her hand in her pocket, pulled two squares of dark chocolate out, and handed one to Bernie. "I wonder what Dad would say about this note?" she mused as she unwrapped her square, then popped it into her mouth.

"Probably the same things we are," Bernie said as she did likewise. She felt the chocolate melting in her mouth and coating her tongue. She gave a small sigh of pleasure. "Do you have any more?"

"I wish," Libby said. She was handing the note back to Bernie when another thought occurred to her. "You do realize that whoever left this on Mathilda was sitting here watching Ada get arrested," she said.

"Not necessarily," Bernie objected.

"But probably," Libby said. Then she made another logical leap. "And maybe he or she was here watching because he or she was the one who had made the call," Libby said as she absent-mindedly smoothed the note out with her thumb before she handed it back to her sister. "And they wanted to make sure the arrest was carried through."

"Which implies they had an inside connection," Bernie pointed out. "On the other hand, they could have arrived when Ada was getting arrested and left us the note because they didn't want to see her getting arrested."

"Well, the one thing we do know is that whoever wrote the note was here sometime between when we went upstairs to talk to Kate Silverman and when the police came down with Ada," Libby said.

Bernie nodded. She agreed with that.

"Which didn't leave them a lot of time," Libby observed. "Like I just said, odds are, they were here before we came. They're probably here watching us now."

"Oh, please," Bernie told her as she folded up the note and put it in her jacket pocket. "Get a grip. You might as well be saying they put a tracker on our van."

Chapter 29

Libby's eyes widened. She put a hand to her mouth. "Oh my God! How do you know they didn't?" she exclaimed. She hadn't thought of that possibility before her sister mentioned it, but now that Bernie had she couldn't get it out of her head. "They could have," she said.

"Why would they?" Bernie countered, sorry she'd opened her mouth. Was paranoia contagious? Bernie wondered. If so, had her sister caught it from Ada?

"Why wouldn't they?"

"Whoever they are."

"We should check."

Bernie groaned as she shook her head. Why had she said anything? Why hadn't she kept her big mouth shut? "I was kidding."

"But I'm not."

"We should go home."

"Oh, now you want to go home, but when I wanted to you told me we had to stay."

"That's not what I said," Bernie protested.

"It's close enough," Libby replied, a mulish look on her face.

"Where do you get this stuff from?" Bernie asked, not that she expected an answer. The one thing she did know was that there was no arguing with Libby when she got this way. It would be quicker to say yes than to spend the next twenty minutes fighting. "Fine," Bernie grumped. "If it'll make you happy."

"It will," Libby said, looking expectantly at her sister.

"What are you looking at me for?" Bernie asked. "You were the one who suggested it. You want to go out in the cold and look for it, be my guest."

"I will."

"Better you than me," Bernie told her her sister as Libby put her gloves back on, zipped up her parka, and put her hood up.

The wind smacked Libby in the face as she got out of the van, making her sorry she'd opened her mouth. As she blinked snow out of her eyes she thought about getting back in the van and forgetting about the whole thing, then ditched the idea. She wasn't about to give Bernie the satisfaction that she'd caved. No. At least she'd make a show of going over the van, because now that she was out here, she thought that Bernie was probably right and she was being paranoid.

Libby told herself to focus. The faster she did this, the faster she'd be back inside Mathilda. What did a tracker look like anyway? Obviously, it had to be a small metal object, but outside of that she had no idea.

And where would someone put something like

that? Where would she put it? Not on the sides of the van. That would be too obvious. Not on the tailpipe in this case. Or near it. The tailpipe would have been too hot. It took about half an hour for that sucker to cool off. Under the hood? Again, no. Because if he or she had raised the hood, the snow would have fallen off and there was more snow on the hood when they came out of the building than there was when they went in.

Which meant there were only two places the tracker could be. Either underneath one of the tire spaces—Libby was sure they had a name but she didn't know what it was—or inside either the rear or the front fender. Libby walked to the front of Mathilda and started looking, but between the dark and the cold it was hard to see. She'd have to go by feel. Cursing under her breath, she took her gloves off and ran her hands over and under the sides of the fender. Nothing was there.

"How's it going?" Bernie asked, rolling down the window as Libby passed by her as she stomped to the back of the van.

"Just super," Libby said, caught in midstomp.

Bernie snickered, which Libby pretended not to have heard. "Want my phone?" Bernie asked.

Libby paused, puzzled. "Why would I want your phone?"

"Duh. Double duh. The flashlight," Bernie said.

"I'm fine without it," Libby replied, feeling like an idiot because she'd forgotten that cell phones had that capability, not that she would ever admit that to her sister.

"Your call," Bernie told her and rolled up the window, glad to not have the wind blowing the snow in her face.

Once Libby got to the back of the van she did the same thing she'd done in the front. She ran her hands over the fender, but she didn't feel anything along the sides or underneath the rear bumper.

She straightened up. She was wrong. Bernie was right, damn it all. Her fingers were killing her from the cold and her lower back wasn't feeling too great, either. Libby was about to go on to the tire openings when she decided to give the fender one last try.

This time when Libby ran her fingers along the inside of the fender, she felt something sitting along the curve of the metal. Obviously, she hadn't been thorough enough the last time. She pulled at it and it came loose. Then she held it up toward the streetlight. Yup. There it was. A tracker. She felt better than she had all day. She ran over to the driver's side, knocked on the window, and held the device up.

"See. I told you," she said to her sister, her voice jubilant with victory. "I'm not crazy after all."

"That's a matter of opinion," Bernie said. She wasn't often shocked, but she was this time. Why would someone have done this? Why had they gone to the trouble? Her mind went into overdrive as she began computing the possibilities. Which might be the reason for what happened next.

When her sister appeared at her window, Bernie rolled it down and held out her hand. "Let me see," she commanded. Naturally, Libby handed the device to her. Unfortunately, at that moment Bernie thought she saw a movement around the left-hand corner of the apartment building out of the corner of her eye. "What's that?" she asked, lifting her hand to point, thereby allowing the tracker to fly into the air.

"Oh no!" Libby cried as she watched the tracker travel three feet and descend into the white morass lying on the ground. She wanted to cry.

"Rats," Bernie cursed as she realized what she'd done. "Don't worry. We'll find it," she told Libby as she opened the van door and jumped down.

"Yeah, in the spring," Libby answered as she walked over to where the tracker had fallen, squatted down, and began to sift through the snow.

"I thought I saw something out of the corner of my eye," Bernie explained. "No. Someone. I thought I saw someone move."

"Who?" Libby asked, looking up. She didn't see anything. Or anyone, for that matter. Just a veil of white. "I don't see anybody."

"There was someone," Bernie insisted as she knelt down and joined Libby in her search for the missing tracker. "I swear there was."

"It could have been a reflection of the light on the snowflakes," Libby replied as she continued to go through the snow with her hand. *There must be a good seven or eight inches of snow on the ground, but it couldn't have rolled that far,* she told herself. If it had rolled at all. She had watched the thing fall. So, it should be there. Unless, of course, they were looking in the wrong spot.

"No, it wasn't a reflection of the light," Bernie insisted as she continued searching. Although had she seen what she thought she had? Was her sister right after all?

"I believe you," Libby said to Bernie, even though she didn't. Not really. The operative word here was *thought*.

It was cold and dark and the snow was swirling around them and after ten minutes, by mutual consent, the sisters gave up looking. There didn't seem to be any point in continuing.

"The important thing is that it's off the van," Bernie said to Libby by way of consolation once they were back inside Mathilda.

Libby grunted. Her teeth were chattering, she couldn't feel her fingers, and her feet were wet from the snow that had found its way into her boots. And on top of that, she was seriously annoyed. She just didn't know who she was more annoyed at: her sister, for dropping the tracker, or whoever put the device on their van in the first place.

"Why would someone do something like this?" she asked as she rubbed her hands together and flexed her fingers to get the circulation in them going again.

"I've been asking myself the same question."

"And?"

Bernie shook her head. "I don't know. But I'll tell you one thing. Whoever it is is really starting to piss me off."

"Me too," Libby agreed as she held her hands in front of Mathilda's heater on the theory that a little heat was better than no heat at all. "You think that person you think you saw . . ."

"Did see . . ."

". . . is the person who put the tracker on the van?"

"And the note. Yeah. As a matter of fact, I do." Bernie tapped her fingernails on Mathilda's steering wheel. The sound echoed through the van.

"Why would he or she still be here?" Libby asked her sister. "Why would they leave a note for us and then stick around and watch us read it? Especially with the tracker on the van. Why would they do that when they'd know where we were going?"

"They might get a kick out of watching our reactions," Bernie told Libby. "You know, the way we like watching someone eat what we bake. For example, Lizzy O's smile of satisfaction every time she eats one of our chocolate croissants definitely makes my day. Maybe whoever is doing this enjoyed seeing our reaction when we read the note he or she left."

"The two things aren't the same!" Libby protested.

"Actually, they kinda are."

"How?" Libby demanded. "Explain it to me."

"Nevermind," Bernie told Libby. It wasn't worth going into. Then Bernie had another thought. "Or maybe we came out sooner than the person expected and he or she didn't want to leave and attract our attention."

Libby gestured to the rows of silent, white-shrouded vehicles, vehicles that were acquiring more snow cover by the minute. "If they are watching us, they're watching us from an apartment window, because they're not here," Libby remarked.

"No. If they're anywhere, they're hiding in the back of the building," Bernie said. "That's the only place they could be."

"Come on, Bernie," Libby said. Her sister was getting a glint in her eye she didn't like. Libby had a pretty good idea where this conversation was going. "My pants are wet, your pants are wet, my hands are freezing and so are yours, and we have to get up at five tomorrow morning. Let's just give it up, go home, and go to bed."

Bernie turned to her sister. "Don't you want to find out who's responsible for this?" she asked.

Libby nodded. "Of course I do." What else could she say? "But just not right now."

"This will just take five minutes," Bernie said.

"Nothing ever takes five minutes."

"This time I promise that it will. Just humor me. After all, I humored you."

"And I was right!" Libby couldn't help herself from exclaiming.

"Which is why we're going to do this. You know the expression hoisted on your own petard."

"Mom used to say that. What is a petard anyway?"

"I don't have a clue," Bernie admitted.

Chapter 30

Libby fastened her seat belt and watched the snow fall, while she tried to ignore the cold seeping up her legs and the snow melting in her boots. The wind had picked up, driving the snow horizontally. The storm was turning into a full-fledged blizzard. She leaned over and turned on the radio, twisting the dial as she hunted for a news station that wasn't staticky. A moment later, she found one. "There," she said after she'd listened to the announcer. "They've declared a snow emergency. We should go home. We have to be off the roads."

"And we will be. This will just take a minute," Bernie reassured her sister. "I just need to do this."

"No. You want to do this. There's a difference," Libby muttered as her sister followed the road that curved around the building complex. Or, rather, Bernie followed what she thought was the road, which by this time was really nothing more than an outline banked by more snow on either side.

The road was narrow, made narrower by the three Dumpsters sitting against the side of the building.

"I don't think this is such a good idea," Libby

told Bernie as Bernie slowed down to go around the next turn. "What happens if we get stuck?"

"Always the optimist," Bernie told Libby. "We're not going to get stuck."

"But if we do?" Libby insisted.

"We'll call AAA."

"They'll take hours to get here on a night like this. If they can get here at all. We might end up sleeping in the van."

Bernie took a deep breath and let it out. "I promise you we're not going to get stuck," she was saying when a black SUV came roaring around the turn from the opposite direction, heading straight for Mathilda. Bernie slammed on her brakes. The SUV did the same. "What the hell?" Bernie cried as she watched the SUV reverse course with a roar of its engine and start backing up.

"They must have thought we left," Libby observed. "You were right. They were hanging out in the back."

"Nice to know I'm not seeing things," Bernie said as she put her foot down on the gas.

"What are you doing?" Libby screeched.

"What do you think I'm doing?" Bernie answered, her attention totally focused on the road.

"Trying to kill us?"

"Ha-ha, Libby. This is the guy who left the note, the guy who put the tracker on Mathilda, and I'm damn well going to find out who he . . ."

". . . or she . . ."

". . . is and why he or she wrote that note if it's the last thing that I do."

"Which it very well might be," Libby said, the words coming out between clenched teeth as she rechecked her seat belt to make sure it was securely fastened. "But what about me?"

"Hold on," Bernie told Libby as she flew around the corner.

Libby reached for the grab bar and white knuckled it as Mathilda skidded sideways. The van was heading for a large oak tree on the right. Libby closed her eyes. She didn't want to see the crash coming. A moment later, she opened them again and let out a sigh of relief when she realized that nothing had happened, that Bernie had managed to wrestle the van back onto the road.

"Oh ye of little faith," Bernie said, nodding to the tree they'd just missed hitting. "We had a foot to go."

"Looks like six inches to me," Libby observed.

"We weren't that close," Bernie protested.

"We weren't that far, either," Libby told her sister as Bernie put on another burst of speed.

The five-second delay had cost her, though, and by the time Bernie got around the next corner, she could see the tail end of the SUV fishtailing around the third corner. She followed, but the

SUV was farther away than it had been before, and by the time she got to the front parking lot it was heading toward the exit. Bernie put her foot to the floor. Mathilda began to rattle. It was not a good sound.

We're going to die, Libby thought as she watched Bernie take one hand off the steering wheel and dig into her parka pocket. *This is so not worth it.* "What are you doing?!" Libby screamed. "Put your hand back on the wheel."

"Obviously, I'm getting my phone out," Bernie explained to Libby as Mathilda hit a bump and Libby's head hit the van's roof. "Here," she said, taking her cell out of her pocket and handing it to her sister.

"What do I want with this?" Libby demanded.

"Take a picture of the SUV's license plate, of course."

"Of course. I don't think I can," Libby said to her sister as Mathilda went over a garbage can cover and Libby's head connected with the van's ceiling again. "It's too dark."

"Whoever is driving is going to have to pass under the streetlight," Bernie said, putting on another burst of speed. "Do it then."

"I'll try, but you're going too fast and I can't keep the camera steady," Libby told Bernie. "Can't you slow down?"

"If I slow down, I'll lose him," Bernie replied, her eyes fixed on the SUV in front of her.

"I feel like a milkshake," Libby complained as she brought the phone up and attempted to look through the camera lens. But the van kept bouncing up and down and she couldn't steady her hands. First, she saw the ground, then she saw the sky, then trees, then more ground. She cursed under her breath. Finally, Libby aimed the lens in the SUV's general direction and started snapping away. A moment later, the van passed out from under the cone of light and into the darkness. Libby put Bernie's cell phone down on her lap.

"Did you get it?" Bernie asked her sister.

"I don't know. I don't know what I got," Libby answered as Bernie tried to coax a little more speed out of their van—and failed. Libby looked over at the speedometer. They were going fifty miles an hour. "I didn't think Mathilda could go this fast," Libby commented.

"Neither did I," Bernie replied.

"It feels as if she's going to come apart," Libby observed as the rattling increased.

By now they were out of the parking lot and Mathilda was making seriously unhappy noises as Bernie kept her foot on the gas and followed the SUV onto the road. The SUV was getting farther and farther away.

"Come on, baby, you can do it," Bernie crooned to the van as she tried to get Mathilda up to fifty-five miles an hour.

Mathilda shuddered, then she slid. Bernie

steered into the slide, but she couldn't regain control. *We must be on black ice,* she thought as Mathilda headed off the road while the SUV pulled farther ahead. Bernie cursed under her breath as she took her foot off the gas and wrestled with the steering, trying to turn the van, but she couldn't. It was like trying to steer an elephant. The van continued its inexorable slide.

"Do something!" Libby cried.

"I'm trying," Bernie replied. She slammed on the brakes.

Which was when she remembered that was the one thing you weren't supposed to do in this situation. The van spun around. Now they were facing the wrong way.

"Oops. My bad," Bernie informed Libby as they headed toward the guardrail on the wrong side of the road.

"No kidding," Libby replied as she closed her eyes again and braced for impact. *What a stupid way to die,* she thought.

Chapter 31

As the guardrail got closer, Bernie recalled what her dad had told her to do in this kind of situation and tapped on the brake. The van started slowing down. Bernie guessed that part of the reason for that was because they were on a slight uphill incline and off the black ice. At least she hoped they were.

"Come on, come on, baby," she urged Mathilda. "You can do this." The van slowed down even more. Finally, it plowed into a pile of snow the plows had left behind and came to rest.

Libby uncovered her eyes while Bernie took a deep breath, sat back, and took her hands off the steering wheel. They were shaking. "Are you okay?" she asked Libby when she could talk.

Libby unfastened her seat belt, turned around, and punched her sister as hard as she could in the arm.

"Ouch. That hurt."

"Good." Libby sat back in her seat. "Now I feel better," she said.

Bernie rubbed her arm. "What did you do that for?" she cried.

"Because you nearly got us killed."

"Not really."

"Yes, really. And I'm not even going to mention

the fact that I probably have a concussion from hitting my head on the van's ceiling twice and that my neck is killing me and that I think I have whiplash and that I thought we were going to die."

"That's all?"

"I'm sure I can come up with a few more things, if you want."

"I don't," Bernie told her. Then she took another deep breath and let it out. *Keep yourself together,* she told herself. *Don't go to pieces.*

"We're lucky we're still here, Bernie," Libby continued. "If a car had been coming in the other direction . . ."

Bernie interrupted. "But there wasn't, Libby."

"But there could have been."

"But there wasn't." *Thank God,* Bernie added silently as she watched the snow fall. She lifted her hands up. They'd stopped shaking. "There aren't any vehicles on the road."

"Which should tell you something," Libby responded. Then she said, "I hope we're not stuck in the snow," the thought suddenly occurring to her.

"Me too," Bernie agreed. She looked up and down the road just to make sure no cars were coming. Then she put the van into reverse and applied the gas.

The wheels spun, but nothing happened. They stayed where they were.

"I knew it," Libby cried.

"Hold on," Bernie told her sister as she gave Mathilda more gas.

"You're going to dig us in deeper," Libby said.

"You want to do this?" Bernie snapped.

"No need to get pissy."

"I wasn't."

"What would you call it? Do we even have a shovel in the back?"

The van started to move.

"Here we go," Bernie said as she slowly backed the van out onto the road and drove a few feet. She couldn't hear anything clunking or clattering or smell any gas. "Seems as if Mathilda is okay, aren't you, girl? I'm sorry," she cooed. "I owe you a detailing job." Then she patted Mathilda's dashboard and apologized to her again for almost getting her into an accident.

"Almost?" Libby echoed.

"Yes, almost," Bernie replied. "Mathilda appears to be fine."

Libby snorted. "And what about me?"

"What about you? You're fine too, withstanding your litany of complaints."

"I'm talking about apologizing to me," Libby said.

"For what?"

"The accident."

"It wasn't an accident. It's only an accident if someone gets hurt or if you have property damage."

"Since when?"

"Since forever. That's the definition of an accident. This was a near accident. Google it if you don't believe me."

Libby turned and stared out the window instead.

"Don't sulk," Bernie told her.

"I'm not sulking."

"You most certainly are," Bernie said stealing a glance at her sister before she turned her eyes back on the road. "Fine. I'm sorry. There. Are you satisfied? Does that make you feel better?"

"Just barely," Libby replied.

"We need to get a faster car," Bernie reflected, thinking about the chase. "I could have caught whoever that was if we had one."

"I'll put it on the list," Libby told her, "along with the jet plane and the chalet in the alps."

"I think I'd prefer a beach house in Santa Cruz," Bernie commented as she leaned forward again to better see out the window. They were the only vehicle on the road. Three miles later, Bernie made a U-turn and drove into a Popeye's parking lot. *Please let them be open,* she prayed. She felt cold all of a sudden. Her hands were shaking again. So were her legs and she could hardly keep her eyes open. *I'm crashing,* she thought. *This is the adrenaline leaving my body.* "I need to get something to eat," she explained to Libby. "Something fried. With gravy. And a biscuit."

"Make that two biscuits for me," Libby replied, suddenly realizing how hungry and tired she was, too.

"Did you get anything we can use, picturewise?" Bernie asked Libby after they'd placed their orders at the drive-thru window.

"I don't know," Libby replied, and she picked up Bernie's phone off the floor—she realized it had slid off her lap during the chase—and clicked on the photos, wondering what she'd snapped because she didn't remember.

Evidently she had taken ten pictures. Five were of trees, one was a white blur—which Libby thought must be the sky, although she wasn't sure—three were of the top half of the SUV, but the tenth pic contained a partial shot of the SUV's license plate. Libby enlarged the photo and handed it to her sister.

"It's something," Bernie said when Libby showed her the two letters she'd managed to capture.

"Not much, but at least this wasn't a total loss," Libby noted.

"Now, all we have to do is find out whose license plate this is and we're in business," Bernie observed. Suddenly she felt a little bit better.

"And how do you propose to do that, Bernie?"

"Ask Dad to ask Clyde."

"And you're going to tell him what?"

"A somewhat censored version of the truth."

"He'll find out the whole truth," Libby said. She was so tired she was slurring her words. "He always does."

"I've been thinking . . ." Bernie began.

Libby interrupted, "Whatever you're thinking I don't want to hear it."

Bernie ignored her. ". . . that Kate Silverman isn't done with her shift yet. What do you say we pop down and talk to her after we eat. I bet the diner is still open."

"What do you say I punch you in the arm again?"

"I'll take that as a no," Bernie said as she drove to the pickup window. Their food was waiting for them. The smell filled the car. "Here," Bernie handed the bag to Libby, and then she pulled into the nearest spot and parked Mathilda. The sisters spent the next five minutes eating.

"God that was good," Libby said as she threw the remains of the chicken thigh into the bag and wiped her hands on a paper napkin. "All I want to do is go home, climb into bed, curl up underneath the covers, and go to sleep."

Bernie couldn't argue with that. She started up the van and as she made a sharp right she heard a clunk coming from the back of the van.

"What's that?" Libby asked.

Bernie shook her head. It wasn't there before. Or maybe it had been and she hadn't heard it.

She had just about decided that whatever it was could wait until morning when she remembered the three cases of wine in the back. The three cases of expensive, hard-to-find wine that they'd ordered for Mr. Wiley's dinner party. She cursed under her breath and stepped on the brake.

"I think it's the wine," Bernie said.

"What wine?" Libby knew she should remember but her brain wasn't functioning very well at the moment.

"The wine for Wiley's dinner party."

Libby frowned. "I thought Googie was supposed to deliver it to their house."

"He was, but no one was home. I said I'd drop it off tomorrow. Hopefully it'll be okay."

"It had better be, considering how long it took to get it," Libby said. The muscles in her legs were aching. She stayed in her seat and watched Bernie get out and go around to the rear of the van. She could feel a slight movement as Bernie opened the van's back doors.

Libby yawned. Despite her best efforts, her eyes started to close. She couldn't help it. They were too heavy to keep open. She was drifting away when Bernie started banging on her door. Libby woke up with a start.

"What?" she cried, disoriented. "What's the matter?"

"Libby," Bernie said. "Get up."

"Huh?" She hugged herself.

"You won't believe what I found." And Bernie opened the door and showed her sister what she'd discovered.

Libby stared at it. She couldn't believe what she was seeing. Suddenly she was wide awake.

Chapter 32

It was ten-thirty in the morning of the following day and Libby and Bernie had come upstairs to eat a midmorning snack with their dad.

"At least it's stopped snowing," Bernie commented as she handed her dad a mug of hot chocolate and a plate with two pieces of crusty French bread toasted, then topped with butter and cinnamon and sugar, and quickly run under the broiler.

This is going to be good, Sean thought, and he wasn't talking about the plate Bernie was holding, either. Then he felt guilty. These weren't suspects after all. They were his daughters. "My favorite," he commented to atone for his thought.

"Mine too," Libby agreed.

Sean looked at his daughters as they sat down on the sofa and began to eat. "Everything okay?" he asked, trying for casual as he remembered the call he'd gotten last night as he was falling asleep.

"Absolutely," Bernie said brightly. "That is if you don't count the fact that we watched Ada get arrested last night."

"So I heard," Sean replied, thinking that he'd need to take a nap later in the day. He'd heard his daughters coming in last night, but hadn't come out to greet them because he'd wanted time to consider the phone conversation he'd had. Then, because he'd been unable to fall asleep until a little after three in the morning, he'd overslept and gotten up after Bernie and Libby had gone downstairs to work.

"Clyde told you?" Libby asked.

"No. Ada's arrest was the lead story on the news this morning." Sean absentmindedly rubbed his cheeks with his right hand. He had to shave. Or maybe he would grow a beard. "Do you still think Ada is innocent in the deaths of Peggy Graceson and possibly Henry Sinclair?"

"I do," Bernie replied.

"Me too," Libby chimed in.

Sean shifted positions, trying to get more comfortable. He'd woken up with a crick in his neck this morning. Probably because of the damp and the cold. Still, it was better than the alternative, as his mom used to say. "And you're continuing on with your investigation as per Ada's request?"

"That's the plan," Bernie said, remembering the expression on Ada's face as the police took her away. She'd seemed so lost. So small. Then Bernie added, "She claims she's being framed."

Sean lifted an eyebrow and reverted to his cop persona. "That's what she's been saying all along."

"So, doesn't that prove that she's right?" Libby asked.

"No. On the other hand, it doesn't disprove it, either. So, let's just say that I'm agnostic on the subject at the moment."

"You told her aunt you'd help," Bernie reminded him.

"And I will," Sean replied. "One thing doesn't obviate the other."

"What would it take to turn you into a believer?" Libby asked as she watched a city snowplow start to widen Longely's main street and thought that they were certainly having a banner year when it came to snow and that they had at least two more months to go.

Sean sat back in his armchair. "Good question. I'll have to think about that." Then he changed the subject. "Are you sure everything is all right?" he asked again, giving Bernie another chance to come clean about last night.

"Positive," Bernie replied, leaning forward. "Why wouldn't it be?"

"Because you don't look as if everything is," Sean told her. Which, he reflected, wasn't exactly a lie. But it wasn't exactly the truth, either.

Libby stifled a yawn. "We just got in late, Dad," she said, shooting a quick look at her sister. "That's all. Really late." And then once she'd gotten into bed, despite being exhausted, she hadn't been able to fall asleep.

Sean took a sip of his hot chocolate. It was perfect. As always. Bernie had melted 80 percent dark chocolate, combined it with gently heated whole milk and cream, and added a dash of cinnamon and two tablespoons of sugar per cup, then topped it off with a tablespoon of whipped cream.

"You girls need to get more sleep," Sean said, putting his mug down on the side table by his chair. "Sleep is the cornerstone of good health."

Libby and Bernie both nodded uneasily. They could tell from the way their dad was talking that he was up to something. They just didn't know what.

"I spoke to McCready last night while you were away," Sean added, trying and failing to keep his tone casual.

"And?" Bernie asked, wondering how much her dad actually knew about last night's misadventures.

"I just wanted to talk to him again and make sure I hadn't missed anything about the two earlier deaths. He's sending me the file, but he's fairly confident that I'm going to come to the same conclusion that he did."

"Did McCready have anything else to say?" Bernie asked. "Any words of wisdom?"

Sean bit into the toast and felt the slight crunch of the bread and tasted the sweetness of the butter and the sugar and the slight heat of the cinnamon. "No, but I do. Be careful."

"We're always careful," Bernie said.

Sean choked on his bread and started coughing. "Really?" he replied after he'd taken a drink of his hot chocolate to wash everything down.

"Absolutely," Bernie lied.

This time Sean raised both eyebrows. "Are you sure there isn't something you want to talk about?"

"Like what?" Bernie asked, acting the wide-eyed innocent.

"You tell me," Sean replied.

"Okay. We could talk about the price of vanilla extract going up if you want," Bernie suggested, employing a diversionary tactic. "It's almost thirty dollars for an eight-ounce bottle. It used to be seven dollars. That's an absurd jump, but all the big companies are using the real stuff now. Hence, the price jump. Talk about the law of unintended consequences. Which means we might have to raise our prices on some of our baked goods." She stopped, took a breath, and chatted on. "Did you know that the vanilla orchid originated in Mexico and could be found only there for three hundred years and that now it only grows in three countries: Mexico, Tahiti, and Madagascar?"

Sean put up his hand to staunch Bernie's flow of words. "Fascinating, but that's not what I meant."

"Sorry," Bernie said, and she began to eat her toast while Libby sipped her chocolate. "I just thought you'd be interested. Then what did you mean?"

"I think you know," Sean told her.

"No, actually I don't," Bernie lied.

"Really?" Sean asked.

"Yes. Really," Bernie lied again, wondering if McCready had filled her dad in. It had been a while since he'd been the Longely police commissioner yet his sources seemed to be intact.

"Interesting," Sean observed as he finished off his first piece of toast.

Neither Libby nor Bernie asked their dad what was interesting because they didn't want to know. Finally, after five minutes of silence Sean spoke.

"Remember Mrs. Sullivan?" he asked his daughters.

"Not really," Bernie said. Which was true.

"Should we?" Libby asked.

"She used to babysit you."

Libby and Bernie both shook their heads.

"Sorry," Bernie said, wondering where this was going. Her dad wasn't one for strolls down memory lane.

"She lives on Livermore," Sean continued.

Bernie took a deep breath. Now she knew where her dad was going with this. Livermore ran parallel to Cleary, the road they'd been chasing the SUV down last night.

"I don't think I'd like to live there," Bernie

said, attempting to redirect the conversation. "Too much noise. And traffic."

Sean went on as if his daughter hadn't spoken. "She was telling me that now that she's older, she has trouble sleeping at night so she spends time with a pair of binoculars looking for deer—evidently there's a herd of them around there—and anything else of interest that comes her way."

"Poor lady. Sounds kind of depressing," Libby noted. "Maybe she should try some melatonin. I hear it's quite effective."

"That isn't the point," Sean said, getting angrier by the second, the fear that something could have happened to his daughters translating into a seething fury. "As I was saying, she called last night to tell me she saw the oddest thing." Sean waited for one of his daughters to ask him what Mrs. Sullivan saw. "Any guesses?" he asked when neither of his daughters said anything. "No? Then I'll tell you. She saw an SUV tear-assing down the road. A minute later, a van with A Taste of Heaven painted on the side careened down the road. She said it looked like the van was trying to catch the SUV. I told her that she must be mistaken, that she'd misread the van logo. But she said she hadn't."

"We were going a little fast," Libby admitted.

Bernie shot her sister a dirty look.

Libby corrected herself. "Very little."

But it was too late. The damage was done. Sean

honed in on Libby's admission. "So, you *were* on the road?"

"Yes," Bernie said, seeing no point in lying now. It appeared that the jig, as they liked to say in the old movies, was up.

Sean took a bite of his second piece of toast, chewed, and swallowed before he continued on with his interrogation. Because, he realized, it was what this had become. "Judging from the time Mrs. Sullivan called me, I'm guessing she saw you after Ada got arrested," he observed.

Bernie didn't say anything.

"I think it's time you told me what's going on, don't you?" Sean's tone of voice was making clear that this wasn't an invitation. But he didn't give Bernie time to answer. Instead he held up his hand and said, "No. Let me guess. You thought the person driving the SUV was the person who called the cops on Ada."

"We think it could be," Libby said, wishing she was somewhere else. She hated when her dad got like this.

Sean steepled his fingers together. "Did you see who the perp was?" His tone was icy.

"No. We couldn't. Too much snow. But Libby managed to get the first two letters of his license plate," Bernie replied. "We were hoping you could get Clyde to run a search."

Sean took a deep breath and told himself to calm down. "Let's suppose Clyde comes up with a license plate number, which I doubt, given the number of vehicles like that around this area— what you're talking about would take a task force. But let's say for the sake of argument that he does. What then?"

"Obviously, we're going to ask the person why they took off when they saw us," Bernie replied. "And if they're responsible for turning Ada in . . ."

Sean interrupted, "What makes you think this person is going to talk to you? What if he or she refuses to speak to you? You do realize he or she doesn't have to answer your questions. You're not the cops. You don't have the power to compel the person to talk."

"We know that, Dad," Libby interjected.

"It's not as if you leave someone shaking at the knees," Sean continued, driving his point home. "What then?"

"I don't know," Libby admitted.

Bernie leaned forward. "We'll think of something."

"Really," Sean said, stretching out the word. He took his time finishing his second piece of toast, after which he wiped his hands on the napkin Libby had thoughtfully provided. "So, then would it be correct to say you almost killed yourselves for nothing?" he observed quietly.

"That's not fair," Bernie protested, straining to hear what her dad was saying. This, she knew, was not a good sign because the angrier her dad got the softer his voice became.

Sean wadded up his napkin and threw it on the side table. "I think it is. What you did was reckless and irresponsible."

"We're fine," Bernie countered.

"Just by the grace of God," Sean snapped. "The county called a snow emergency last night."

"We didn't know," Libby protested, throwing an I-told-you glance at her sister.

"Well, you should have," Sean told her. "You shouldn't have been out on the road at all, let alone chasing someone. Especially in that van of yours. Which—correct me if I'm wrong—doesn't handle itself well in the best of times, let alone in a blizzard. Jeez, you'd think you'd know better by now. How old are you two?"

Bernie looked at Libby and Libby looked at Bernie.

"Dad . . ." Libby began.

"What?" Sean growled.

Libby made her voice louder, more assured. "There were extenuating circumstances."

Sean crossed his arms over his chest. "Really?"

"Yes, really." And Libby told Sean what they were.

Chapter 33

"You should have said something when you came in last night," Sean complained. How was he to know that something was wrong, he thought. After all, he wasn't a mind reader.

"You were asleep," Bernie said.

Which wasn't true, but he didn't say that. "Then you should have woken me up," he told Bernie instead.

"Here," she said, handing him the crumpled piece of paper with the smeared writing.

Sean put on his reading glasses. "The ink's run," he noted as he held the note up to the light hoping it would help, but it didn't, so he brought it back down. Fortunately, he could still make out the letters. "Odd," he said after he'd read and reread it.

"The note?" Libby asked.

"Yes," Sean said. "It's almost . . ."

"Schizophrenic," Bernie said.

"I was going to say it's like the person who wrote this couldn't decide what he wanted to say, but your word works, too." Sean paused for a minute. "And the tracker. That's even stranger."

"In what way?" Bernie asked.

"The tracker and the note are almost an embarrassment of riches."

Libby cocked her head. "How do you mean, Dad?"

Sean took a sip of his hot chocolate. "It's as if someone wanted you to find the tracker. I mean if they hadn't left the note you wouldn't have thought about a tracker. And as for the tracker, there are a lot better places to hide it than the one this person picked. So did they want you to find the tracker or not? That's the question."

"I say not," Bernie said. "I'd say whoever did it was a rank amateur."

"Which means they wanted to scare you off," Sean pointed out as he put his mug down. "Which means you're on the right track."

"I don't see how," Libby protested. "We don't know anything."

"We know less than nothing," Bernie seconded.

"Well, the person who wrote the note and put the tracker on Mathilda thinks that you do," Sean answered.

Bernie sighed. "Is there any chance at all we could get fingerprints off the note? Or DNA?" she asked her dad.

"I'm no expert, but probably not," Sean replied. "Too much water."

Bernie sighed again. She and Libby seemed to be hitting one dead end after another. She was thinking about that when Libby told their dad about the notebook.

"May I see it," he asked.

"Certainly," Bernie replied, handing it over.

Sean weighed it in his hand.

"Well, at least we know Kate Silverman didn't put it in the van," Libby observed as she watched her father.

"No we don't know that," Bernie said.

"Yes we do, Bernie. Kate was at work when we left the van."

"You're right, Libby. Actually, come to think about it that notebook could have been in Mathilda for a while. Ada could have put it in there when she ran out of the house on New Year's Eve."

"True. And we wouldn't have seen if she shoved it under the van bed liner."

"You would if you cleaned out and vacuumed the back of the van more frequently," Sean couldn't resist saying as he opened the notebook and skimmed through it.

"The back of the van isn't that bad," Libby protested.

"It's not that good," Sean replied. He pointed at the notebook. "So, this is the notebook Ada read from on New Year's Eve?"

"Yes," Bernie said.

"You're positive?"

"Absolutely," Libby replied.

"The one that Ada said contained proof that her dad was murdered?"

"Yes, Dad," Bernie assured him.

Sean began to read. Bernie and Libby watched. The noises from the store percolated up from downstairs as they waited. Libby reached over, picked up her cup, and finished the last of her hot chocolate, while Bernie ate her second piece of toast even though she'd told herself she'd eat only one. Five minutes later, Sean looked up.

"I can't make any sense of this," he said.

"I know," Libby agreed. "Neither can Bernie or I."

Sean continued to read. Ada's father's notebook was filled with random notes, doodles—Ada's dad seemed to favor rocket ships and trucks—comments on the weather, and the places he'd gone for dinner and lunch. The entries were in ink and pencil. None of them were dated.

"I don't see anything here," Sean said, stopping midway.

"There wouldn't be," Bernie said and she told her dad what Ada had told her.

Sean leaned down and massaged his left calf. Recently, those muscles had been cramping up on him. "Do you mind if I keep the notebook for a while?" he asked after he'd straightened up.

"Of course not," Bernie said. "What are you planning to do with it?"

"Look it over a bit more," Sean lied, running his thumb over the notebook's black and white cover. He had an idea. But it was far-fetched. Really far-fetched. And he didn't want to put it out there until he was sure. But if he was right . . . If he was right, it would send everyone down a very different path. He was thinking about how he was going to get what he wanted to do done when he realized that Bernie was talking to him.

"Sorry, I missed that," he told her.

Bernie repeated herself. "Now you know why we were chasing the SUV."

Sean leaned back. "I do. But I still think it was extremely reckless behavior on your part and I want you to promise me you won't do anything like that again."

"I promise," Libby said, noticing as she spoke that the steely glint in her dad's eyes had disappeared and his voice had returned to normal.

Sean looked at his younger daughter. "And you?"

"You would have done what we did," Bernie said.

"But you're not me," Sean pointed out, thinking that maybe his wife had been right after all about filling his daughters' heads with his stories.

"Okay," Bernie said.

"Okay what?" Sean asked Bernie.

"What you said."

"Say it."

"Dad, I'm not sixteen anymore," Bernie protested.

"I'm aware of that," Sean said, folding his arms across his chest and staring his daughter down.

"Then why are you treating me as if I am?"

"Because you're acting as if you are. You're not invulnerable, you know."

Bernie stopped slouching and sat up straighter. "I know."

"Sometimes I wonder," Sean muttered.

Bernie studied her father's face, the worry lines around his eyes and mouth, and felt bad. "Fine," she said after a minute had gone by. "I promise not to indulge in any high-speed chases in a blizzard. Happy now?"

Sean wanted to say, "Don't take that sarcastic tone with me, young lady." But he didn't. Instead he said, "Yes, I am happy. Very happy."

Libby looked from her sister to her father and back again and decided that a little lightening up of the atmosphere was in order. "What would you do now?" Libby asked Sean while he took another sip of his hot chocolate.

Sean put down his mug and marshaled his thoughts as he looked out the window and watched Mrs. Crook park her Kia in front of A Taste of Heaven. A moment later, Amber scurried out of the shop with Mrs. Crook's weekly order of a dozen triple ginger chocolate cupcakes with chocolate frosting and eight almond croissants in hand.

"What are you thinking, Dad?" Libby asked.

Sean turned back toward his daughter. "I'm thinking that I'm grateful my ankle is better and I can walk without a cane again." Last week, he'd watched Mrs. Crook almost take a tumble when her cane had slipped on a small patch of black ice, which was why Amber had run out to Mrs. Crook's car to deliver her order today.

"I'm glad too, Dad," Libby said. "Now about those suggestions of yours . . ." she said, letting her voice trail off.

"Ah, yes." Sean took another moment to strategize before turning to her and saying, "As far as I can see, we have three basic lines of attack. The first one being the SUV you were chasing last night, but as I said earlier, I don't think that Clyde's going to turn anything up. I can't even begin to guess how many registered black SUVs there are in this area, that's if the vehicle even comes from this area."

"And the second line of attack?" Bernie asked.

"The cyanide. But you're not really equipped to investigate that, either, so if I were you I would concentrate on Peggy Graceson and go from there. See what you can find out about her. See what you can find out about the argument between Peggy Graceson and Ada."

"Which means we need to talk to Ada's aunt, Sheryl," Libby said.

"Evidently she was there when it happened," Bernie informed her dad.

He nodded and went back to looking out the window.

"What are you going to do, Dad?" Bernie asked.

"I'm working on it," he told her as he continued studying the street. It was still empty except for people parking and hurrying into A Little Taste of Heaven to get an early lunch and mothers with children going into the kiddy barber three stores down. The weather didn't encourage strolling.

Once his daughters went back downstairs, Sean picked up his phone, called McCready, and asked him about an old case he remembered Ada's dad, Jeff Sinclair, had been involved in.

"That was a long time ago," McCready replied. "What's leaving the scene of an accident when you're drugged to the gills got to do with anything?"

Sean told him what it had to do with. Then he made his request. McCready squawked, but eventually relented and agreed to meet Sean at the Sunset Diner. After that, Sean called an old friend and colleague and asked him to join them there as well. He grinned when he hung up the phone. This was going to be fun.

Chapter 34

The Sunset Diner was located midway between Hollingsworth and Longely which was why Sean had chosen it. The diner was nothing to write home about visually speaking. It had been years since the diner's owner had put any money into it. The neon sign had been missing its *S* and its *i* for the last ten years, and the place hadn't been repainted for as long as Sean had been going there. In the interval, the silver paint had gone from bright to a dull grayish brown that blended in with the evening dusk.

Inside, the booths' red seats were crisscrossed with black tape, which covered the cracks in the leather, and the counter and tables were nicked and full of scribbles, courtesy of the people who had sat there over the years, but the coffee was strong, the pancakes were good, the bacon was crisp, and the waitresses let you sit for as long as you wanted to.

"I used to come here a lot when I was working," Sean remarked as he joined McCready in a booth at the back of the diner. It was between lunch and dinner and except for an elderly couple studying cruise brochures the place was empty.

"Me too," McCready said. "Where's your chauffer?" he asked.

"I Ubered," Sean told him.

"I'd go nuts without a vehicle," McCready noted.

"I am going nuts," Sean told him.

"I got my ex-daughter-in-law's father's vehicle in the garage and he's not coming back from Oakwood cemetery for it. Neither is she, for that matter. Interested?"

"I wouldn't mind taking a look," Sean said. Then the waitress came over and Sean told her there'd be one more.

"Good. Who's coming?" McCready asked as the waitress left. She came back a minute later with another place setting, plus three white coffee mugs, set them on the table, and left.

"Eckleburger," Sean said.

"I thought he was dead."

"No. He's ninety."

"Close enough," McCready said.

"He opened an agency in Yonkers when he retired from the Longely PD," Sean said.

The waitress returned with a carafe of coffee and began to pour. Sean added milk and sugar to his mug and took a sip. He loved his daughters' coffee, but there was something about diner coffee that was special. He just couldn't figure out what it was.

"So, did you bring it?" he asked McCready as he studied the menu. He was trying to decide between the corned beef hash and a sausage and pepper two-egg omelet when McCready pushed a manila envelope across the table.

"Here," he said.

Sean opened the envelope and shook out the pages. A residue of dust came with them.

"I need those back," McCready said as Sean looked through them.

"I assumed," Sean said. "Not that anyone will miss them."

"Probably, but why take a chance," McCready replied. He'd had to go into the old records storeroom to get what Sean had asked for. Fortunately, the records were housed in a former warehouse a half a mile away from the police department. "Just be glad Hollingsworth PD hasn't gotten around to digitizing their records yet."

"Believe me, I am. I'm surprised you found them," Sean told him, thinking about the state of the Longely PD record storage room.

McCready shrugged. He was too, but he wasn't going to say that. Instead he said, "I take it you don't think she did it?"

"She, meaning Ada? Obviously not," Sean answered. "Do you?"

McCready shook his head. Sean noticed he hadn't hesitated. "I can't see her for this."

Sean took a sip of his coffee. "Then who do you like?"

McCready added another packet of sugar to his

coffee while he considered his answer. "If I were betting I'd say the stepmother," he answered after a minute had gone by.

Sean raised an eyebrow. "Why Vicky?"

"Because she and Peggy Graceson hate—hated—each other."

"How do you know that?"

McCready stirred his coffee. "They had a big fight two years ago come March. Lots of yelling and screaming. My guys were called. They calmed everything down. Then that evening, Graceson went over to the stepmother's house and rammed the stepmother's Mercedes with her car. Claimed it was an accident. Her foot accidentally pressed down on the accelerator instead of the brake."

"Seems to be a family pattern," Sean observed.

"Yeah. They have a thing with cars. Anyway, those two hate each other."

"Fine. Two questions."

McCready polished his fork with the paper napkin in front of him. "I'm waiting," he said, looking up.

"One. Why kill the uncle?"

McCready shrugged. "I heard the stepmother had a beef with the uncle, too. He scammed some money off of her. A lot of money."

"Predictable," Sean said, thinking of Rose and the twenty grand. "But still . . ." His voice dropped off. Everything about this case was too much. It was like it was hyped up on steroids.

McCready continued. "Plus, he had one of her kids arrested for taking his car. The kid got community service, but she never forgave him."

"Yeah, but why now?" Sean asked.

McCready frowned. "Who the hell knows. The only thing I do know is that I don't know how that company has stayed in business all these years. No one talks to anyone else. Second question?"

"Why make Ada the fall guy, or gal, if we're being PC."

"Because Ada is the official weirdo of the family. Not that the others aren't in their own unique ways," McCready said. He sat back. "And then there's this. With three people gone there's more money for everyone when the company goes public."

"But that's true for everyone," Sean pointed out.

"Yeah, but some people need more money than others and I happen to know that Vicky Sinclair is up to her eyeballs in debt. More so than the other family members. In fact, the word is she's going to sell her house and move into an apartment. She likes blackjack and she's not very good at it," McCready concluded.

Sean was about to ask McCready how he knew this when Jack Eckleburger walked through the door. As Sean watched him approach, he reflected that Eckleburger used to be a lot taller, but then he supposed that that applied to him as well. He only hoped that when he got to Eckleburger's age his gait was as steady and his back was as straight as Ecklebergur's was. Maybe the trick was to keep working. Eckleburger had opened his agency the day after he'd retired from the Longely Police Department.

"That's quite the jacket," McCready noted as Eckleburger reached their table.

"Pendleton," Eckleburger answered as he took off the white wool jacket with the wide yellow and blue stripes, and hung it on a hook. Then removed his cap, hung that up on the lower hook, and sat down. "Warmest thing I own. I've had it for fifty years."

"Looks like you're wearing a blanket," McCready observed.

"Good to see you, too," Eckleburger retorted as the waitress filled his mug with coffee.

McCready smiled. "Always a pleasure." He'd thought of Eckleburger as a snotty know-it-all, so he was surprised that he was as glad to see him as he was.

"Ready?" the waitress asked as she stood there, pencil poised above her pad.

"Yes," Eckleburger said and ordered the corned beef hash with an egg on top without looking at the menu. The other men did the same.

"This is the only place I eat it," Eckleburger explained.

"Me too," Sean said, wondering why his daughters didn't serve it. Maybe he'd suggest it to them.

"Definitely an old-school dish," McCready observed. "My mom used to make it every Sunday morning."

The men spent the next half hour eating and exchanging war stories, talking about the times before DNA testing, before cell phones, before texting and computers and surveillance cameras, when all you had to rely on were your instincts and your smarts to solve cases.

"We should do this more often," Sean said after he'd eaten the last speck of hash on his plate.

Eckleburger nodded. So did McCready. It felt good to talk to people from the old days, they all thought. To remember who they'd been and what they were instead of what they were becoming.

"I'll tell you one thing I don't miss," Eckleburger said as he pushed his plate back. "Testifying on the stand.

"Me neither," McCready said.

Sean cocked his head. "I don't know. I kinda enjoyed screwing with the defense."

Eckleburger shook his head. "You always were a competitive son of a bitch." He leaned forward. "So, what have you got for me?"

"This," Sean said and he took the notebook Bernie had given him and the pages McCready had filched and placed them in front of Eckleburger.

"I didn't know you'd gone private," Eckleburger said while he glanced at what Sean had given him.

"I haven't," Sean told him. "My daughters are working this. I'm just helping them out."

Eckleburger smiled. "You didn't say that last night."

"Why?" Sean replied. "Does it make a difference?"

"Not in the least." The corners of Eckleburger's mouth went up. "I like being back in the business. Taking the cases I want. Maybe you would too."

"Could be," Sean said.

Eckleburger tapped the papers in front of him with his fingers. "You know what I'm doing has no legal status," he told Sean.

"Obviously. Do I look that far gone?" Sean demanded.

"Frankly, yes, you do," Eckleburger shot back as he opened the notebook.

Sean smiled and signaled the waitress for more coffee. He decided it felt good to be insulted again. He was tired of being mollycoddled.

"This is Jeff Sinclair's writing?" Eckleburger asked after the waitress left.

McCready nodded. "Yeah. His written statement from a past case."

"Is it enough?" Sean asked anxiously.

"Yes," Eckleburger said. "It should be fine." And he got to work.

Sean and McCready watched Eckleburger's finger moving along the lines of writing, his eyes darting from a page in the notebook to Jeff Sinclair's statement and back again. Occasionally, he would murmur something to himself like "interesting" or "aha." then take a sip of coffee and return to what he was doing.

"So?" Sean asked after five minutes had elapsed.

Eckleburger held up his hand. "Give me a few more minutes."

Sean did. Finally, Eckleburger looked up and cleared his throat. Then he began.

"I think I can say with a certain amount of surety that the person who wrote the notebook is not the same person who wrote the statement," Eckleburger asserted. "There are numerous inconsistencies. To mention just a few, the *a*'s are different, the *p*'s have different loops, the writer of the notebook puts a lot of pressure on his pen, whereas the writer of the statement doesn't. I could go on and on, but I don't think I have to."

Sean leaned forward. "You're positive?"

"I'm seventy-percent confident."

"That's good enough for me," Sean told him as he put his hand over his coffee cup to indicate to the waitress he didn't want any more. "So," he asked, thinking out loud, "if we know that Ada's dad wrote the statement, then who the hell wrote the entries in the notebook?"

"An interesting question," Eckleburger said, pushing the papers and the notebook back across the table.

Sean turned to McCready. "I need to talk to Ada."

McCready shook his head. "Don't look at me."

Sean held up his hand and wiggled his fingers. "Five minutes. That's all I'm asking."

McCready pointed to the papers on the table. "That's what you said about getting you Sinclair's statement."

Sean drew himself up. "I didn't say that."

"Maybe not the five-minute part, but definitely the this-is-all-I'm-ever-going-to-ask-you part."

"You know what they say," Sean told McCready. "In for a penny, in for a pound."

"Yeah, McCready," Eckleburger said, his eyes sparkling. "Be a mensch. Help the man out. You know you want to."

"Even if I did, I can't," McCready said.

"Sure you can," Sean replied.

"Things are different. I'm not in charge anymore."

"But it wasn't that long ago that you were, McCready. You still have friends," Sean told him.

"Admit it," Eckleburger said to McCready, "you haven't had this much fun in years."

Which, McCready had to confess, was true. *What the hell,* McCready decided and made the call.

"Rodriguez says Ada doesn't want to see you," McCready informed Sean after he'd made his request to the deputy sheriff and the deputy sheriff had spoken to Ada Sinclair. "She says you were mean to her."

Sean snorted. "Tell her to get over it. Doesn't she realize I'm trying to help her?"

"Evidently not." McCready grinned. "You always were the charmer. So, what do you want me to do?" he asked when Sean didn't say anything else.

"I'm thinking," Sean snapped.

"Think faster," McCready told him.

Sean straightened up. "Okay. Ask Rodriguez to ask Ada if she'll answer a question for me."

McCready relayed Sean's request. "She wants to know what kind of question," McCready told him a moment later.

Sean contained his temper. "Tell her a simple one."

McCready did. A minute later, he handed his cell to Sean. "Keep it short," he told him.

Chapter 35

Bernie pulled Mathilda into Linda Sinclair's driveway, put the van in park, and looked to her left. Peggy Graceson's house was empty at two in the afternoon, which was what Bernie had anticipated considering that Peggy had lived there by herself. More importantly, Linda Sinclair's house and the house on the opposite side of Peggy Graceson's home appeared to be empty as well, as did the other houses on the block.

The street looked forlorn in the dim light of the dreary, gray January day, with only an occasional holiday light remaining to brighten the gloom. It was silent. No one was out. Its inhabitants were either at work, at school, or in day care, the empty trash cans littering the sidewalks and driveways bearing witness to the fact that no one was home to put them back in the garage, where they belonged.

"I'm surprised there aren't more robberies here," Libby observed, surveying the scene. "The block is deserted. It's a thief's paradise."

Bernie smiled. "That's why we're here," she noted. "And the word you want is *burglary*. A burglary is when you break into a place, a robbery is when you take something by threats or force."

"It's not going to matter what the correct word usage is if someone calls the police," Libby retorted.

Bernie reached over and turned off the van. "Look around. Who's going to call? There's no one here."

Libby finished the last of her coffee, crumbled up her paper cup, and stuffed it in the trash bag by her feet. "We don't know that. Someone might be home and see us."

"Like who?" Bernie demanded.

"Like someone who's sick with the flu. Or pneumonia."

"Or the bubonic plague. Or ebola."

Libby shook her head. "I'm serious."

"I know you are. Unfortunately."

Libby thought of another possibility. "Graceson's house could be alarmed."

"If it was there'd be a sign out front," Bernie told her sister.

"Maybe Graceson didn't use a company," Libby replied. "Maybe she was a do-it-yourselfer. Maybe she installed cameras herself. Have you thought of that?"

"But she's not here to watch the feed. Have you thought of that?"

"Other people are, though."

"Look," Bernie said, deciding that this conversation could go on forever if she let it. "Do you want to help Ada or not?"

"Of course I do," Libby protested. "How could you ask that?"

"I just did. Especially since Clyde can't identify the SUV for us and it wasn't in the Sinclair Enterprises parking lot."

Libby took a triple ginger butter cookie out of the bag by her side, broke it in half, and offered one of the halves to Bernie. She and Bernie had spent the last hour and a half driving over to and around the parking lot of the Sinclair factory and had come up empty-handed. If there was a black SUV with the license plate they were looking for, they hadn't seen it.

"Perfect," Bernie noted, referring to the cookie after she'd eaten her half. They'd added freshly grated ginger to the recipe and that had made all the difference. "Listen," she said as she held out her hand for another one and thought, *Damn these are good,* "Peggy Graceson's house is a good place to start. Even Dad said that."

"No. What he said was she was a good person to start the investigation with, by which he meant talking to people about her. He didn't mean breaking into her house," Libby told her sister as she gave Bernie another cookie and took the last one for herself.

"That's all well and good, but no one is going to talk to us. Why should they? We're not cops. And even if they will, we don't know enough to ask the right questions. We need more information to do that."

"That's for sure," Libby muttered.

"Who knows," Bernie continued, "maybe there's something in her house that will point us in the right direction, because we're definitely floundering around now."

"I'm sure the police have gone through the place already," Libby objected.

"Probably. But they could have missed something. Listen, Libby, if you have any other suggestions, I'll be happy to hear them."

"I don't," Libby admitted after a minute had gone by.

"Fine," Bernie said, slipping the van key into her jacket pocket. She was wearing her winter burglary outfit—black jeans, a navy hoodie, a black pea coat—and she'd tucked her hair into a navy wool watch cap. When in doubt, always go with the classics clotheswise. That was her motto. "Then let's do this," she told her sister.

"At least park around the corner," Libby pleaded.

"This is better," Bernie replied. She planned to cut across to Peggy Graceson's house once she got to the end of Linda Sinclair's driveway. The two houses were literally just a stone's throw away from one another, separated by a line of scraggly fir trees. "This way we can claim we've come back to pick up a pan we've forgotten—in

333

case anyone asks. It looks less suspicious that way."

"In your opinion."

"Yes. In my opinion. Obviousness is the best antidote to suspicion."

"Says who?"

"Sez me."

"I don't know about that, but I do know that Dad would not approve," Libby noted.

"Where we parked or what we're about to do?" Bernie asked, playing the innocent.

"Both," Libby replied. "And we did promise him."

"To state the obvious, we promised Dad we wouldn't chase anyone. We're not chasing anyone."

"That's rather disingenuous, wouldn't you say?" Libby protested.

"No, Libby. I would say that's what we call a loophole."

Libby frowned, annoyed at being one-upped. "You know, Bernie, sometimes you're too smart for your own good."

Bernie turned and faced her sister. "Funny, that's what Mrs. Pimplé said before she sent me to the principal's office." Actually, it was one of many times, but she didn't say that. "But if you had a name like that, wouldn't you change it? Especially if you were a teacher. All I did was ask her why she hadn't. After all, you don't hear Crapper being used as a last name since he invented the flush toilet, do you?"

"There was an actual person named Crapper?"

"Thomas Crapper, to be exact. He was a plumber."

"Wow," Libby said. "Who knew?"

"I think he was even knighted or something."

Libby was about to ask another question about Thomas Crapper, realized her younger sister was trying to divert her, and got back to the matter at hand. "That's very interesting but what will we say if someone calls the police?" she demanded. "Or if Linda Sinclair comes home early?"

"I told you. We'll say we came to pick up a pan that we forgot."

"And if we're in Peggy Graceson's house at the time?" Libby asked.

"We'll say we thought we heard someone and that the door was open so we went in because we were concerned that there was a robbery in progress."

Libby snorted. "And you're going to say that with a straight face?"

"Yup. That's my story and I'm going to stick with it," Bernie told her. "Say something enough and people will believe you." Bernie reached out and patted her sister's arm. "Come on, Libby. Are you coming or staying? The longer we sit here like this, the more suspicious we look." When Libby didn't answer right away, Bernie said,

"Hey, you can stay in the car if you want. In fact, maybe you should. That way you can warn me if anyone comes home."

Libby thought it over and shook her head. She was tempted but two people could go through the house faster than one. And then there was the fact that she couldn't talk her way out of things as well as her sister could. She didn't have the gift of gab. "That's okay. I'll come."

Bernie shrugged. "Suit yourself. Just remember I made the offer," she said as she got out of the van and quietly closed the vehicle door behind her.

Libby did the same. "Why are you always so confident everything is going to be okay?" she demanded of her sister as she zipped up her parka once she was outside. The wind had started to pick up, making it seem even colder than it already was.

Bernie grinned and put her hood up. "My natural charm and grace."

"Really."

"Okay, then let me ask you something. Why are you always so sure that things won't work out?" Bernie countered.

"I don't know why," Libby answered truthfully. "It's just the way I am. It's the way I've always been."

"I could say the same thing," Bernie replied as she turned and started walking up Linda Sinclair's driveway. Libby followed.

The sisters were just getting to the end of the driveway when they heard the sound of a truck coming up the street. Bernie stopped and turned. It was a UPS truck. *Damn,* she thought as it stopped in front of Linda Sinclair's house. Libby gasped as the driver emerged with a package a moment later.

"Relax," Bernie told Libby out of the side of her mouth as she watched the driver start up the driveway.

"Hey," the driver called, catching sight of the two sisters. "I've got a package for a Linda Sinclair."

Bernie faked a smile. "We're old friends come to surprise her," Bernie said, trotting down the driveway to meet the driver. That seemed like the safest explanation. She held out her hand. "I can take it for you."

The UPS man smiled in return and held out his clipboard.

"We just drove in from Buffalo," Bernie improvised as she scrawled the name Evita Horowitz on the line the driver had indicated and took the package he was holding out to her.

"Snowy up there," the driver noted.

Bernie laughed. "Tell me about it."

"Well, have a nice visit," the driver told Bernie, touching his hand to his hat before he turned and hurried toward his truck.

"And you have a nice day," Bernie called after him.

The driver waved, indicating he'd heard her, jumped in his vehicle, and drove away, the noise of the truck receding as the driver headed toward his next stop.

"See," Bernie said to Libby, once she had walked back up the driveway. "I told you. People see what they expect to see." Then she put the package on the top of the steps leading up to Linda Sinclair's back porch and proceeded to Peggy Graceson's house.

Chapter 36

As it turned out, Bernie didn't have to use her lock picks after all. For which she was extremely grateful. They required a sensitive touch. It was hard enough using them when her fingers were moving like they were supposed to, let alone using them when her fingers were stiff from the cold even with her gloves on. It would have taken her forever to open the door. Instead, she used Peggy Graceson's spare key, which was where Bernie had hoped it to be—right under the garden gnome by the back door.

Here goes nothing, Bernie had thought as she'd bent down and brushed the snow off the gnome. Then she picked the gnome up and gently shook it. "Good heavens, methinks I hear a clink," she observed as she straightened up. She looked at the gnome carefully and noticed a thin line separating the gnome's hat and hair.

"Aha," she said. "I do believe we're in business." She tried lifting the gnome's brown hat up and when that didn't work she tried unscrewing the hat, which did work. A couple of twists and Bernie took the hat off and handed it to Libby. Then she removed her glove and thrust her hand into the opening. A moment later, she came out with the key.

"How did you know there'd be a key there?" Libby asked Bernie as she handed the gnome's hat back to her sister.

"My brilliant powers of deduction," Bernie replied as she replaced the gnome's hat and put the gnome back where it had been. "All garden gnomes contain keys. It's what they were made for."

Libby raised an eyebrow.

"Well, they are."

Libby crossed her arms over her chest and snorted. "Try again, Bernie."

"Okay. I overheard Peggy telling Linda that's where she'd left the key for the cleaning service. I was just hoping that it was still there," Bernie said as she climbed the two steps leading to Peggy Graceson's back door and inserted the key in the lock. She twisted it and the door swung open. "And if the key wasn't there"—she patted the right-hand pocket of her pea coat—"I brought along my . . ."

". . . Brandon's," Libby corrected.

"Don't be so literal," Bernie chided.

"I believe *accurate* is the word you want."

". . . lock picks, just in case. Now that that's settled, shall we go in?" asked Bernie, bowing and extending her arm.

Libby nodded and the sisters stepped into a small hallway, Libby making sure to close the door after herself. She looked around. Judging by the coats hanging off of hooks on the wall and the shoes neatly arranged on the mat on the floor, this space functioned as a mudroom and it led directly into the kitchen.

Bernie sniffed. The place smelled stuffy, as houses that aren't occupied even for a short time have a tendency to do. A Styrofoam box half full of congealed Chinese takeout sat on the counter, while a couple of dried-out looking tangerines and a half-finished bottle of Coke Zero sat on the kitchen table next to a stack of five magazines and a small stack of mail.

"I wonder what's going to happen to the house?" Libby said, looking around.

"I imagine it'll go up for sale once Peggy Graceson's estate is settled," Bernie replied as she walked over to the kitchen table and went through the mail. Like the takeout, it was old. The postmarks on the envelopes were dated from a couple of days before the day of Peggy's death.

Evidently someone had either stopped the mail or was collecting it. Otherwise, the mailbox would have been overflowing by now. To make sure, Bernie walked to the front of the house and peeked out the window on the door. Nope. The mailbox was empty. Which meant she was correct. The mail had been stopped or it was being collected. Probably by Linda Sinclair.

Or maybe Peggy didn't get a lot of mail. That

was a third possibility. A cursory glance showed there was nothing of interest in the mail from Bernie's point of view. Just bills for Peggy's car insurance and utilities, and some junk mail, mostly fliers for upcoming sales.

Evidently Peggy shopped at Macy's, Lord & Taylor, and Kohl's. *But, realistically, what did you expect? A letter that said: Prepare to die?* Bernie asked herself as she put the mail back where it had been and looked at the magazines. Two were shelter magazines, while the others dealt with travel. She picked them up and leafed through them one at a time. The shelter magazines looked as if they hadn't been touched, but the travel magazines were dog-eared and food stained. As Bernie paged through them, she noted that Peggy had dog-eared articles about New Zealand and Australia.

"I wonder if Peggy was thinking about taking a trip to Australia and New Zealand?" Bernie mused while Libby picked up a couple of travel guides that were lying on the kitchen counter and went through them.

"From these guides, I'd say it certainly looks as if she was," Libby observed, not bothering to glance up.

"I wouldn't mind going there," Bernie commented.

"Me neither," Libby replied. "I just don't know if I could sit on a plane for twenty-four hours."

"Twenty-two hours," Bernie corrected absent-mindedly.

"Because at that point two hours is going to make a big difference," Libby said as she began reading the notes Peggy had scrawled in the margins of the travel guides. The notes dealt with visa and currency regulations, citizenship requirements, names of people to get in touch with who were currently living in New Zealand and Australia and had moved from the States, ways to mail packages abroad, health care, and work requirements for noncitizens.

"It looks as if Peggy was planning on moving there," Libby observed as she showed Bernie the notes in the margins.

"Interesting," Bernie commented after she'd read them. "How old do you think Peggy was?"

Libby thought for a minute. She'd never been good at guessing other people's ages. "I don't know. Midforties, early fifties maybe. Why?"

"I just didn't figure her for someone to pick up and move to Australia, that's all. Especially at her age. Maybe buy a better house in Westchester or a second home in the country, but that's it. When is the IPO coming out?"

"Soon," Libby replied. "Like in the next month or two. Obviously, she was planning ahead," Libby said. "Maybe living in Australia and New Zealand was her childhood dream and now that she was getting some money she could quit her job and move there."

"I don't know." Bernie thought back to her conversation with Peggy Graceson on New Year's Eve. Nothing about her had suggested a person who wanted to uproot herself and start all over again. At least not without a good reason. "She just didn't strike me as the adventurous type."

"Me neither," Libby agreed, thinking back to that evening as well. "But it looks like we're wrong. Or she could have just been planning on taking a long vacation."

"But if that was the case why find out about citizenship requirements?" Bernie asked.

"Curiosity? For a friend?"

"Or because she was afraid something was going to happen to her if she stayed here and she wanted to get as far away as possible from Westchester," Bernie posited. "And she was right. Something did happen to her. The question is, why did she feel that way?"

"Why indeed," Libby said as she put the travel guides back where she'd found them. "I didn't see any sign of anything at New Year's Eve. Did you, Bernie?"

Bernie shook her head. "No. She didn't seem nervous."

"Maybe she thought she'd taken care of the problem," Libby suggested. "She had to have thought that, because if she was scared, why didn't she leave sooner? Unless she was waiting till after the IPO offering before heading out."

"Wire transfers work all over the world."

"Maybe there was some sort of agreement in place saying she had to be here to collect her share of the money," Libby speculated. "Or we could just be reading things into this, making it more complicated than it is."

"Considering someone poisoned her, I don't think that's the case," Bernie observed as Libby turned and studied the refrigerator.

The door was covered with magnets, most of which held up a variety of reminders, business cards, and ads. According to the reminders, Peggy was supposed to have had a manicure in the coming week, and a hair appointment for a trim and color tomorrow. For some reason, the thought made Libby feel sad. Then Libby's eyes fastened on a torn piece of paper with some writing on it. She took the note off the refrigerator and read it. Then she read it again and tapped her sister on the shoulder.

"It looks as if our Peggy was in love," she said, handing the note to her.

"This is a flight confirmation number," Bernie said after she read it. "She was going to Sydney from JFK."

"I can read," Libby said, as she pointed to the writing on top. Peggy had written "Peggy and

Red" and drawn a heart around them with an arrow next to it. "She was going with someone," Libby surmised.

"I used to do that when I was in high school," Bernie reminisced.

"Or, she was meeting someone in Sydney."

"Also a possibility," Bernie said. "In either case, I'd say it's fair to state she definitely had a thing going with Red."

"Whoever that is," Libby said.

"Who indeed," Bernie said as she carefully folded up the piece of paper, and tucked it in her jean's pocket. Then she opened the refrigerator door. The only thing in it was a six-pack of soda, a container of orange juice, and half a loaf of raisin cinnamon bread.

"I wonder what she planned to do with the house?" Libby asked Bernie as she turned toward the cabinets and began to open doors and pull out the drawers. Except for a few dishes and plates and a couple of boxes of cereal and tins of tuna fish, they were empty. "Maybe Peggy was like your friend Penelope," Libby suggested.

"Perhaps," Bernie said, remembering.

Penelope was a friend of hers who had lived on the West Side in New York City in a small one-bedroom apartment and stored her sweaters in her oven and had her coffee delivered from the diner down the street. The only eating-related things Penelope had had in her kitchen were a set of silverware, five mismatched plates, four mugs, and a single small saucepan, just in case, as Penelope liked to say.

"Or she could have been moving," Libby said.

"You wouldn't ship your kitchen stuff to Australia," Bernie objected. "Too expensive . . ."

"Or she could have been getting ready to put her house on the market," Libby countered.

"Makes sense," Bernie agreed. "Or she could have been getting her kitchen remodeled." She nibbled on her lower lip while she thought. "Linda Sinclair would have known," she declared a moment later.

"Known what?" Libby asked, turning toward her sister.

"That something was happening. Linda Sinclair's house is practically on top of Peggy's. She would have seen Peggy dragging in packing cartons. She would have seen stuff in her trash can."

"So?" Libby asked.

"So she would have figured something was up," Bernie said, playing out the scenario in her mind.

"Or Peggy could have told them she was getting the kitchen painted," Libby replied. "Or remodeled."

"And what if Linda didn't believe her? What if Linda thought she was heading out of town?"

"You're saying that Linda killed Peggy?"

"Possibly. Or Linda could have told people at work."

Libby raised an eyebrow. "And her murderer—whoever that is—decided to kill Peggy before she left?"

"In a word, yes."

"Why?" Libby asked.

"Maybe whoever killed her wanted to stop Peggy from doing something," Bernie hypothesized. "Maybe she had threatened them or maybe they found out she was going to do something to stop the IPO."

"Why would she?" Libby asked. "Then she'd be out the money, too."

Bernie brushed a lock of her hair off her face. "This is true."

"And what about Henry?" Libby added.

"Let's concentrate on Peggy for the time being," Bernie suggested. "We have enough stuff to sort out as it is."

"Agreed," Libby said as she stood there trying to put herself in Peggy Graceson's shoes. "Did she know she was in danger or didn't she? If she did, why didn't she throw some clothes in a suitcase and get out of town?"

"Obviously, because she was waiting to go to Australia," Bernie said. "Love will get you every time."

"You should know."

"Ha. Ha."

Libby looked at her watch. "We should speed things up."

"Yeah. It's getting close to the witching hour," Bernie agreed and they headed upstairs. "Maybe we can find out who Peggy's secret admirer was."

But they didn't. There was nothing on the second floor that told the sisters anything they didn't already know. The three upstairs bedrooms were painted a pale blue. All of them had white lace curtains and area rugs in different shades of blue. The two guest bedrooms had twin beds. The first one also had a sewing machine, a large work table piled high with scraps of fabric, and a half-finished quilt lying across the bed, while the second bedroom contained a treadmill, a set of weights, and a TV. Peggy Graceson's bedroom was furnished with a double bed; a dresser, which was piled high with Peggy Graceson's clothes; a wooden rocking chair, also piled with more clothes; and an empty closet.

"She must have been going through her wardrobe," Bernie said as she stepped over a pile of shoes on the pale blue rug. "Deciding what to toss and what to keep."

Libby lifted a Victoria's Secret catalog from the nightstand and put it down. "Too bad she didn't get a chance to wear what she ordered," she said, gesturing to a black lace bra and a pair of black lace panties that were spread out on top of the pillow. The price tags were still on them.

"Yes, it is," Bernie said as she looked out the window. It was getting dark outside. It was time to finish up and get out of the house.

As they walked down the stairs, the sisters decided that Bernie would take the basement and the garage while Libby would go through the rest of the first floor. Once they got downstairs, Libby turned her attention to the dining and living rooms. She expected it would take her ten minutes at the most.

The two rooms were furnished in mid-twentieth-century knockoffs. The sofa and the chairs were low and square with a slim profile, while all the wood in the living room and the dining room was teak. The pictures on the wall were framed posters from the works of Degas and Renoir, while the inexpensive rugs on the floor were blue and aqua tweed.

A large television hung on the wall opposite the sofa, while two art books sat on the coffee table. The whole effect was cheerful, but oddly impersonal, like a hotel room or an upscale doctor's office, Libby thought. She was just about to tell Bernie she was done, when Bernie called Libby on her cell.

"Get down here," Bernie told her. "You won't believe what I've found."

"A giraffe?"

"Nope. You have to see it to believe it."

Chapter 37

"What am I looking at?" Libby asked Bernie after she'd walked through the basement door that led to the garage.

Bernie didn't say anything. She just pointed.

For a moment, Libby couldn't speak. She was too stunned. "Oh my God," she cried after she got her voice back. "Is this what I think it is?"

"I'm pretty sure it is," Bernie answered as Libby walked down the two steps and squeezed by a row of metal shelves filled with cartons.

"Good parking job," Libby commented about the SUV as she walked to the front of the vehicle. The space between the vehicle and the wall was so tight she had had to flatten herself out to get through.

When she got to the front she studied the black SUV's license plate. The first two letters on it matched the ones she had captured on Bernie's phone. This was the SUV she and Bernie had chased, the one whose driver had put the note and the tracking device on Mathilda, the one they'd almost died trying to catch. Okay. Slight exaggeration.

"No wonder we couldn't find the SUV in the factory parking lot," Libby noted. "It's probably been here all the time. But what the hell is it doing in here?"

"Hiding, I'd say."

"Well, whoever put it here, picked an excellent spot," Libby observed as she watched Bernie try the door handle on the driver's side. The door opened.

"Let's take a look, shall we," Bernie said as she plopped herself down in the seat, leaned over, opened the glove compartment, and began taking stuff out of it. She took out a jumble of candy wrappers, a pack of tissues, a bottle of Advil, and a small prescription pill bottle full of oxycodone. Bernie read the label on the bottle. It read: VICKY SINCLAIR. FOR BACK PAIN. TAKE NO MORE THAN TWO AT A TIME TWICE A DAY. "Interesting," Bernie said, showing the bottle to Libby.

"You think this is her vehicle?" Libby asked.

"Well, I don't think it's Harry Potter's," Bernie said, going back to digging through the SUV's glove compartment. Out came more candy wrappers, a couple of pens, the owner's manual, and finally the thing she'd been looking for: the insurance card.

Bernie glanced at it and handed the card to Libby. Libby read it and handed the card back to Bernie.

"I'd say this proves it," Bernie commented.

"So, what's Vicky Sinclair's SUV doing in

Peggy Graceson's garage? Why isn't it in her garage?" Libby wondered out loud.

"Because that would be the first place someone would look," Bernie guessed as she put everything back in the glove compartment and closed the door. "Which means Vicky Sinclair had a key to this house. Or," Bernie added, "she knew where to find it. Obviously, the location of Peggy Graceson's house key was not a closely guarded secret. Probably everyone knew."

"And the code to the garage door opener?" Libby asked. "Does everyone know that as well?"

"Why not? And if Vicky Sinclair didn't she could have come in through the house and opened the garage door from the inside," Bernie replied as she went through the rest of the SUV, but there was nothing in it aside from a couple of empty cans of Pepsi and a half-eaten bag of potato chips, the fancy kind made out of beets and sweet potatoes. Bernie reached in, took a handful of chips, and ate them.

"Bernie," Libby cried, horrified.

"What?"

"How can you eat those?" Libby protested.

"Easy," Bernie answered. "I'm hungry."

"The bag is open. You don't know where they've been or how long they've been sitting in the SUV."

"And I don't care," Bernie told her as she ate another handful. "I'm hungry." She held the bag up. "Now if we were the police, and could get DNA and/or fingerprints off of this, that would be a different story."

"But we're not," Libby said as she walked over to the blue Honda Civic that was parked next to the SUV. "And I don't think that Clyde would be able to get that information for us."

"No, he won't," Bernie agreed as she got out of the SUV and joined her sister by the Civic. "And I wouldn't ask him to." It was one thing to get her dad's friend to run a license plate through the DMV database and quite another thing to have him submit something to the police crime lab under false pretenses.

Libby tried the Civic door. It too opened and she got in. "I'm guessing this is Peggy's vehicle," she said, looking around.

Unlike Peggy Graceson's house, the vehicle had that lived-in look. The front seat was festooned with a couple of empty fast-food bags from McDonald's, two empty coffee cups, a bunch of wadded-up Kleenex, a bag of cough drops, as well as a stack of local newspapers, a couple of romance novels, a pair of sheepskin gloves, a wool scarf, and a bottle of eye drops.

"It looks as if Peggy lived in her car instead of her house," Libby observed as she pushed the newspapers aside and came up with a pair of binoculars; a small spiral notebook, the kind you buy in a drugstore; and a birding book. "Go figure," Libby announced, showing the birding book to Bernie. "I never would have taken her for a bird-watcher."

"And I never would have thought she'd be running off to Australia. Or getting murdered," Bernie said as she took the binoculars out of her sister's hands and examined them. "These are really high quality, Libby. I think they cost a little over two thousand dollars," Bernie noted as she handed the binoculars back to her sister.

"How do you know that?"

"Brandon won a pair like it in a poker game last year. Can I see the notebook?" Bernie said, reaching her hand out for it. Libby handed it to her and Bernie leaned against the garage wall and began to page through it.

"There's nothing in here except bird-spotting notations," she noted while Libby opened the Civic's glove compartment.

Unlike the inside of the vehicle, the inside of the glove compartment was pristine. There were a couple of pens, a pair of nonprescription sunglasses, a cloth for cleaning them, the driver's manual, an insurance card, and a small manila envelope. Libby took the envelope out and showed it to Bernie.

"I wonder what's in this?" she said.

Bernie was just about to tell Libby to open it and find out when she heard a noise. "Do you hear that?" she asked.

Libby shook her head. She didn't, but a moment later she heard what her sister had. People talking. The voices were coming from the street. "That's Linda Sinclair," Libby said, identifying the person speaking.

"I guess we overstayed our welcome," Bernie observed.

"Ya think?" Libby shot back.

"They're here somewhere, Rick," Linda was saying to her son. "They have to be. Their car is here."

"I told you parking the van in Linda's driveway wasn't a good idea," Libby hissed.

"Let's leave the recriminations until we get out of here," Bernie said to her sister.

"If we get out of here," Libby said as she got out of the Civic and carefully closed its door so as not to attract any attention.

"No problem. We'll go out through the window in the basement."

"Does it open?" Libby asked.

"Of course it opens," Bernie told her. "All windows open."

Libby was about to say *not necessarily* when the back of Linda Sinclair's head and those of her son and daughter popped up in front of the garage door window. Bernie ducked down. So did Libby. They both held their breath.

"Where are they?" Bernie and Libby heard Rachel ask her mom.

"Heaven only knows," Linda Sinclair replied.

"Why the hell couldn't Ada leave things alone?" Rick complained.

"Your sister has problems," Linda Sinclair answered, her voice sharp.

"But, Mom, she was doing okay or as okay as she ever does," Rachel said. "What set her off?"

Linda Sinclair shook her head. "Your guess is as good as mine." Then she turned and walked out of Bernie and Libby's line of sight. A moment later, Rick and Rachel followed her lead.

"Now what?" Libby whispered to Bernie after another minute had gone by and she was sure Linda Sinclair and her children weren't coming back.

"We try that window," Bernie said as she headed toward the door that led into the basement. She had her hand on the doorknob when she heard a sound coming from inside the house, one that a door opening and closing would make. "Or maybe not," she muttered.

"They're in the house," Libby said. She could hear muffled voices.

"It's time for Plan B," Bernie said.

"What's Plan B?" Libby asked.

Her sister gestured toward the garage door.

"But they'll see us coming out," Libby objected.

"Not if we're fast," Bernie told her. Then she turned and headed for it. When she got there, she looked up searching for the red handle that would allow her to manually open the door. It was attached to a rope that was hanging above her head. It was high and she had to stand on her tiptoes to reach it.

"Here goes nothing," Bernie declared, grasping the red handle with both hands and pulling. Nothing happened. She tried again. Still nothing.

"Why isn't it working?" Libby demanded.

"It will," Bernie asserted, and she wiped her hands on her parka jacket, took a deep breath, grabbed the handle, straightened her arms, and using her abs pulled down with all her might.

"Yes," Bernie said as the door went up three inches. And groaned. Loudly.

"What is that noise?" Libby asked.

"The mechanism needs oil," Bernie explained as she got ready to try again.

"They'll hear us," Libby said, referring to Linda Sinclair and her children. "Everyone on the block will hear it."

"Hopefully not, but as they say, in for a penny, in for a pound."

"Where do you get these sayings from?"

"Mom. She used to say that all the time."

"I don't remember that," Libby replied.

"Trust me, she did," Bernie replied as she took a deep breath and pulled down on the rope again. The door made another groaning noise and rose six inches. Bernie assessed the space. It was going to be a tight fit, but it would have to do. She didn't want to risk making any more noise. "Come on," she gestured to Libby, who was standing right next to her. "You first."

"Why do I have to go first?"

"Because I got the door opened."

Libby was about to say something but decided this wasn't the time for arguing. Instead, she looked at the space between the door and the floor and wished she was twenty pounds lighter. "I don't think I'll fit."

"You'll fit," Bernie assured her. "Just think thin thoughts."

"All I can say is I'm glad I don't have big boobs," Libby noted as she got down on the floor, lay on her back, and sucked in her stomach. Then she put the manila envelope she'd grabbed out of Peggy's car over her chest as an additional layer of protection. "Here goes nothing," she grumbled as she began to wiggle through. She had to turn her face to the side so the bottom of the garage door wouldn't hit her nose.

Bernie went after her. "That wasn't so bad, was it?" Bernie said as she sprang up and pushed the garage door closed.

"That depends how you define bad," Libby said, examining the mark on the manila envelope. At least her parka wasn't ripped.

Bernie didn't reply. She was busy brushing the snow off the back of her jacket and jeans when Libby coughed and pointed. Bernie turned. *Damn,* she thought as she saw Linda Sinclair and her two children standing there. All of them had their arms folded across their chests and unpleasant expressions on their faces.

"So, what exactly is it that you two are doing?" Linda Sinclair asked.

Bernie smiled her most ingratiating smile. "Would you believe, looking for one of our pans?"

"No, I would not," Linda Sinclair snapped. "And neither will the police."

Chapter 38

Bernie forced a laugh. "I was kidding. Actually, my sister and I were looking at the vehicles in Peggy Graceson's garage. My dad needs a new car and we figured maybe we could get a good deal on Peggy's Civic, but then we saw the SUV and we decided that that might be a better bet. Did Peggy own that, too?"

"No. That's Vicky's," Linda replied.

"Great," Bernie said. "You probably don't know if she wants to sell it or not. I guess we should call." She started to walk away. "Thank you for your help. We'll be in touch."

"Not so fast," Linda said, putting out an arm to block Bernie from getting to Mathilda. She pointed to the manila envelope Libby was holding. "Where did you get that from?"

"Oh, this old thing," Libby said, looking down. "It's nothing."

"Then why does it have Sinclair Enterprises stamped on the left-hand corner?" Ada's sister, Rachel, asked. Both she and Rick were dressed in office casual. It looked as if they'd both come home from work.

Libby couldn't believe she hadn't noticed the stamp before.

"They're recipes Peggy Graceson sent us,"

Libby blurted. She knew it was a bad answer, but her brain had gone numb and this was the best she could come up with.

Linda Sinclair tsk-tsked. "You do know that Peggy didn't cook, right?"

"That's what makes them so unique," Bernie piped up.

Linda Sinclair narrowed her eyes and turned toward her son. "Rick, call the police and tell them we caught someone breaking into our neighbor's house."

"Let's not be hasty," Bernie said.

"And why shouldn't we be?" Rachel demanded. "You've been nothing but trouble since the day—"

"Evening," Bernie corrected.

Rachel glared at her. "Whatever—you came into my house."

"For one thing," Bernie said, "we didn't break into Peggy Graceson's house; we used the house key."

"Peggy told us where it was," Libby added.

"Tell that to the police," Linda Sinclair said. "Though, frankly, I don't think they're going to care."

"Fine," Bernie said, "I admit we may have overstepped a bit."

"You think?" Rick said.

"Okay. We did," Bernie allowed. "But don't you want to hear why?"

Rachel sniffed, read a text on her cell phone, and looked back up. "Not really," she said and yawned, already bored with the conversation.

"I think you should listen. We're very close to finding Peggy Graceson's killer," Bernie lied, "and we were hoping to find some evidence in the house to corroborate our theory." She looked Linda Sinclair in the eye while she went for broke. "Do you really want to see your daughter go to jail for a murder she didn't commit?" Bernie asked softly. "Because I don't think you do."

Linda Sinclair's face collapsed. "You're right. I don't," she admitted.

"And at this point, we're the only chance she's got," Libby said.

"That's a frightening thought, but you may be right," Linda allowed.

"Mom," Rick whined.

Linda shushed him with a look and invited Bernie and Libby inside.

Ten minutes later Rick and Rachel had gone off to meet their friends and Bernie and Libby were sitting in Linda Sinclair's kitchen waiting for the kettle to boil.

"I swear this family is cursed," Linda Sinclair confided as she got out the tea canister, a canister that Libby was gratified to learn contained oolong tea.

Bernie didn't reply. She was too busy studying the contents of the manila envelope, now spread out on the kitchen table. Among other things, the envelope had contained Peggy Graceson's passport and eight thousand dollars in one hundred–dollar bills.

Bernie reached over, picked up the passport, and opened it. "Peggy just got this," Bernie said, noting the issuing date as she looked at Peggy Graceson's picture. She looked happy, Bernie decided. As if she was heading off on an adventure. Because she was. Then Bernie took out the piece of paper lodged between the last page and the back cover and unfolded it and smoothed it out with the edge of her hand. It was an itinerary.

"According to this, it looks as if Peggy was going to Australia on February twenty-eighth," Bernie noted. "She was landing in Sydney and then going on to Perth. Do you know who her boyfriend was?" she asked.

Linda Sinclair turned from the stove, a bemused expression on her face. "If she had one, it was news to me. What makes you think she did?"

Bernie reached into her pocket and took out the note that had been on the refrigerator. "This."

"Wow," Linda said as she read it. "I remember writing 'Jimmy's the Best' all over my notebook and drawing hearts all around his name when I was in sixth grade. I had such a crush on him."

Bernie smiled, remembering her first crush. "So, she never said anything to you about her trip or who she was going with?"

Linda shook her head. "But then I'm not surprised. She and I . . . kept strictly to business stuff. We didn't get along too well."

"How come?" Libby asked as Bernie leafed through the third item in the envelope: a bunch of papers that had been paper clipped together.

"She wasn't nice to my kids," Linda replied. "She called the cops on them a couple of times. I got really mad and probably said some things I shouldn't have."

Bernie lifted her head. "Did you know Peggy sold her house?" Bernie asked Linda Sinclair.

Linda shook her head. "She told me she was remodeling her kitchen."

Bernie held up a sheaf of papers. "According to these she was living there on a postpossession agreement."

"Then where was she going to put all of her stuff?" Linda asked.

Bernie shook her head. "Maybe in storage."

"So, she really was getting out of town," Libby said.

"It would appear that she was," Bernie replied.

The teakettle whistled and Linda Sinclair poured some of the water into the teapot, swished it around, poured it out, measured out the tea into the pot, and poured in the water. Then she brought the pot to the table, along with three cups and a plate of biscuits, and went back for the sugar and the milk and set those down on the table as well.

"Do you like your tea strong?" she asked Bernie and Libby.

Both of them nodded.

"You know, it was your mother who taught me about brewed tea," Linda Sinclair reminisced. "Until then I'd only drunk tea from tea bags." She sighed. "I'm sorry about what happened," she continued. "I reached out a couple of times and tried to explain that Ada's dad was desperate for money at the time. But your mom didn't want to listen."

Bernie nodded. "She could be like that. Why do you think Peggy Graceson was killed?" she asked Linda Sinclair, changing the subject.

Linda Sinclair shook her head. Her expression gave nothing away.

"Surely you must have some idea," Bernie insisted.

Linda Sinclair sat down, poured a little tea into her cup, tasted it, and said, "It needs a little more time, and in answer to your question, I really don't know."

Bernie took a biscuit off the plate in front of her and ate it, deciding as she did that it really wasn't worth the calories. "Not even an inkling of an idea?" she insisted.

"Over the years, I've found it best to stick to my business and not mind other people's. We're not exactly a close-knit family," Linda Sinclair explained.

"So it would seem," Bernie replied. "But even so, perhaps you know why Vicky Sinclair's car is parked in Peggy Graceson's garage."

Linda Sinclair brightened. "That I do know." Bernie and Libby waited for her answer as Linda Sinclair poured herself a little more tea and tasted it. Then she nodded and poured some into Bernie's and Libby's cups before filling her own. "Even though the SUV is registered to Vicky it's really a company car in the sense that anyone can use it. Probably Peggy had to use it for something and left it in her garage," she said as she added a lump of sugar and poured a little milk into her tea.

Libby leaned forward. "I don't think that's the case," she said. "The timing's all wrong. And anyway, she had her Civic."

"Well, Vicky's kids borrowed the SUV a lot even though they weren't supposed to," Linda said, a malicious smile on her face. "Perhaps you should talk to them."

"Thanks for the tip," Bernie said as she finished her tea. "That's very helpful. Now, what about yours?"

Linda took a biscuit and ate it. "My what?" she asked after she swallowed.

"Your kids," Bernie explained, even though she was sure Linda Sinclair knew whom she was referring to. "Did they use the SUV, too?"

Linda Sinclair took a sip of her tea. "Why would they? They have their own vehicles," she replied.

Ten minutes later Bernie and Libby were out the door.

"Do you believe her?" Libby asked her sister as they walked down the front steps.

Bernie considered her answer. "I think I do," Bernie said, heading toward Mathilda. Bernie had just gotten into the van and inserted her key in the ignition when her dad called. A minute into the conversation, Bernie put the phone on speaker so Libby could hear what their dad was saying.

"You think Eckleburger is right?" Libby asked Bernie after their dad had hung up.

"Yeah," Bernie said as she got out of the van and walked back to Linda Sinclair's house. "He was an expert witness before he retired. He testified all over the country. I don't think he's likely to make a mistake." She rang the bell. Linda Sinclair answered the door a minute later.

"What do you want now?" she demanded, looking annoyed.

"This." And Bernie relayed the question her father had told her to ask.

Linda Sinclair's eyebrows shot up. "Funny you should ask," she said when Bernie was done talking. "I've been wondering about the notebook since Ada found it."

Chapter 39

It was almost four-thirty when Libby and Bernie arrived at Sinclair Enterprises. Located a couple of miles off the thruway, the building was low and squat, made of preformed concrete panels with a sign on the top spelling out the company's name in blocky, bright blue letters that stood out in the afternoon dusk. There were few windows in the building and those were oblong instead of rectangular.

The building was surrounded by a parking lot that was mostly empty, and as Bernie and Libby walked in they couldn't help wondering whether the parking lot had been built with an excess of enthusiasm or if the place was being run with a bare-bones crew. Since there was no receptionist at the window clearly marked "Reception," they walked down a short hallway until they couldn't go any farther.

"Right or left?" Libby asked.

"Right," Bernie said, hearing voices coming from that direction.

The first two offices were empty but the third one was occupied by Vicky Sinclair and her two children, Lance and Erin. The three were gathered around a large metal table in the center of the room when Bernie and Libby walked in.

"Hi there," Bernie said.

The three Sinclairs stopped and stared.

"What do you want?" Erin demanded.

"Who let you in?" Lance said, walking toward the sisters.

Bernie put on her best smile. "We let ourselves in. No one was at the reception desk so we followed your voices and here we are."

"That certainly makes my day," Erin sneered. Unlike Rachel, Erin was wearing a designer dress more suitable for cocktail hour than work.

Vicky straightened up. "Why are you here?"

"We've come to talk about the car," Bernie said as she reflected that Vicky looked wearier than the last time she'd seen her. Her face was drawn and she had circles under her eyes that her makeup wasn't hiding.

"What car?" Lance asked.

"The SUV in Peggy Graceson's garage," Libby replied.

"An SUV isn't a car," Erin asserted. "It's a light truck."

Vicky Sinclair shot a warning glance in her daughter's direction before speaking to Libby. "And what, pray tell, does that have to do with us?" Vicky Sinclair asked.

"Linda told me your children drove it from time to time," Bernie answered.

"Everyone drives it from time to time," Lance

told her. "You should talk to Rick and Rachel. They were in it all the time," he asserted.

"Funny. That's what Linda Sinclair said about you," Libby observed.

"Why do you care?" Vicky Sinclair asked.

"Yeah, why?" Lance echoed. "It's none of your business."

"It is if the people driving it were the people who put a tracker on our vehicle," Libby said.

"And the note," Bernie added. "Not to mention probably being the ones who called the cops on Ada."

Vicky's eyebrows shot up. She looked surprised. "You're accusing my kids?"

"Not accusing. Asking," Libby said.

"Why would we do that?" Erin demanded.

"That's what we want to know," Libby said.

"You should ask Rick and Rachel," Lance said.

"We did," Bernie told him. "They said to ask you."

Lance snorted. "What's your problem?" he demanded of Bernie, taking another step toward her.

"I don't have one. What's yours?" she replied.

Lance opened his mouth to say something but before he could Vicky Sinclair intervened. "You'll have to excuse my children," she said. "Everyone's on edge these days, what with Henry's and Peggy's deaths and the company going public and all."

"It's a simple question," Bernie said. "We're just looking for a simple answer."

"Right." Vicky snorted. "First of all, they didn't have anything to do with Peggy Graceson's SUV; second of all, we're done talking here; and third of all, I'm going to call the police if you don't leave."

"On what grounds?" Bernie challenged.

"Trespassing," Vicky Sinclair shot back.

"This is a business," Libby protested. "I can walk in here if I like."

"And now I'm asking you to leave," Vicky Sinclair said, and she reached for the phone sitting on her desk.

"Fine," Bernie said, and she motioned to her sister. "Come on, Libby, let's go."

"My pleasure," Libby replied, turning toward the door.

Vicky joined Bernie and Libby as they walked down the corridor.

"What?" Libby said. "You don't trust us to walk out by ourselves?"

"Not really," said Vicky Sinclair.

"What are we going to find that you're so worried about?" Bernie asked.

"I'm not worried," Vicky Sinclair told her. "We're busy and you're taking up time."

"So, tell us what you know and we'll go away," Libby promised.

"I don't know anything," Vicky Sinclair said

exasperatedly. "How many times do I have to tell you that!"

"But you suspect," Bernie said softly.

By now they were at the reception desk. A plump woman in her forties was sitting behind it.

Bernie pointed to the woman. "She wasn't here before."

The woman looked sheepish. "I had to pee."

"It's okay, Maggie," Vicky said to her. Then she gestured to Libby and Bernie. "These two are just leaving." And with that she turned and marched away.

"Have a good day," Bernie called after her.

Vicky Sinclair didn't answer.

"No manners," Bernie commented as she was getting her gloves out of her jacket pocket. That's when she noticed the large framed color photo hanging on the wall opposite the reception area. She must have missed it when she and Libby had come in. Bernie stepped closer and studied it. An oval plaque on the bottom read, SINCLAIR ENTERPRISES. Everyone in the photo was young and smiling.

"I think I know who Red is," Bernie said, turning to Libby.

Chapter 40

Two days later, at three in the afternoon Bernie and Libby knocked on Sheryl Sinclair's door. Her house, a modest cape, was set in the middle of a cul-de-sac off Winton Road. As the crow flies, it was three blocks away from Linda Sinclair's house, but due to the street patterns considerably more if you walked or drove.

"Here goes nothing," Bernie said as she waited for Sheryl to answer the door. She and Libby had spent the last couple of days talking to Ada, Vicky Sinclair and her children, as well as the rest of the people at the party on New Year's Eve, and now they were hoping to fit the last piece of the puzzle into place. At the very least.

"Are you sure she's home?" Libby asked.

"That's where Maggie said she was," Bernie answered, thinking about their dad and what he'd said about vanity.

"And your phone is fully charged?" Libby asked.

"For the third time, yes," Bernie told her sister as she knocked on the door again.

"And we have a good fifteen minutes on it?"

Bernie snorted. "How many times do I have to repeat myself?"

"I was just making sure," Libby said as she

studied the statues of the three LED reindeer standing in the front yard. She was deciding they must be pretty at night, all lit up, when Sheryl opened the door.

"What are you doing here?" she asked, looking surprised to see them.

Bernie handed her a box of shortbread cookies dipped in dark chocolate that they'd made this morning. "We just wanted to give you this and tell you how sorry we are for your loss."

"It's a little late, but thank you," Sheryl said, taken aback.

"I wonder if we can come in," Libby continued.

"This really isn't a good time," Sheryl demurred and began to close the door.

"It'll just take a minute," Bernie said quickly.

"We just want to put the last pieces together. To try to understand why Ada did what she did," Libby added.

Sheryl's eyes widened. She opened the door back up. "That's interesting. I thought you were on her side," she said.

"We were. We thought she was innocent," Libby replied, "but after talking to everyone we realized that we were wrong. We just want to know what she and Peggy Graceson fought about. For our own peace of mind, you understand. My sister and I are just trying to grasp why Ada did what she did. It's so hard to believe."

Sheryl fingered the top buttonhole of the red

cardigan she was wearing. "Well . . . I don't know. . . ."

"Please," Bernie begged in the face of Sheryl's dubiousness. "I know my father would be very grateful. He doesn't understand, either."

Sheryl relented. "I suppose I owe you that much," she allowed, stepping away from the door and beckoning the sisters in. "Coffee?" she asked.

"Just some water please," Libby replied.

"Me too," Bernie replied. "I think I've had my quota for the day."

As she and Libby passed through to the kitchen, Bernie could see that the inside of the house was as modest as the outside was. It was smaller on the inside than the outside had led Bernie to believe, or maybe it just looked that way because all the furniture belonged in a bigger space. The living room was cluttered with mismatched sofas, settees, and coffee tables, while the dining room had a large table, a cabinet, a desk, and twelve chairs crammed into it.

"My husband liked to buy things," Sheryl explained, correctly reading the expression on Bernie's face.

"You must miss him," Bernie said, nodding to the framed photo of her husband sitting on top of the cabinet.

Sheryl let out a sigh. "Yes, we were together for a long time. I don't think I'll ever forgive Ada for what she did to my Henry."

"So you don't think it was a hit-and-run?" Libby asked.

Sheryl gave her a how-stupid-are-you look.

"No, I don't."

"Why did Ada kill him, if you don't mind my asking?" Bernie inquired as she took the seat Sheryl had indicated at the kitchen table.

"No, I don't mind at all," Sheryl replied. "Obviously, because he knew that Ada had killed Peggy and she was afraid he was going to go to the police."

"When do you think he knew?" Libby asked as Sheryl, ignoring what Libby and Bernie had both said, poured them coffee from the coffeemaker on the counter. Then she took the box of cookies they had brought, opened the top, and put those on the table.

"I'm not sure. I did tell him about the fight Peggy and Ada had. Perhaps I shouldn't have. But it was terrible." Sheryl sighed, poured herself a cup of coffee, and sat down. "Really frightening to watch. They almost came to blows."

"That must have been scary," Bernie said as she took a cookie and bit into it. It practically melted in her mouth. That was one of the joys of these cookies. Their "mouth feel."

"It was," Sheryl said. "I thought I was going to have to call the police."

"So, what now?" Libby asked.

"In what sense?" Sheryl asked.

"Now that your husband has . . . passed."

Sheryl put on a sad face. "It's going to be hard, but I suppose I'll just have to carry on. For everyone's sake. Henry would have wanted me to."

"That's so brave of you," Bernie said. She leaned over. "I'm told he was quite the ladies' man," she confided. She watched Sheryl flinch, then recover. "You know, really good in bed."

"How dare you," Sheryl snapped.

"Easy." Bernie rummaged around in her bag. "Here it is," she said, coming up with a Kleenex. "I think I'm getting a cold."

"Who said that?" Sheryl demanded, her voice getting louder.

Libby jumped in. "I'm sorry if what my sister said upset you. She didn't mean to."

"No, I certainly didn't," Bernie agreed. "But to answer your question," she lied, "Kate Silverman said something. So did Vicky and Linda, for that matter. I mean to look at him you wouldn't think he was such a Casanova, but what do they say about never judging a book by its cover? I guess it's true."

"No it's not," Sheryl said, her face getting paler.

"So you and he didn't have a good sex life? I'm sorry. It must have been hard to be married to someone who gave his best, so to speak, to someone else. If I were you I'd certainly want a little payback."

Sheryl got up slowly. Her jaw was clenched and her eyes had narrowed to slits. "What do you think you're playing at?"

"Nothing." Bernie ate another cookie. "I'm giving you a compliment. I think you did the right thing."

"What right thing?"

"You took care of the problem. Sometimes a final solution is the best solution."

"You're saying I murdered my husband?" Sheryl demanded of Bernie.

"And Peggy Graceson," Libby added helpfully.

"All I'm saying," Bernie continued, "and I think this goes for my sister as well, is that if my husband was leaving with someone else, I'd be pretty upset. At least, I imagine I would, not being married and all." Bernie finished her cookie and brushed the crumbs off the front of her pale blue angora sweater and adjusted the cameo she had pinned to its neckline. "I can certainly understand why you did what you did. Bad enough he was seeing Peggy. But running away with her? To Australia no less. I have to say I really admire you. It took a lot of work to forge Ada's dad's notebook. And making Ada the fall guy. Brilliant. She has a history. She's easily influenced."

"And no one likes her, whereas everyone likes you," Libby observed, "so it was only natural that they'd blame her. But what I really don't understand is why . . ."

Bernie interrupted, ". . . you left the note and the tracker? That was overkill."

"Up until then you had us in the palm of your hand," Libby added.

"I want you to leave." Sheryl's face had turned sheet white.

Interesting, Bernie thought. Up until now she'd thought that was just an expression.

"Libby and I didn't mean to upset you." Bernie stood up and lifted up her sweater. "See," she said, "I'm not wired."

Libby rose and did the same. "Neither am I."

She and Bernie both sat back down.

"This is just between us girls," Bernie said.

"The police have already arrested Ada," Libby said.

"Your execution was flawless except for that. Tell us," Bernie urged. "We can't do anything. You've won. We just want to know. For our own satisfaction."

Sheryl bit her lip. "You're both crazy," she said. "I don't know what you're talking about."

"Of course you do," Bernie said. She leaned forward, reached out, and put her hand over Sheryl's hand and patted it. "You know," she said to Sheryl, "I just want to repeat that I really do admire you. I think you did the right thing."

"I think so too," Libby said as her sister sat back in her chair. "What you did took real guts. You shouldn't have to stand by and be a victim, take abuse. Both of them got what was coming to them."

Bernie nodded vigorously. "I hope I have the guts to do what you did if I ever get in that situation. You made the world a better place. I mean, running away to Australia. That must have been the final straw."

"It was," Sheryl admitted, the dam breaking.

"After everything you did for him," Bernie replied.

"I did do a lot," Sheryl said.

"That's what everyone says," Bernie assured her.

"I was a good wife." Then Sheryl sat back in her chair and studied the kitchen walls. Bernie noted that her color had returned to normal.

After a moment, Sheryl spoke. "The notebook was pretty good, wasn't it?" she allowed, pride shining through her voice.

"It was excellent," Libby said.

Sheryl smiled. "It took a long time to do."

"I bet it did," Libby told her. "But how did you get Ada to go up to the attic and find it?" Libby asked. "That's the part that puzzles me."

"That was the simple part," Sheryl replied. "I told her I'd been up there and found one of her dad's notebooks and I thought there was something in it she should see. Then after she found it—I hid it in a box of old clothes—I pointed the pages out to her and told her the whole thing was in code. I told her if she read certain passages out loud the guilty party would reveal themselves."

"Kind of like that scene in *Hamlet*," Bernie noted.

"I don't know what the hell you're talking about," Sheryl told her.

Bernie waved her hand in the air. "Forget it," she said. "It's not important."

Libby leaned forward. "But there was no guilty party, was there? Ada's dad died a natural death, didn't he?"

"Ada never believed that," Sheryl said. Then she pointed to Bernie's and Libby's cups of coffee. "You haven't had any."

Bernie smiled at her. "Give us a moment. We had a cup before we came."

Sheryl nodded.

"So why the tracker and the note?" Libby asked.

"I got nervous," Sheryl admitted. "I thought it would be good to have a backup subject. Just in case."

"That was your Plan B? It was as simple as that?" Bernie asked.

"It was," Sheryl answered. Then she blinked. "Do you hear that?" she asked.

Bernie and Libby both shook their heads.

"I don't hear anything," Bernie said, silently cursing under her breath.

"Neither do I," Libby agreed, backing up her sister.

"Well, I do," Sheryl said. "Maybe it's the UPS man. I'm expecting a package." And she got up to take a look.

Libby and Bernie exchanged a glance as they rose and accompanied Sheryl to the door. They were a little behind her, but they could see three cars; one was blocking the driveway while the other two were parked in front of Sheryl's house. McCready and three other men were getting out of their vehicles and heading for the house.

Sheryl spun around. "And I believed you," she growled. "Oh my God," she said as a realization dawned on her. "What an idiot I am." And she dashed into the kitchen, grabbed Bernie's bag, and turned it upside down. Everything in it fell onto the table and Sheryl pawed through the contents until she found Bernie's phone.

"Hey, give that back," Bernie cried as Sheryl grabbed it.

"You recorded me, didn't you?" Sheryl said.

Instead of answering, Bernie grabbed onto Sheryl's wrist and tried to pry the phone out of Sheryl's hand, but Sheryl was stronger than she looked. She twisted away from Bernie and ran to the sink and dropped the phone into the garbage disposal and flicked the switch. There was a terrible rattling noise. Bernie reached for the switch but Sheryl took hold of Bernie's arm and bit it. Bernie screamed and pushed Sheryl away. Sheryl fell into Libby as Libby was reaching for the off switch, knocking Libby's hand away, but Bernie managed to get to the switch and turn the disposal off.

"No you don't!" Sheryl yelled, picking up a paring knife that was on the counter and lunging at Bernie. Bernie sidestepped and Sheryl whirled around and went for Libby. Libby took a couple of steps back, but her progress was blocked by a chair, and before she knew it Sheryl was standing in front of her holding the knife to her throat.

"Turn the disposal back on," she told Bernie, "or I'll stab your sister."

Bernie put both hands in the air. "Let's all relax," Bernie said in as calm a voice as she could manage.

"Do it!" Sheryl screamed.

"Listen to her," Libby managed to get out.

"Yes, do," Sheryl told Bernie.

"Fine," Bernie said. She was reaching for the switch when there was a loud crash. Sheryl startled and Libby grabbed her arm and tried to wrestle the knife out of Sheryl's hand as McCready; Chuck Pullman, the current head of the Hollingsworth PD; and two detectives came charging into the kitchen.

"Drop the knife!" one of the detectives yelled

as he reached under his coat and took out his gun.

Sheryl ignored the order and kept trying to stab Libby.

"Do what he says," Bernie told her.

"Go to hell," Sheryl spat out.

"Okay, but just listen," Bernie said, trying to keep her voice from shaking. "You destroyed my phone."

"That's true," Sheryl said.

Bernie smiled encouragingly. "So there's no record of what you said. There's just a you said/we said sort of thing."

McCready nodded. "She's right."

"Yes, she is," Pullman said.

"Go on," Sheryl said.

Bernie nodded and continued. "But, if you don't put that knife down there's a strong possibility that one of the gentlemen over there"—Bernie nodded in the detectives' direction—"is going to shoot you. At this point in the game, all you'll be charged with is . . ."

"Aggravated assault," Pullman said.

"So put the knife down," Bernie said.

"Please," Libby told Sheryl, Libby's voice coming out in a croak.

Sheryl did. Libby rubbed her neck as the detectives moved in. While they were taking Sheryl into custody, Bernie stuck her hand into the garbage disposal and pulled out her phone. The blue plastic case was nicked and scored and the glass was cracked. Bernie held her breath and turned it on.

"Oh my God, it works," she said as the screen lit up. She entered her password, then went to video, pressed the icon, then pressed video. A moment later, Sheryl's voice floated out into the air.

Bernie looked at Sheryl and smiled. "I guess what they say in their ads about this case being indestructible is true."

Sheryl screamed and lunged at Bernie, but it was too late. Her arms had already been cuffed behind her back.

The Hollingsworth chief of police nodded at the uniforms and they marched Sheryl out to the squad car.

"You said you were going to give us a half hour," Bernie said to Pullman.

Pullman shrugged. A tall man who always gave the impression of bending down to hear what people were saying, he pointed to McCready. "It was my predecessor's call."

McCready nodded. "Blame your dad. He said he'd shoot me if I let anything happen to you, and I think he would."

Bernie was going to say she agreed with McCready when a black Infiniti screeched to a halt in front of the car blocking Sheryl's driveway. The passenger door opened and Ada got out. A moment later Linda Sinclair and her two children joined Ada. The four of them ran over to Sheryl, who was standing next to the vehicle in the driveway.

"I'm going to kill you!" Ada screamed at her.

"How could you?!" Linda yelled. Her face was red.

Ada lunged at Sheryl and the two officers standing there moved between them and told Ada to step back.

"Dad must have told Ada," Libby said as she watched the scene outside unfolding.

"Probably not the smartest thing to do," Bernie observed as the shouting continued.

By now Rick and Rachel had gotten embroiled in the dispute as well.

"Maybe Dad was right after all," Bernie said, watching the Sinclairs screaming at Sheryl and the officers trying to keep them away from her. "Maybe people don't change after all."

"At least not these people," Libby said.

"Remind me not to answer if Ada calls," Bernie told Libby.

"Don't worry," Libby replied. "I will."

Chapter 41

Sean whistled as he parked the car he'd bought from McCready, in the parking lot near Gossman's dock. "There she is, ladies," he said, pointing to the *Mary Jane* as he got out of his car. The fishing boat was cleated in the fourth slip on the dock. "Isn't she a beauty?"

"Be still my heart," Libby muttered as she looked at the forty-foot wooden-hulled fishing boat bobbing up and down in the water.

Sean gestured to the sky above them. It was a bright blue and the sun was shining. "It's going to be a great day," he announced. Then he turned and patted his new vehicle. It was a pale green 2005 Buick LeSabre. "And we got to come here in my new car."

"Your new old car," Libby pointed out.

"An oldie but a goodie," Sean said, grinning. He knew his daughters' opinion on his recent purchase and he didn't care. "You know," he reminisced, "being here brings back memories of me and your mom."

"You and Mom came here?" Bernie asked.

Sean nodded. "All the time. Your mom loved Montauk."

"Did you go fishing?" Libby asked.

Sean nodded. "For tuna. In the beginning of

389

June. Just like we're doing now. We'd rent a motel room—I think the motel was called the Dusty Rose; it was right on the beach—and spend a couple of days fishing, and then we'd hang out at some dive bar at night and shoot pool. Of course, the place was different then. Not all built up and fancy. That was the Hamptons. This was a fishing community. A lot of those guys were Portuguese. There was a bakery up the street"— Sean waved to a line of stores on the left—"that made the best sweet rolls."

"Maybe they still do," Bernie suggested.

"Nah," Sean said. "They've been gone a long time."

"We could make them," Libby said.

Sean grinned and turned back to get the thermos of coffee and his daughters' blueberry muffins that he'd forgotten to get out of the LeSabre. "That would be nice," he said. "I would like that." Then he started for the boat. This one wasn't big; he'd been on those. This one just took on six people. Which was good, he thought. The girls would like that better.

"Got your bands?" Sean asked Libby.

Libby nodded. She heard they were better than Dramamine for seasickness. She guessed she'd find out.

"It's just a matter of willpower, you know," Sean said to Libby. "If you think you're going to get sick to your stomach you will be."

Libby was just about to answer and not in a nice way, but Bernie got there first and changed the subject.

"How did you know?" she asked her dad.

He looked at her. "How did I know what?"

"That Sheryl forged Ada's dad's notebook? That she was behind the whole thing?"

"She was too nice," Sean declared.

"That's it?! She was too nice?! What does that even mean?"

"Exactly what I said. From what you told me, everyone else at the New Year's Eve party was groaning and moaning and trying to prevent Ada from reading from her dad's notebook. Sheryl was the only one who was telling everyone to let her. If she hadn't done that, there was a good possibility, from what you said, that everyone else would have shouted Ada down."

"But why did you hit on the notebook?" Libby asked. "How did you know it was a forgery?"

"I just kept thinking about it. About everything. Nothing made sense. It was like there was too much, and then I started thinking that judging by what you said nothing in that notebook pointed to a motive for murder. It was all dates and observations and then I thought about how sure Ada had been that her dad had gotten murdered and how easy she was to mislead. She was like a sitting duck waiting to have her neck slit."

"Graphic," Libby murmured.

"But true," Sean said. "Ada would have believed anything that pointed to her dad being murdered, and once I decided on that and you found the plane tickets and Linda finally remembered that Sheryl had gone into her attic to supposedly get an old picture for a promo—a promo that wasn't on the books—well the whole thing made sense."

"So, Sheryl did this because her husband was leaving her." Libby shook her head. "Killing two people and framing another one seems a bit excessive. Most people would get a divorce."

"But not the Sinclairs," Sean replied. "They always took and obviously continue to take things to the limit. And then there's the money. With two more people gone Sheryl stood to get a bigger percentage of the money, and she needed it. Evidently, she owed a fair chunk of change to the bookies. At least that's what McCready managed to dig up."

The three walked on in silence for a little while. Then Bernie said, "I was right about where she got the cyanide."

"I just never thought Sheryl even knew about the dark web, much less how to get on it. Evidently I was wrong," Libby said.

"Yes, you were," Bernie couldn't resist saying. She turned to her dad. "But why did Henry come looking for Ada? Why did he want the notebook?"

Sean pulled the brim of his hat down to block the sun. "I think he suspected the notebook was a forgery and wanted to get hold of it so he could take it to the police. I think he knew that his wife had killed Peggy Graceson and was afraid that he'd be next. And he was right. He was."

"But why didn't he go to the police?" Libby asked.

"And say what? He probably didn't think they'd believe him. Would you have?"

"No," Bernie said. "I wouldn't."

"Exactly," Sean said. They were now at the dock. He breathed in the smell of the ocean and listened to the caws of the seagulls circling overhead. God, he was happy. "Here we go, girls," he said as he stepped onto the dock. "We're going to have a good time. You'll see."

"From your mouth to God's ear," Libby muttered.

"You know," Sean reflected while he walked toward the *Mary Jane*, "the trick in life is to keep things simple. That goes for crime as well as anything else. As O. Henry wrote, 'It was beautiful and simple, as all truly great swindles are.' "

"Amen to that," Bernie said as she saw McCready, Eckleburger, and Clyde coming toward them out of the corner of her eye.

"I figured we owed them something," Sean explained.

"I figure you're right," Bernie agreed.

Recipes

It is traditional on New Year's Eve and New Year's Day to serve something like lentil soup or Hoppin' John (made with black-eyed peas) to ensure a prosperous new year. This recipe for lentil soup comes from renowned children's book author Bruce Coville. It's delicious and worth making any time of the year.

Ingredients

1 very large onion (or two medium ones), chopped

¼ cup olive oil or more if needed

2 large carrots, diced

2 large stalks celery, chopped

3 cloves garlic, minced

1 teaspoon dried oregano

1 bay leaf

1 teaspoon dried basil

1 (14.5-ounce) can crushed tomatoes

2 cups uncooked lentils

8 cups water (or 1 quart water and 1 quart low-salt chicken broth)

½ cup spinach, rinsed and thinly sliced

2 tablespoons vinegar or more to taste

Salt and ground black pepper to taste

Kielbasa, ½ standard ring. Optional, although the soup is more popular with than without. If using peel, slice and cut those slices into smaller pieces.

Directions

1. In a large pot, heat oil over medium heat. Add onions, carrots, and celery and stir until onion is tender. Stir in garlic, bay leaf, oregano, and basil. Cook for 2 minutes.
2. Stir in lentils and add water and tomatoes and kielbasa. Bring to a boil. Reduce heat and simmer for at least 1 hour. When ready to serve stir in spinach and cook until it wilts. Add vinegar and season to taste with salt and pepper and more vinegar if desired.

This is another variation on lentil soup. Made with coconut milk and lots of ginger, it's my new favorite.

Ingredients

1 large onion
6 cloves garlic
1 4-inch piece of ginger, peeled
2 tablespoons virgin coconut oil, more if needed
¼ teaspoon cayenne pepper, or to taste
1 13.5-ounce can unsweetened coconut milk

1 cup red lentils (you can use whatever kind you want but the cooking time might be longer)

5 cups water, vegetable broth, or chicken broth, or any combination

2 teaspoons kosher or sea salt, more if needed

1 bunch fresh spinach, rinsed and sliced fine

1 15-ounce can crushed tomatoes

½ cup shredded coconut

Salt and ground black pepper to taste

Directions

1. Chop onion and dice garlic and ginger. Heat coconut oil in Dutch oven, add onion, and cook, stirring, until translucent, 6 to 8 minutes.

2. Add ginger and garlic, and continue stirring until the garlic turns golden. Add cayenne pepper and stir. Add coconut milk; lentils; shredded coconut; 2 teaspoons salt; and five cups of water, vegetable broth, or chicken broth, or any combination thereof. Bring to a boil. Then lower heat and allow to simmer for half an hour or until the lentils are soft.

3. Add tomatoes, spinach, and salt and black pepper to taste; reheat; and serve. This soup also reheats well. For variation, you can substitute a half cup of fresh basil for the spinach.

At the conclusion of the Jewish High Holy Days, which mark the beginning of the Jewish New Year, it's traditional to serve apples and honey or honey cake at the celebratory meal to make sure that the new year is sweet. Here is a recipe for a steamed honey cake from my friend Sarah Saulson, who is an excellent cook and baker. She has adapted it from Gil Marks's "Lekach" from his *The World of Jewish Cooking*.

Ingredients

4 eggs
¼ cup sugar
3 teaspoons baking powder
3 cups all-purpose flour
½ teaspoon salt
1½ teaspoons cinnamon
1½ teaspoons cardamom
1 cup honey
¼ cup canola oil
2 tablespoons coffee
1 teaspoon vanilla
Optional: ½ cup chopped walnuts

Directions

1. Generously grease a 2-quart steaming mold.
2. Beat together eggs and sugar until light and fluffy. In a separate bowl combine flour, baking powder, salt, cinnamon, and cardamom. In another separate bowl combine

oil, honey, coffee, and vanilla. Add wet and dry ingredients to egg mixture alternately, mixing well after each addition. Stir in walnuts if using.

3. Spoon batter into steaming mold. Place a canning ring or canning jar ring in base of a large pot. Put mold on ring. Fill pot with water up to half the height of mold. Place a lid on large pot. Bring water to a simmer and simmer for 2½ hours. Remove from water. Place mold on cooling rack and remove top. Unmold once cool. Note: Our favorite way to eat this is toasted with butter.

Center Point Large Print
600 Brooks Road / PO Box 1
Thorndike, ME 04986-0001 USA

(207) 568-3717

US & Canada:
1 800 929-9108
www.centerpointlargeprint.com